I'll never forget the feeling of that punch, when my fist actually connected on his exposed flesh and it yielded just a bit. I had often heard people talk about a punch "connecting," and I finally understood what that really meant. The punch had mass and weight, and a wonderful electric thrill ran down my hand and across my body as I sensed his muscles tighten. He even gave a small grunt.

Also by Robert Sharenow

MY MOTHER THE CHEERLEADER

The Berlin Boxing Club

Robert Sharenow

HARPER TEEN
An Imprint of HarperCollinsPublishers

For Stacey,
who is always in my corner.

HarperTeen is an imprint of HarperCollins Publishers.

The Berlin Boxing Club
Copyright © 2011 by Robert Sharenow
All rights reserved. Printed in the United States of America.
No part of this book may be used or reproduced in any manner whatsoever without
written permission except in the case of brief quotations embodied in critical articles
and reviews. For information address HarperCollins Children's Books, a division of
HarperCollins Publishers, 195 Broadway, New York, NY 10007.
www.epicreads.com

Library of Congress Cataloging-in-Publication Data
Sharenow, Rob.
  The Berlin Boxing Club / Robert Sharenow. — 1st ed.
    p. cm.
  Summary: In 1936 Berlin, fourteen-year-old Karl Stern, considered Jewish despite
a nonreligious upbringing, learns to box from the legendary Max Schmeling while
struggling with the realities of the Holocaust.
  ISBN 978-0-06-157970-7
  1. Berlin (Germany)—History—1918–1945—Fiction. [1. Berlin (Germany)—
History—1918–1945—Fiction. 2. Germany—History—1933–1945—Fiction.
3. Family life—Germany—Fiction. 4. Boxing—Fiction. 5. Schmeling, Max, 1905–
2005—Fiction. 6. Nazis—Fiction. 7. Jews—Germany—History—1933–1945—
Fiction. 8. Holocaust, Jewish (1939–1945)—Germany—Fiction.] I. Title.
PZ7.S52967Ber 2011   2010024446
[Fic]—dc22   CIP
                                                                      AC

Typography by Jennifer Rozbruch
15 16   CG/RRDC   10 9 8
❖
First paperback edition, 2012

"There is one kind of sport which should be especially encouraged, although many people . . . consider it brutal and vulgar, and that is boxing. . . . There is no other sport which equals this in developing the militant spirit, none that demands such a power of rapid decision or which gives the body the flexibility of good steel. . . . But, above all, a healthy youth has to learn to endure hard knocks."

—Adolf Hitler, *Mein Kampf*

PART I
1934-1935

"The first and hardest lesson for young boxers is learning how to take a punch. If you cannot master this skill you will never have success in the ring. Even the greatest champions must absorb countless blows."

Helmut Müller, *Boxing Basics for German Boys*

How I Became Jewish

As Herr Boch finished the last lecture of the school year, I sketched one final caricature of him into the margins of my notebook. He had bushy gray hair, and long muttonchop sideburns framed his jowly face. I enjoyed drawing his exaggerated features, and it helped me endure even his most tedious classes. One day I drew him as the kaiser, the next as Napoleon. Today, though, I simply depicted him as an enormous walrus, which was the animal he most closely resembled. He was one of our school's more kindly instructors, known as much for his love of tales of Teutonic knights as for the copious piles of dandruff that collected on his jacket. So sometimes I felt bad about my cruel creations, although not bad enough not to do it. I was just completing the drawing when the bell rang, ending the class and the term.

"Please remember to leave your final essay books," Herr Boch said, closing the book he had been reading from. "And enjoy your summer."

"*Danke*, Herr Boch," most of the boys replied as we rose, moved to the front of the room, and dropped our essay books onto a pile on his desk.

I shoved the rest of my books into my rucksack and quickly turned to join the flow of boys exiting the room, anxious for vacation to begin.

"Stern," I heard Herr Boch call to me.

I froze and turned toward him.

"*Ja*, Herr Boch?" I said.

"Stay back a moment."

I slowly moved to the front of the room, a lump forming in my throat. Had he finally caught me? I stopped in front of his desk.

"I'd like you to help alphabetize the essay books for me."

"Of course," I said, exhaling with relief.

When I finally walked out of the classroom, all of my friends had gone and the hall was eerily quiet and empty. A door creaked in the distance. Probably just the old building groaning in the wind, I thought, but some instinct sent a chill through my body, and the small hairs pricked the back of my neck.

I moved to the back stairwell and picked up the faint sound of whistling. As I descended the stairs, the whistling grew louder until I could discern the guttural melody of the

"Horst Wessel Song," the unofficial anthem of the Nazis. If I hadn't known better, I would've sworn it sounded like a group of nature scouts on a hike in the Bavarian Alps. Then I heard the slap of leather soles hitting the floor in time to the music, like an approaching squadron of soldiers.

Suddenly I knew exactly who it was. And I knew they were after *me*.

My brain screamed at me to run, but something, fear probably, kept my legs from accelerating. I slowed down until I was nearly tiptoeing down the steps, hoping against hope that I could sneak by them. Yet as I got to the second floor, the door to the hallway opened, and the group of boys poured out onto the landing.

There were three of them, all a year older than I was: Gertz Diener, Julius Austerlitz, and Franz Hellendorf. I quickly averted my gaze, looking down at my feet, as I tried to continue my descent to the first floor. But before I could take another step, the whistling stopped, and they abruptly blocked my path. Short, wide, and angry, Gertz had a shock of spiky blond hair and spoke with the slightest lisp. Julius stood a foot taller than Gertz and had an extremely thick torso, as if he were wearing a small barrel under his shirt. And Franz was skinny and dark, like a junior version of Josef Goebbels. In the past when they had walked down the hall together, I had thought they looked funny, with their distinctly small, medium, and large outlines. But at this moment there was nothing comical about them as they fanned themselves around me like a tight human fence.

They called themselves the Wolf Pack; really, though, they were a makeshift National Socialist club, and they had been terrorizing the handful of Jewish students at our school over the past several months. Each of the four other Jewish students at my school, the Holstein Gymnasium, had received at least one violent hazing from the Wolf Pack, except me. Up until that moment I had managed to avoid them, assuming that I had kept my background hidden.

"*Guten Tag*, Stern," Gertz said, mock-politely.

"*Guten Tag*," I managed to stammer.

"We know your little secret," he said.

"What secret?"

"Oh, you know. You should have been honest with us, Stern."

"After all, we might've wanted to borrow money from you, Jew," Franz added.

I stiffened with fear. I didn't really consider myself Jewish. Raised by an atheist father and an agnostic mother, I grew up in a secular household. I had absolutely no religious background or education. I also had been blessed with a religiously neutral name, Karl Stern. "Karl" had no Jewish connotation, and as for "Stern," you could find Jewish Sterns, Lutheran Sterns, even some Catholic Sterns. And of all the members of my family, I was by far the least Jewish looking. Tall and skinny with fair skin, dirty blond hair, and a small, thin nose, I was told that I most closely resembled my only non-Jewish grandparent, my mother's father, a tall blond Dutchman. How had they discovered my secret? Had they seen my father or my sister?

"I don't know what you're talking about. I'm not Jewish," I stammered.

"Oh, no?" Gertz said. "Then what are you?"

"I wasn't raised with any religion."

"So you're a Red," Gertz sneered. "That's even worse."

"All the Reds are Jews anyway, aren't they?" Franz said.

"Communist *Schwein*," Julius said.

"Jews are destroying our country."

"Dirty pig."

"But I'm not—"

"Pull down his pants!" Gertz barked.

Before I could react, Julius grabbed my arms. I strained against his grasp, but he easily held me firm. Franz roughly unbuckled my belt and unbuttoned my trousers. Three buttons snapped off in the process and clicked down the stairs that I wished I had run down earlier, descending with sharp little pings. All that school year I had managed to guard my nakedness from my classmates. Athletics were not stressed at our gymnasium, so we had physical education only once a week, and in the locker room I always managed to shield my incriminating penis behind a towel. But now Franz pulled down my pants and underwear so they hung around my ankles, and my penis bobbed in front of them in all of its circumcised glory. My father had explained that the procedure had been done for health reasons and that lots of modern people were circumcising their children in Europe and the United States. Whatever the reason, no matter how much the rest of me looked and felt like a gentile, I had a penis that was undeniably Jewish.

"There it is, boys," Gertz declared. "A one-hundred-percent authentic kosher wurst."

"But I'm not Jewish," I quickly said. "I've never even been to synagogue."

"That doesn't matter," Gertz said. "You have Jew blood."

"There's only one thing worse than a Jew, and that's a Jew who tries to pretend he's not a Jew," Fritz added.

"Sneaky little shit," Julius hissed. "Hitler was right about you."

I longed to confess that not only did I not consider myself Jewish, but I disliked Jews as much as they did. I didn't identify with them at all, and I was furious at having to be associated with them. To me, most of the Nazi propaganda about Jews had a ring of truth to it. There were lots of Jews in banking and finance. Jews generally lived in their own neighborhoods, separate and apart from "real" Germans. My family didn't live in a Jewish section of the city, and my father used to complain about religious Jews when passing through their neighborhoods. When he'd see them on the street, he'd mutter, "Here come the undertakers." Once I heard him comment, "We finally live in modern times when we can throw off all of that primitive *Scheiss* and live like everyone else. Yet *they* still live in a ghetto."

Many of the religious Jews I had seen had large noses, thick red lips, and small dark eyes, and they wore black hats and coats. I found it more than slightly ironic that my father also possessed these basic physical characteristics, save for the black hat and coat.

Jews sounded different. They acted different. They were different. And just like Adolf Hitler, I believed they were ruining everything. Only Hitler saw the Jews as ruining Germany, while I merely saw them as threatening my standing at school and with my friends. I stood in the stairwell wondering how the Wolf Pack had found out about my background.

Franz lunged forward and spat directly in my face. A thick line of hot spittle ran down my right cheek until it dangled off the side of my face. Gertz cleared his throat and shot his own wad of phlegm onto my other cheek. They all laughed. My limbs felt numb, as if my body had suddenly turned liquid. And then the fear so overwhelmed me that I totally lost control. A small stream of urine trickled down the side of my leg and onto my pants, which were bunched at my feet. I felt the warm wetness on my legs.

"Verdammt!" Gertz yelled. "He's pissing himself."

Julius let go of my arms.

"Get away from me, you Jew pig!"

He kicked me from behind, sending me crashing to my knees and into the small puddle of piss I had made. The moisture seeped into the wool of my pants leg and crawled up the side of the fabric. As the three boys closed in around me, I looked up at them and muttered weakly: "But I'm not a Jew."

"Get up!" Gertz commanded. "Get up and fight!"

First Round Knockout

THE WORD "FIGHT" STUNG MY EARS ALMOST AS BADLY AS the word "Jew." I had never been in a fight before, always avoiding any sort of conflict out of fear of getting hurt. I lay there silently, hoping that spitting in my face, pulling down my trousers, and watching me piss myself would be enough to satisfy them.

"Pull up your pants and fight like a man," Gertz commanded. *"Schnell!"*

I struggled to my feet, pulling up my pants with as much dignity as I could muster. As I rebuckled the belt, moisture soaked my crotch, and I felt like a baby wearing a wet diaper.

"Look, I don't want to fight," I stammered.

"Of course you don't," Gertz sneered. "All Jews are cowards."

I resisted the urge to tell them that two of my uncles, my father's older brothers, had been killed in World War I. Uncle Heinrich had even been posthumously awarded the Iron Cross.

"Franz, you take this one," Gertz commanded.

Franz Hellendorf, the smallest of the group, inched forward, and in that moment I saw something familiar in his dark, moist eyes. Fear.

He was scared too.

A coward knows another coward when he sees one. Franz shot a look up and down my body and measured himself against me. I was at least six inches taller than he was. His eyes met mine, and he blinked nervously. I must have looked like a gangly giant to him.

"Go on." Julius pushed Franz toward me. "You can take him."

As Franz inched forward, I instinctively jerked back. Gertz and Julius laughed.

"Look at that, he's scared of little Franz," Gertz said.

Even Franz smiled a bit at my reaction, and I could see his fear receding; the black pool in his eye dried into something hard.

"Put up your fists and fight," he said.

I tried to react, but I could not will my arms to move.

Franz lurched forward and shot a fist at me that landed at the bottom of my rib cage. It was a light punch, but it still cut some of the wind out of my lungs. I coughed. The others laughed, so he punched me again, this time catching me on the edge of my chin and sending my head snapping back. More laughter. Franz then threw several punches at my face, landing on my eye and the side of my mouth. My top lip caught on the corner of my right canine tooth, and blood gushed out of my mouth and dribbled down my chin, eliciting more howls. The sight of my blood gave Franz an even bigger shot of confidence, and he danced around me like a prizefighter, taunting me to defend myself.

"Come on, let's go."

Suddenly I heard the voice of Herr Boch from the stairwell above us.

"*Hallo?* What's going on down there?"

The stairwell's twists and turns prevented him from seeing us. Gertz, Julius, and Franz shot one another quick looks of panic. My labored breath was the only sound in the stairwell.

"*Hallo?*" Herr Boch called again as he began to descend the stairs. Unfortunately he was one of the oldest teachers at our gymnasium and couldn't move very quickly.

Gertz grabbed me by the shirt and hissed into my ear: "You fell down the stairs. Understand?"

Before I could reply, he pushed, and I fell hard against the side of the stairwell, knocking my face against the metal handrail as I went down. I slid down a few steps until I came to a stop face-first on the landing. My mouth filled with blood as one of my lower teeth came loose and dangled against my tongue. The fall hurt more than all of Franz's punches combined.

The Wolf Pack sprinted past me down the stairs and disappeared out the door before my teacher came into view.

"Stern!" he cried when he saw me. "Are you okay?"

He rushed to my side.

"Du lieber Gott!" he said. "My God! What happened?"

He gave me his hand and helped hoist me back to my feet. It was then that he noticed the stain on my trousers, and his nose twitched at the stench of me. My whole face throbbed as if tiny bicycle pumps were inflating thin balloons under my skin and against the bones in my head. The dangling tooth fell out, but I tucked it under my tongue, not wanting Herr Boch to see.

"What happened?" he asked again.

I knew he was fond of me, as I was a top history student. I wanted to confess, but while Herr Boch never spoke about politics, I was afraid that if he found out I had Jewish blood, he would turn against me and give me poor marks.

"I fell down the stairs," I managed to say through my swollen mouth.

"Stern, I heard other boys with you. Who was with you?"

"I fell down the stairs," I repeated. *"Danke,* Herr Boch. I'm fine."

I quickly retreated down the stairs before he could continue his questioning. As I pushed my way through the doors into the first-floor hallway, I half expected to see Gertz and the Wolf Pack waiting for me. But the hallway was mercifully empty. My body reacted with a shudder of relief. A sob escaped my mouth from deep within me. I longed to cry, to let it all out, but I swallowed that urge and buried it back in my gut. I had to get home. I was already an hour late. I spat the tooth and a mouthful of bloody saliva into the gutter and ran.

Winzig und Spatz

I TRIED TO BE ABSOLUTELY SILENT AS I ENTERED OUR apartment building, carefully maneuvering up the winding staircase that twisted through its center. We lived in a large three-bedroom flat on the top floor of a four-story brick building in a quiet middle-class neighborhood. Each floor housed one apartment. I knew my parents would already be at the gallery, setting up for the opening. My sister and Frau Kressel, our housekeeper, were home waiting for me; I needed to get to the bathroom and clean up before they saw me. I turned the key in the lock of our flat as slowly as possible and felt the gears tumble and rotate with a few audible clicks. The door opened with a small squeak. The entry hall was dark and quiet, and I saw the dim glow of light from down the hallway toward the living room.

As I took one step inside, the wood floors groaned under my weight. Almost instantly I heard a small voice calling: "Spatz? Spatz, is that you?"

My sister, Hildy, called me Spatz, and I sometimes called her Winzig after her favorite book series, *Die Abenteuer von Winzig und Spatz*—*The Adventures of Tiny and Sparrow*—by Otto Berg. The books featured woodblock-style illustrations of Winzig, a tiny mouse dressed in lederhosen, and Spatz, a large sparrow who wore an alpine-style hat with a feather. They spent their adventures trying to scrounge up food and outwit Herr Fefelfarve, the obese stationmaster at the Düsseldorf railroad station, where they lived.

Like most boys, I preferred Karl May's cowboy adventures set in America, but for Hildy, there was only Winzig und Spatz. In her pretend games, Hildy cast me as Spatz, the brave and mighty sparrow who fearlessly soared aloft scouting for food and rescuing them from danger, while she was Winzig, the small, resourceful mouse who had a knack for escaping from tight corners and a penchant for sweets. I aspired to be a cartoonist, and I would draw Hildy original Winzig und Spatz comic strips to entertain her, creating new gags and adventures for the duo.

At eight years old, Hildy stood barely four feet tall. Like our father, she had, curly black hair and a small hooked nose, and she already wore glasses for acute nearsightedness. I used to imagine that her eye problems gave her a distorted view of the world that made everything appear in reverse. She was always upbeat and cheerful even when there was

SPATZ

WINZIG

FEFELFARVE

ONE DAY AT THE STATION FEFELFARVE FALLS ASLEEP WHILE EATING HIS BRATWURST LUNCH.

WINZIG SNATCHES THE WURST...

WHILE SPATZ REPLACES IT WITH A PINECONE

LATER

AGGH! THIS IS THE WORST BRATWURST I'VE EVER TASTED!

TASTED PRETTY GOOD TO US ... HEE HEE

BURP!

nothing to be cheerful about. Most of all, she had a completely backward view of me. To Hildy I was strong, smart, confident, handsome, heroic, and capable of nearly any intellectual or physical feat. I certainly didn't want her to know that my schoolmates had just used me as a punching bag and spittoon.

I shut the front door and moved quickly toward the bathroom at the end of the hall.

"Where have you been?" she called. "We haven't done the wine yet."

As she came into view, I turned my face down and moved to the bathroom.

"I had an accident at school. Just let me go to the bathroom and then we'll take care of the wine."

She flicked on the light, caught a glimpse of me, and let out a sharp scream.

"What's going on?" I heard Frau Kressel call from down the hall.

"I fell down the stairs," I said, moving toward the bathroom.

I tried to shut the door behind me, but Hildy pushed it open and followed me inside. Frau Kressel appeared behind her and gasped.

I looked at my reflection in the bathroom mirror. The right half of my top lip had swollen to triple its normal size, and a dark red scar lined the soft pink skin along the top of my teeth. Dried blood formed a patchy goatee around my mouth, and a purple bruise framed the entire right side of my face, punctuated by large red mounds of raised flesh near my eye and my chin where I had been hit.

"Does it hurt?" Hildy asked.

"No," I lied. My entire head pulsed as if a swarm of angry hornets had stung me.

"Hildegard, wet a cloth with warm water," Frau Kressel said. "Karl, you sit."

A stout countrywoman in her sixties, Frau Kressel had been cooking and cleaning for our family for as far back as I could remember. She lived in a small spare room off the kitchen with just a single bed, a dresser, and a tiny sink. She was a woman of few words, but she was an anchor for Hildy and me. While both my parents were intellectuals who talked at length about anything and everything, Frau Kressel rarely spoke beyond the simplest sentence, but when she did say something, Hildy and I listened.

I obediently sat on the toilet seat while Frau Kressel took the wet washcloth from Hildy and gently cleaned the blood from my face. She tried to do it softly, but each swipe felt like the jab of a small penknife. She managed to clean away most of the blood, and I ran my tongue over the scar on the top of my lip and the raw hole where my tooth used to be. I knew Papa would be mad that I looked so horrible for a gallery opening.

"What's that awful smell?" Hildy said.

The pain had so distracted me that I had forgotten about my soiled pants.

"It's nothing! Just go get the wine bottles set up, and

we'll mix them in a minute."

I pushed Hildy out of the room. Frau Kressel stared at me.

"Do you want to tell me what happened?"

I paused for a long moment and then shook my head. "No."

"Are you sure?"

I nodded and she sighed.

"Give me the pants. I'll have them clean for you by morning."

I stripped off my pants and underwear and handed them to Frau Kressel. She had bathed and changed me since I was a baby and taken care of me whenever I was sick. So she was one of the only people in the world I could be naked in front of without being embarrassed.

"Don't forget to clean yourself or you'll get a rash," she said, and then exited the bathroom.

As I cleaned my crotch and legs with a wet cloth, I caught a glimpse of myself in the mirror and shuddered at the pathetic image. For years I had been able to pass as a gentile, which allowed me to walk the streets and the hallways of school without being taunted for being a Jew. Now everything would be different.

Hitler had come to power the previous year, and I knew that things were getting bad for Jews all across Germany. Yet because of my religious anonymity at school, Hitler and the Nazis ranked only fifth on the list of my biggest concerns in life:

1. *Finding a way to gain weight*
2. *Getting rid of my acne*
3. *Getting inside Greta Hauser's pants and having her find her way into mine*
4. *Papa's financial situation*
5. *Hitler and the Nazis*

I was tall and extremely thin. Too thin. Thin was not the German ideal that Hitler and his propaganda machine promoted. Yet no matter how much I ate, I couldn't put on weight. I was also plagued by acne. Despite diligent thrice-daily washing, small red patches of acne relentlessly sprouted on my forehead and cheeks, and sometimes on the tip of my nose.

I was also obsessed with the recently bloomed chest of Greta Hauser, who lived with her family in our apartment building. My father's art gallery and his finances rounded out my list of worries. He never seemed to sell any paintings, and I could not figure out how we survived on his meager earnings.

Yet all of those concerns were trumped that day, because I knew that from now on I'd have to guard against future attacks. I turned away from my own reflection, finished cleaning myself, and went to my room to change into my serving whites.

Hildy and I always worked as staff when our father had an opening at the gallery. We donned white shirts and white pants to make us look official and helped to serve the wine and cheese and to hang coats. When I arrived in the kitchen, Hildy was already dressed in her whites and waiting with ten wine bottles arrayed before her on the kitchen table. Seven of the bottles were full of cheap white wine, while the other three were empty. It was my job to redistribute the wine from the full bottles into the three empty bottles and then fill up the difference with water. Business at the gallery had been extremely slow, and Papa had been adding water to his wine for the past couple of years, first only adding one bottle of water out of ten; then gradually, as business got worse, the number rose to three out of ten. I opened the bottles and used a funnel to evenly distribute the liquids. Hildy held the funnel while I poured. In order to make sure the wine still had enough flavor, I added a half teaspoon of sugar to each bottle. Hildy followed me down the line and put the corks back in and shook up the bottles.

When all of the bottles were mixed, I took a small taste from each one. The ten quick sips helped numb the pain in my head and made my legs feel more solid and warm.

"Can I try some, Spatz?"

"When you're thirteen," I said. "Now, let's trim the cheese."

Hildy hoisted a ten-pound wheel of Muenster onto the kitchen table. It was coated with a thick fuzzy layer of green and white mold. Our father could afford only the poorest wheels of cheese from the market, so it was our job to make them look presentable. I took a paring knife and cut away the moldy outer layer.

"Ugh," Hildy said as she cleared away the green debris. "Rats got at this one. Look, there are teethmarks."

"When I'm done with it, they'll never know."

After a few minutes of cutting, I had carved the ten-pound hunk of mold into what I hoped would pass for a seven-pound wheel of Muenster. I cut us each a slice to taste.

"Not bad," she said.

"Okay, put it in the bag and let's go."

Hildy hesitated.

"Come on—we're already late," I said.

"Do you think Papa will sell any paintings tonight?"

"With the crap he's showing these days—it's not likely."

"Spatz, I'm scared. I heard Mama say we might have to move, if Papa—"

"Don't worry. We'll be fine. Papa always figures something out."

"But what if he doesn't?"

"He will," I said, not believing it. "Now, *mach schnell*. If we're any later, Papa will kill us both, and then you'll have nothing to worry about."

In every Winzig und Spatz book, they would say the same thing whenever they set off on an adventure. Spatz would begin and Winzig would complete their call to action. So mustering as much enthusiasm as I could, I said to my sister, "Come on, Winzig. There's adventure in the air . . ."

She looked at my bruised face, and she could tell I was scared too.

"Karl. What will we do if—"

"There's adventure in the air . . . ," I persisted.

"And cake to be eaten." She finally chimed in.

I placed the bottles in a wire carrying bin along with a stack of paper cups. We said good-bye to Frau Kressel and hurried out of the apartment.

Galerie Stern

WE DIDN'T ARRIVE AT THE GALLERY UNTIL PAST EIGHT, and when we walked in, it took only one look to tell my father was fuming, despite his attempt to appear the perfect host. A few patrons already milled around the space, looking at the paintings by an Austrian artist named Gustav Hartzel. Papa didn't even notice my injured face; he just gestured sharply with his chin toward a table where we were to set up the refreshments. Papa's hair was slicked back perfectly, and he wore his freshly pressed tuxedo, accented by a blue silk scarf. He turned to talk to one of the patrons, flipping the scarf around his neck with a dramatic flourish. He always wore the blue scarf for openings, and seeing him in it made my skin crawl. I scanned the crowd, and as always, no other men were wearing silk scarves. The only other scarf wearer was an elderly woman in a long velvet dress. Mother was nowhere in sight.

My father founded the Galerie Stern in the 1920s to specifically showcase expressionist artists, like Otto Dix and George Grosz. Harsh, raw, and abstract, their work depicted everything from the bloody trenches of World War I to the street life of Berlin. "The time for pretty pictures of flowers and kings has passed," my father explained. "Art needs to show life, real life, in all its wonders and horrors." My father had served with Dix in World War I. He never spoke about his experiences during the war. When I asked, he simply showed me some of Dix's work and said, "This is all you need to know about life during wartime."

I often practiced drawing by sitting in the basement of the gallery and copying works from my father's collection. All the expressionist artists had different styles, but they tended to use thick, harsh paint strokes or thin, jagged pen lines. There was nothing smooth or easy about any of their work or the worlds they depicted. I preferred their paintings and drawings of whores, exposing themselves to men on the street and in brothels.

But Dix, Grosz, and most of the other modern artists my father represented had fled Germany since the Nazis' rise to power. Hitler had deemed their art degenerate, and galleries were forbidden to show their work. Many artists were arrested for public indecency or on political charges. On the day George Grosz left Berlin, he came to say goodbye to my father.

"Time to go, Sigmund," Grosz said. "A good artist knows how to read the landscape. You should get out too."

"This will pass," my father said. "Politicians come and go, but art—art endures."

"Well, my art will endure somewhere else. They're burning paintings, Sig," he said with a sigh. "Did you hear that they melted down Belling's sculptures? Melted them down like they were worthless scrap. Think about that: They're melting art to make bullets. These are savages we're dealing with."

Against Grosz's advice, my father had stayed, and instead of closing the gallery, he began showcasing government-approved artists. Most of the paintings featured boring landscapes or apple-cheeked workers plowing their fields in heroic poses. My father mustered as much enthusiasm as he could when selling these works, but I could tell his heart wasn't in it. In the past, gallery openings were times of celebration and his adrenaline would run so high that he would barely sleep at night after premiering a show. Now the openings left him drained and dissipated, his smile fading as soon as the door was shut.

Hartzel, the artist being featured that night, had long hair and a beard and wore a bright green untucked cotton shirt. His large canvases depicted purple and brown Bavarian mountains under dramatic blue skies with billowing clouds, the kind of art my father used to dismiss as "pretty flower paintings."

He and my father stood in front of one of the paintings,

talking to a potential buyer.

"The strength of the mountains has always inspired me," Hartzel said.

"Yes," my father added, "the natural beauty is symbolic of the strength of the German people."

The patron gave a polite smile and moved on to the next canvas, clearly not impressed. Hildy and I stood by the door, taking coats and offering refreshments.

"Karl! Bring Herr Hartzel some wine."

I fetched a cup of wine. Hartzel took it from me and downed it in one gulp.

"We'll never make a sale with this crowd," Hartzel said.

"Patience," my father said. "The night is young."

Hartzel noticed my face.

"What happened to you?"

"I fell down some stairs. At school."

"*Wunderbar,*" my father said. "We've got an important opening and you look like Frankenstein's monster. Go down and get the artists' biographies that are on the press. And be careful on the stairs."

As I descended the stairs, a light was on in the basement, and I expected to see my mother printing the artists' bios, one of her jobs at the gallery, but the room was empty. I moved to the back of the cold stone room and then into the printing room, where I found the papers I was looking for piled in a neat stack beside the printing press. A large iron contraption stained with rust, years of ink, and large globs of thick grease, the old press was used to make up posters, catalogs, and flyers for my father's artists. I was grabbing the stack of pages about Hartzel when a crumpled sheet lying on the floor caught my eye. I picked up the page, which was half smeared with ink.

BERLIN IS STILL HOT, LADIES—
YOU JUST HAVE TO LOOK IN THE RIGHT CRACKS. THE COUNTESS HAS JUST WHAT YOU'VE BEEN WAITING FOR. . . .

The ink smear prevented me from reading the rest of the page. My face flushed as I reread the sexy message. This clearly had nothing to do with gallery business. Who were these ladies? Where were the cracks? And who was the Countess? An image formed in my head of a mysterious woman with long hair and a slinky cocktail dress.

"Karl!" my father called from upstairs. "Karl, where are you?"

I stuffed the paper into my pocket and trudged back up the stairs to discover that the gallery had filled up nicely. I placed the pages on Hartzel on the table beside the wheel of Muenster, which had several significant pieces cut out. I glanced around to make sure that no one was retching from consuming the rotten cheese, but everyone seemed to be fine so far.

Hildy excitedly wound her way through the crowd toward me.

"Karl, have you seen?"

"What? Is Mama here?"

"No—*der Meister*," she said.

"Huh?" I said, not understanding.

"The champ is here. He's really here!"

I turned and saw the imposing figure of Max Schmeling standing by the door.

Der Meister

THE AIR CURRENT IN THE ROOM CHANGED AS SOON AS the champ walked in, as if a breeze had directed everyone to turn his way. Heads and necks craned, people subtly pointed, nodded, and whispered excitedly, everyone confirming for themselves and one another that yes, he was really there. He stood very straight and tall, looming over those around him. His wide face was bright despite his dark brows and deep-set eyes. In America they called him the Black Uhlan of the Rhine, a nickname his manager had invented to instill fear in his opponents. The name fit. Uhlans were elite horseback-riding soldiers. And he did look like a dark warrior. But his big, inviting smile surprised me, a strange contrast to the hulking fighting machine that was the rest of him. He wore a large trench coat and a tuxedo with a crisp white shirt and a silk kerchief in his pocket.

Beside him stood his wife, the Czech actress Anny Ondra, who wore a long white gown with a small white fur jacket over her shoulders. She also radiated with the special glow of the famous, as if a spotlight were on her at all times, accentuating her tight, shiny blond curls, her sharp red lips, and her perfectly angled thin eyebrows, which sat above large, confident eyes. She was one of Germany's most famous movie stars and had recently starred with her husband in a boxing movie called *Knockout*, in which she played an aspiring actress who falls in love with Max, a backstage worker at a theater.

Anny greeted someone by the door with two quick kisses on either cheek. And Max shocked me by striding right over to my father and giving him a warm handshake and a short manly hug.

For years my father had claimed to be friends with the former heavyweight champion, but I had never quite believed him until that night. "He used to come by the gallery all the time," my father boasted. "You were just too young to remember."

"Was he an artist?" I asked.

"Only with his fists." My father laughed. "But he loved the artists, and the artists loved him. Berlin was a different place then, Karl. Everyone mixed with everyone: artists, musicians, film stars, athletes. It was a different time. A grand time."

As I stood with Hildy, watching them greet each other, I

wondered what someone like Max would have to say to my short, intellectual, art-obsessed father. My father said something, and Max laughed. What could he have said to amuse Max Schmeling?

Then my father quickly scanned the crowd until his eyes found Hildy and me. He signaled to us with a snap of his fingers. I was so lost in observing the scene, I didn't realize he was trying to communicate with us until Hildy nudged me with her elbow.

"Karl, he wants us."

We both made our way toward them. As we did so, Max turned and looked at me. I felt his eyes fall on me. It was the first time I had been gazed upon by someone famous, and it felt as if I were caught in the periphery of the warm glow of his spotlight.

"Max, this is my son, Karl, and my daughter, Hildegard."

"Hildy." She quickly corrected him.

"A pleasure to meet you, Hildy," Schmeling said, gallantly taking her hand and giving it a small kiss. Her face flushed bright crimson, and he turned to me, offering his hand. I extended my own, and we shook.

"What happened to you?" he said, nodding toward my face.

"I fell down some stairs," I responded quickly.

"I'm afraid my son was not blessed with the grace of an athlete, Max," my father added. "He comes by it honestly, though. I was never much for sport either."

My face burned a deeper red than Hildy's. How dare my

father lump me in with himself as an uncoordinated non-sportsman? In fact, I was a decent football player, although my father would never have known that. We had never played ball together. "We are people of the mind," he once explained when I asked him to kick a ball with me. "Our brains are not in our feet."

"How old are you, kid?" Max asked me.

"Fourteen."

"Why, he's big for fourteen, Sig," Max said. "He must get that from your wife's side. And look at his reach. You've got a born fighter here."

He lifted my arms and extended them out to their full length, so my body formed the letter *T*. He measured my arms' combined length with his eye.

"His reach must be at least seventy-two inches already. And what are you, five foot nine? Ten?"

"Ten," I said.

"He's got the reach of a champion, Sig," Schmeling said conclusively, letting my arms fall back down to the side.

My heartbeat quickened. I had never even heard of "reach" before that night, but now I wanted to have good reach more than almost anything in the world. He said I was a "born fighter." Could that possibly be true? My father seemed to have missed the entire miracle.

"Karl, please take Herr Schmeling's coat and offer him some refreshments." He turned to Schmeling. "I must greet your beautiful wife. Hildy, come with me and help with Frau Ondra's jacket."

My father and Hildy moved off toward Anny, leaving me momentarily alone with Max, who was slipping off his overcoat.

"Here, let me take that, Herr Schmeling," I said.

"*Danke*," he replied, handing me the coat. "And call me Max."

"Okay, Max," I said, although the word sounded too informal.

"So who got you, kid?" he said.

"Pardon me?"

"Who were you fighting?"

"I—I fell . . . and—"

"I've been in the ring for most of my life. You may have fallen down some stairs, but you were also in a fistfight. I know a bruise from a punch when I see one. Looks like someone got you with an uppercut to the chin and a right cross just below the eye."

I had no idea how to respond. I didn't want my father to know, to think I had drawn attention to my problems and myself on the night of an opening.

"Look, there's no shame in taking a beating," he said. "I've had my fair share. As long as you fight back, there's no shame. Right?"

As long as you fight back, there's no shame.

My Adam's apple lodged in my throat, and moisture clouded my vision. I quickly looked down at my feet, feeling an even deeper shame than when I had received the beating by the Wolf Pack. Just a few seconds earlier Max

Schmeling had anointed me a potential champion with great reach, yet now he knew me for what I really was: a weakling and a coward. I quickly looked up at Max.

"Please don't say anything to my father."

The champ's eyes connected with mine just as my father came toward us with Schmeling's wife.

"Max, I don't know how she does it, but Anny just keeps getting more and more beautiful."

Max gave me a furtive wink as he handed me his coat. "I'm a lucky man, Sig."

The Barter

AS THE NIGHT WORE ON, I KEPT MY DISTANCE FROM Max as best I could. My head throbbed from the combined weight of my injuries and my shame. My father made sure that Max and Frau Ondra always had a full cup of whatever they were drinking, but I would force Hildy to make the deliveries. Because he was in training, Max would not drink alcohol, so he contented himself with water.

Questions whirled in my head. How could you tell if a fist had hit a face as opposed to the railing of a staircase? How had my father ever gotten to be friends with Max? Did Max know my father was Jewish? And where was my mother?

My father was standing with the artist Hartzel, Anny, and Max in front of one of the paintings. My father called

38

me over to fetch Max more water. I avoided eye contact with him as I brought over the pitcher and refilled his cup.

". . . and wouldn't you love to own one of Herr Hartzel's landscapes, Max? I think Anny took a shine to this one."

My father gestured to the canvas, a simple image of a pasture and rolling hills.

"It is nice, Max," Anny said. "Might look good in the country house."

"Yes, your paintings are very accomplished, Herr Hartzel," Schmeling said. "Perhaps this one would look good in the library. We'll take it."

"Wunderbar!" my father said.

"I'm honored to have you own a piece of my work, Herr Schmeling," Hartzel said, bowing slightly.

"There is one other painting I'm interested in," Max said.

"Oh, yes, the mountain scene you admired over here," my father said, gesturing to another bland canvas.

"No," Max said. "The painting I'm interested in isn't on your walls tonight."

Hartzel's face fell.

"The portrait Grosz painted of me," Max continued. "You know I've had my eye on that one."

"Ah, Max, but you know that's not for sale," my father said.

"There must be a price," Max said.

"It is my last painting by Grosz," my father explained. "I always try to keep at least one painting by each artist I work with."

"Bring it out for me. Anny's never seen it."

My father rolled his eyes. "If you insist." He turned to me. "Karl, go bring up the portrait of Herr Schmeling by Grosz. It's downstairs in bin seventeen."

I went back down into the basement, where one wall was lined with high wooden storage bins filled with canvases. Flipping through bin seventeen, I saw several canvases by George Grosz, and I knew my father had claimed it was his last to establish a bargaining position. In truth no one was buying anything by Grosz, Dix, Max Beckmann, Emil Nolde, or any of the other expressionist painters my father used to represent because of the Nazi ban. The bins were filled with their unsold work.

I finally came to Grosz's portrait of Max, a stark oil of him bare-chested, standing in profile, wearing royal blue fighting trunks with his blunt fists extended. His head was tilted down, his eyes darkened in menacing shadows, and thick black brushstrokes accentuated his arm muscles. I knew the painting well because it had been one of the works I had copied into my journal. Everything about the image seemed to convey strength, confidence, and menace. I wiped a thin layer of dust off the top of the canvas and carried it upstairs.

Everyone gathered around as Max, Anny, and my father approached me. I held up the painting like a human easel.

"Ah, there it is!" Max exclaimed.

"Oh, Max, it's beautiful," Anny cooed. "You look thinner."

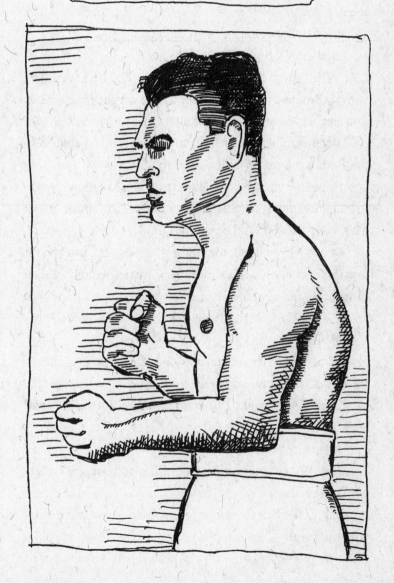

MAX BY GROSZ

"It was painted some years ago," Max said with a laugh, jokingly rubbing his biceps. "I've put on more muscle since then."

"I love it," she said.

"How much, Sig?"

"Well," my father said, "you know I don't want to part with it. Besides, you have mirrors around your house, Max. You can admire yourself anytime."

"But in a mirror, it's hard to see myself in profile like this," Max countered with a sly grin.

The gallery patrons laughed at their sparring.

"It's for me, Herr Stern," Anny said, "to remind me of Max when he's off on the road fighting."

As far as I could tell, the Hartzel canvas Max had bought was the only one sold that night, and we desperately needed to make a sale.

"Please, Herr Stern," Anny said.

"Well . . ."

Before my father could name a price, I felt Max glance at me. I was still too afraid to meet his eye.

"Wait!" Max said. "I have an idea. We'll make a barter arrangement."

"A barter?" my father said.

"Yes. We get the painting and I'll give your son private boxing lessons."

The gallery patrons reacted, nodding and whispering with approval.

"Surely you can't put a price on private boxing lessons

with Europe's greatest heavyweight."

"Boxing lessons?" my father said, aghast. "My son will be entering the art world, not the ring."

"A great fighter has plenty of artistry," Max countered.

"What does he need fighting lessons for?" my father asked.

"Every boy should learn to defend himself, Sig," Max replied. "Looks like he could use the lessons."

He gestured to me, still holding the painting. A few of the patrons tittered. My head tingled even more than it already had, as more blood rushed to my face and seemed to swirl in and out of the bruises. I felt like hiding behind the canvas, but I was also intrigued by the idea. What kid wouldn't want to learn to box from a champion?

"Well, boy," Schmeling said, "do you want to learn?"

All eyes fell on me, waiting for a reaction. I wanted more than anything to scream out "yes," but I knew my father still held the hope of getting cash for the painting. My father stared at me most intensely, willing me to refuse with his eyes. Max looked at me with an amused smile, clearly not seeing the rope of tension that bound my father and me. Although my voice stayed silent, my head instinctively nodded yes. I saw my father's mouth momentarily curl into a snarl and then flatten.

"Ah, see. Of course he wants to learn to box. How about it, Sig?"

All eyes turned to my father, and I knew he would have no choice but to agree.

"If Frau Ondra wants the painting," he said, "I must bow to the will of a beautiful lady."

"Then it's done," Max said, coming forward to shake my father's hand to seal the deal. "When I am in Berlin, your boy will join me at my training gym, the Berlin Boxing Club, for lessons."

A few people clapped my father and Max on the back, congratulating them on the deal. Some patrons also approached me and patted me on the shoulder as I stood there, still holding the painting.

Boxing Lesson No. 1

THE CROWD BEGAN TO THIN AROUND ELEVEN, AND there was still no sign of my mother. At the end of the night, Hildy and I returned to the basement and wrapped up Max's two paintings in brown paper, the only canvases sold the entire evening. Hildy held the twine in place with her little thumb as I tied the bows binding the wrapping in place. My mind raced with excitement about training with Max. Could he mold me into a champion? Would we become friends?

"She's so beautiful," Hildy said wistfully.

"Who?"

"Frau Ondra. She looks even prettier than she does in the cinema. I wish Papa had bargained for beauty lessons for me, along with the fighting lessons for you."

"Beauty lessons?"

I realized that Hildy had been thinking about Frau Ondra as much as I had been thinking about Max. She loved the cinema, and we attended weekend matinees at the grand Nollendorfplatz Theater as often as possible. Hildy liked to sit close so her whole field of vision got swallowed up by the gigantic screen.

"She just looks so perfect. She's the opposite of me."

She cast her dark eyes down. I hadn't realized that Hildy was conscious of her own looks in that way. She was only eight years old.

"You don't need beauty lessons, Winzig," I said.

"But I'm so dark."

"There's nothing wrong with that."

"Easy for you to say. You're light."

"What about Claudette Colbert and Myrna Loy?"

"Claudette Colbert has red hair."

"Well, how about Louise Brooks? She's got even darker hair than you."

"I guess so."

"If you ask me, Frau Ondra could use beauty lessons from you," I said, lifting her chin.

"Thanks, Spatz." She gave me a weak smile.

"Come on, we'd better get back up there."

When we got back upstairs, most of the patrons had cleared out, and Max and Anny were putting on their coats by the door. I brought them the two paintings.

"*Danke,*" Max said. "Now for your first lesson."

He reached into his pocket and pulled out a small red

rubber ball, which he quickly bounced off the floor toward me. I reached to pluck it from the air, momentarily bobbled it, but then held my hand tightly around it.

"Good. You've got decent reflexes," he said. "Keep this ball in your pocket and take it out and squeeze it whenever you're walking somewhere. A fighter needs strong hands and fingers."

I gave the ball a few quick squeezes and felt the muscles across the back of my hand flex in a pleasing way. I hadn't even known I had muscles back there. The night wasn't over and already I felt that I was getting stronger.

"Next," he continued, "do you have coal or wood in your house?"

"Our building has a coal furnace."

"Good," he said. "I want you to talk to your building superintendent and tell him you want to shovel the coal into the furnace every morning and every night. I'm sure he'll agree; it's dirty hard work, but great for the arms and shoulders."

"Okay," I said.

"Finally, you need to be able to do the three hundred."

"The three hundred?"

"It is the basic building block of becoming a boxer. Every day you must be able to do one hundred push-ups, one hundred sit-ups, fifty pull-ups, and fifty minutes of running, which all adds up to three hundred."

"What about a punching bag or something like that?" I asked.

"We'll worry about that once you can do the three hun-dred. Once you can do that, you'll be ready for your first lesson in the gym. I'll be back in Berlin in a couple of months, which should give you some time."

My father approached with Frau Ondra and Hildy to say good-bye.

"A pleasure, as always, Sig," Max said, extending his hand. They shook.

"Thanks for coming, Max, even though you robbed me," my father replied.

"You have beautiful children, Herr Stern," Anny said. She leaned down and gave Hildy two small kisses, one on each cheek. "Especially this one."

Hildy blushed and took in a sharp, pleased breath.

Max held out his hand to me, and we shook.

"Remember the three hundred."

"I will."

"*Gute Nacht!* See you soon!" he said.

My father placed a hand on my shoulder and wore a small smile, which quickly faded as soon as they passed out the door. I felt his hand press sharply on my shoulder as he turned away.

"Now, where is your mother?"

Uncle Jakob

WHEN WE ARRIVED BACK AT THE APARTMENT, IT WAS approaching midnight. Hildy had fallen asleep and my father had to carry her in his arms the final few blocks and up the stairs. Stepping inside our flat, I was relieved to hear muffled voices coming from the kitchen. Then I heard a grunt of pain, and I recognized the voice of my uncle Jakob.

"Gently!"

"I'm trying," my mother replied. "Hold still."

Frau Kressel hurried down the hall to greet us.

"*Gott sei Dank!*" she said. "You're here."

"What's going on?"

"The kitchen," she said. "I'll take Hildy."

She plucked Hildy out of my father's arms and carried her to her room. My father and I continued down the hallway. As we entered the kitchen, I was shocked to be confronted by Uncle Jakob bending over the sink with his bare ass hanging in the air. A small dark bloody hole had punctured his left buttock, which my mother was probing with a long tweezers. A bottle of my father's brandy sat open beside Jakob, and he clutched a glass of the brown liquid in one hand.

"*Scheisse!*" he gasped as she moved the tweezers.

"I said hold still."

"What are you using?" he said. "A soup ladle?"

"What the hell is this?" my father demanded.

"Oh, I thought I'd just stop by and say hello, Sig." Uncle Jakob quipped through gritted teeth. "It's been a long time since my sister poked me in the ass with a sharp object. Agh!" he screamed. Even in intense pain, Uncle Jakob could make me laugh.

Before I'd met Max Schmeling, Uncle Jakob had been the person I most admired. In his late twenties, Uncle Jakob was confident, funny, and rebellious, and he always sparred with my father about everything from sports to politics, even the weather. We shared a love of American cowboy movies, and he would often pepper his speech with western slang and call me buckaroo. Tall and lean like me, he had bright red hair and pale gray eyes.

The older sibling by four years, my mother was the more serious and studious of the two. She stood five feet eight, tall for a woman, and she wore her hair pulled back in a modest bun that fully revealed her pretty features and smooth skin that reminded me of a porcelain doll. She rarely used any makeup, save for some lipstick. Her one indulgence was an expensive face cream in a large white glass tub with a silver top, which she spread on herself every evening.

People who knew her superficially would've said that she was quiet and almost submissive. But I understood that her quietness was really a pensive quality. She was prone to blue periods that my father described as "one of her moods," though this phrase seemed far too lighthearted to describe these deep bouts of depression. When a mood came on, my mother would take on a glassy-eyed expression and retreat to her bed for hours and sometimes days, sleeping up to twenty hours at a stretch, emerging only to use the toilet and retrieve a glass of water or piece of bread. Other times she would soak in a hot tub for hours.

"She needs rest and quiet," my father would say. "That's all. She'll be back on her feet in no time."

And usually he was right. She would suddenly emerge from her slumber as if nothing had happened, as if someone had lifted a lead cloak off her body and she could finally move again. These episodes were scary and painful, but they did not affect our day-to-day life much because Frau Kressel was always there to cook, clean, and take care of our needs.

I rarely saw my mother cross or question my father about anything. Tonight was a rare exception.

"Shhhhh!" my father hissed. "The neighbors."

"Put the towel back in your mouth and bite," she told Jakob.

"I told you I'm not hungry, dear sister."

"Do it!" she said. He dutifully stuck a wadded-up towel into his mouth.

"Hold still!" she said. "I think I got it."

Uncle Jakob bit down on the towel, muting his deepest grunt yet.

"There," my mother said, slowly extracting a small black bloody pebble from inside him. She placed it in a ceramic mixing bowl with a sharp wet clink. Frau Kressel entered, and my mother handed her a towel.

"Hold this against the wound while I get some thread."

Frau Kressel pressed the towel against the wound, sending a small trickle of blood coursing down the back of his leg.

"Why, Kressel, we hardly know each other," Jakob joked.

"*Stillschweigen!*" she said, and pressed a bit harder to shut him up.

My mother finally broke her concentration and turned to look at us, her eyes bulging as they fell on me.

"What happened to you?"

"Him?" my father gasped. "He'll be fine. Now what the hell is going on here?"

My mother ignored him and came toward me, still holding the bloody tweezers. She lightly caressed the uninjured side of my face.

"Are you okay?" she asked.

"Yes." I nodded. "I tripped down some stairs."

"Hope you gave the stairs a good licking, buckaroo,"

Uncle Jakob cracked. "Looks like you got smacked by a whole house."

"Will one of you please explain?" my father demanded.

My mother turned to her sewing kit and retrieved a needle and thread.

"We were having a meeting," Jakob started. "A simple meeting—"

"Wait," my father interrupted. "Karl, go to your room."

"What?" I whined. "I'm old enough—"

"No," my father said.

"Sig, he's fourteen," Jakob countered.

"You, say nothing," my father said, pointing an angry finger at him. "This is my house."

"He should know what's happening—"

"He knows enough," my father said. "You're already putting us in danger just being here."

"We're all in danger, Sig."

"I decide what's right for my—"

"Enough," my mother interrupted. "Karl, go to bed."

"Mama . . ."

I looked at my mother, but she just came over and gave me a light kiss on the forehead, careful to avoid the bruised areas.

"Just go," she said. "It's been a long night. You need rest. We all do."

I hesitated and looked at Uncle Jakob in the hope that he'd fight for me to stay. He just winked at me.

"One of my girlfriends found out about one of my other

girlfriends, and the next thing I knew I had a hole in my *Hintern*. I bet that's what happened to you too, and you're just too embarrassed to say in front of your mother, right, buckaroo?"

Reluctantly I turned and retreated down the hall to my room.

Drawing In on Max

I LAY AWAKE IN BED, TRYING TO EAVESDROP, BUT FROM my room, I couldn't hear a thing that was going on in the kitchen. I already suspected exactly what had happened. From whispered conversations I had overheard in the past, I knew Uncle Jakob was a member of an underground Communist group that was trying to organize against the Nazis. I assumed he was part of a secret meeting that had been broken up by the Gestapo and that he'd gotten shot while he fled the scene. My father hated politics and always shouted Jakob down whenever he tried to talk about his "group."

"I learned everything I needed to know about politics and religion during the war," my father said. "They're all worthless."

About an hour after I had retreated to my room, I heard Jakob leave.

My own fantasies far overpowered everything else that night, even the fact of my uncle's getting shot. I kept replaying the events of the evening over in my head and felt a strange rush of excitement as I remembered every detail of my encounter with Max. After Adolf Hitler, he was probably the most admired man in Germany. He had been the first German to capture the world heavyweight title in 1930, after beating Jack Sharkey. Even though two years later Max lost the title in a rematch with Sharkey, he was still considered one of the best fighters in the world. In his book *Mein Kampf,* Hitler specifically advocated for boxing to be part of the standard physical fitness program for all German boys. Propaganda Minister Goebbels used Max in the Nazi press as an example of the ideal German man for boys to emulate.

My parents' bedroom was next to my own, so later, when they got into bed, I leaned my head against the wall behind my bed to better hear the sound vibrating from their room. They were no longer arguing about Jakob. My father talked about the disappointing sales at the gallery, despite Max's and Anny's appearance, and finally the bargain for my boxing lessons.

"Boxing lessons?" My mother reacted with as much dismay as my father had when he'd first heard the idea. "He'll get hurt. Sig, you shouldn't have let it happen."

"You think I'm happy about it? We could've used that money."

"Just tell Max that Karl changed his mind and doesn't want the lessons," my mother countered. "I'm sure he'll pay you something for the painting."

My entire body tensed. I had already started to imagine myself as Max's protégé and becoming a warrior, the envy of every boy in Germany. Now she threatened to end my dream before it began. I held my breath.

"It's too awkward, Rebecca," my father said. "We shook on it. A deal's a deal."

"Why can't you just tell him Karl doesn't want to do it?"

"But he does want to do it," my father said.

"How do you know?"

"What boy in his right mind wouldn't want boxing lessons from Max Schmeling?" My father continued: "And just look at him. He's a piece of straw. He walks around as if a breeze might knock him over. He needs to be able to defend himself."

As much as it hurt to hear my father's unflattering evaluation of my stature, I knew he was right.

"What happened to my pacifist husband?"

"Did you see his face tonight?"

"He said he fell down some stairs—"

"Perhaps he did, but only after he was beaten and pushed," my father said. My mouth fell open in surprise that he had known the truth all along.

"Who?" my mother gasped.

"I don't know," my father said. "Maybe the Hellendorf kid. His father's one of them. He's got some new job working with the government. With the way things are right now, it couldn't hurt for Karl to learn how to use his fists."

"But our son wants to be an artist. He has my father's gift."

Although he died before I was born, I knew my grandfather had been a well-known artist. He was even commissioned to paint a portrait of the kaiser that hung in his private home for years. As a young woman my mother had also been a gifted painter. She was studying at the art institute at the time she met my father, who picked her up at a student exhibition by offering to represent her. They married while my mother was still a student, and she dropped out of the institute to make a home for our family. After that, she didn't pick up a brush again. Whenever it came up, she'd simply say she'd "lost interest." When I asked my father, he replied that she "didn't have the temperament to be a painter."

Art had always come naturally to me. Since I was ten years old, I had kept a sketchbook journal in which I recorded little illustrations and cartoons of what was going on around me or inside my head. My parents hoped I'd become a painter or perhaps an architect. But I was mad for the newspaper comic strips that were becoming popular and dreamed of working as a newspaper cartoonist or illustrator. My father hated cartoons and thought they were lowbrow and beneath me. This was a constant source of friction between us.

"Why would you want to waste your talent on cheap

laughs about mice and children?" he'd say dismissively. "Art should elevate humanity. It should be more than just pie-in-the-face nonsense."

Despite his disapproval, I loyally practiced my cartooning and held on to the fantasy of working for a big newspaper one day.

I couldn't get to sleep that night. So to relax myself, I found a photograph of Max in a book of great German sports heroes I had and sketched a caricature of him into my journal. As I drew the deep manly lines and shadows of his face, something became clear to me: Max did not fit the stereotype of a blond, blue-eyed Aryan superman. He had dark hair and eyes, thick eyebrows, and a wide nose. He also tended to grow a heavy five-o'clock shadow. He resembled a Jew more closely than any Nordic hero. This made me feel closer to Max and his world. As the picture came together, a new dream formed in my head as I imagined myself transforming into a champion boxer.

I put down my pen and pad and held up my arms in the darkness and looked at the thin silhouettes of my fingers. Then I curled them into fists and was pleased by the transformation as each delicate finger disappeared into a small, blunt shadow. Max had praised my reach. So I extended my arms in front of me and out to the side and for the first time noticed how long they were, as if I were a bird opening its full wingspan. Perhaps I really was the mighty Spatz, like Hildy imagined.

I picked up the small rubber ball Max had given me from

MAX

my night table and gave it a series of squeezes, one hundred with each hand. I vowed to follow every piece of advice Max gave me to the letter, thinking that if I did, I would be transformed into something more like him.

My parents finally drifted into silence in the next room, and I set the ball back on my night table. In my half-awake dreams I saw myself in a boxing ring, squaring off against the Wolf Pack. I fought them one at a time, dancing around the ring and dispatching them with an expert series of blows. I moved with ease, as if I were spinning around them on ice skates, moving in to punch and then gliding back. First Franz fell, then Julius, and finally Gertz also collapsed in a heap. I stood above their prone bodies and heard the crowds cheering wildly. I raised my long arms over my head in victory. They seemed to reach all the way to the clouds.

Greta

AT FIVE-THIRTY THE NEXT MORNING MY ALARM CLOCK jolted me awake. I typically slept until at least seven, and at first I was so foggy, I couldn't remember why I had set the alarm in the first place. Then I felt my bruised face throb as I shifted my head against the pillow, and the events of the previous day came rushing back to me: my beating at the hands of the Wolf Pack, meeting Max Schmeling, and the barter. And I sprang up out of bed determined to fulfill Max's training regimen to the letter, including the daily three hundred. When he called for my first lesson, I would be ready. I vowed that every morning I would do sit-ups and push-ups as soon as I got out of bed; then I would run to the park near my house, which had a chin-up bar. The run to the park and back would equal about fifty minutes of roadwork.

It sounded simple. Yet when I got out of bed and tried to do the push-ups, I barely hit ten before my arms started to wobble. By the fifteenth, I could feel my chest and shoulder muscles shake, and by number seventeen I had collapsed. I was able to complete eighty sit-ups, just twenty shy of my goal.

I quickly got dressed in lightweight pants and a blue sweatshirt and ran to the park. The sky was just beginning to lighten, and the streets were relatively empty and quiet at that hour. As I passed the newsstand on our corner, a deliveryman unloaded bound stacks of morning papers onto the sidewalk. He nodded to me as I passed and watched me run by with a look that I took to be respect. I nodded back, straightened my posture, and ran a little faster. Along my route, I passed a milkman in a donkey cart making deliveries, a shabby old street sweeper pushing a rusted dustbin on wheels, even a weary prostitute walking home from a long night. I felt a satisfying surge of adrenaline at being the only person out there in training, seeing a side of the world I had never seen before. I was already someone different, someone special. The run to the park left me winded but still standing.

I stood in front of the bar, examining it. I had never tried to do chin-ups before. But how difficult could they be? I reached for the bar, which was cold and unforgiving. I pulled mightily, and my arms shook with the effort. I just barely got my chin over the bar once when my muscles gave out and I swung back down. I dangled from the bar for a few seconds, trying to find the strength for another pull, before falling to the ground, feeling utterly defeated. All of my energy from the run drained away as I picked myself up off the dirt and cursed my weakness. I might have good reach, but I was no athlete. I ran home, determined at least to fulfill the running portion of the three hundred.

Unfortunately, I ran out of steam and had to walk the last five minutes of the trip back to the apartment, leaving me with a total of 45 minutes of roadwork, 1 chin-up, 17 push-ups, and 80 sit-ups, for a grand total of 143. Not even half of the coveted 300. I sketched diagrams of the basic exercises into my journal, careful to capture what I thought was the perfect technique. Then I dutifully recorded my workout totals, disappointed at my poor results but determined to shovel the coal so at least I would have succeeded at one of my tasks.

Next I went to the basement to see our building superintendent, Herr Koplek, who lived in a small room adjacent to the furnace room. He was also an avowed fan of Hitler and kept a Nazi flag pinned to the outside of his door. He loyally read the Nazi tabloid, *Der Stürmer*, which featured the most virulent anti-Semitic articles and cartoons. I secretly swiped Herr Koplek's old copies of *Der Stürmer* and kept them under my mattress, but because of the pinups, not because of the Nazi propaganda.

My mother and father thought Herr Koplek an imbecile. When he first hung the Nazi flag on his door, my father said, "Koplek is just the kind of idiot who falls for that kind of

DAILY WORKOUT

sword rattling and chest pounding."

I hesitated for a moment but then took a deep breath and knocked on the door in the center of the swastika flag.

"*Ja?*" a gruff voice called from inside.

"It's Karl Stern, Herr Koplek."

I heard rustling from inside and then the door swung open, revealing Herr Koplek, a squat man with a thick red neck and a bristly gray brush cut, standing in his undershirt, looking annoyed.

"Well?" he asked impatiently.

"I wanted to see if you you'd allow me to shovel the morning coal for you?"

"Shovel the coal?" His eyes narrowed.

"Yes . . ."

"I'll not have you stealing from the building's supply for your stove," he said, shutting the door.

"No, Herr Koplek," I said, grabbing the door before it could close. "I'm in training."

"Training?" He paused. "Training for what?"

"To be a boxer."

He laughed. "A skinny thing like you would get snapped in half."

"That's why I need to shovel the coal, to build up strength. Herr Schmeling suggested it."

"Herr Schmeling?" he said, raising an eyebrow.

"Yes. He's going to teach me."

"Max Schmeling?"

"He's a friend of my father's."

"Why would a good German like Schmeling be friends with someone like your father?"

"My father sold him a painting just last night."

"Yes. I'm sure your father found a clever way to take his money."

"Can I shovel the coal? *Bitte?* You can watch me to make sure I don't steal."

He crossed his arms, his slow brain considering.

"Won't it save you work?" I added. "And give you time to tend to more important matters?"

"The coal pile is here," he said, indicating a large mound in the corner of the basement near the bottom of the chute that led up to the street. "You fill the wheelbarrow just to the top and load the furnace once in the morning and once in the evening."

"*Danke*, Herr Koplek."

"But if I find you stealing so much as a single piece, I'll have you dragged away by the police. Understand?"

I rolled up my sleeves, grabbed the shovel that stood against the wall by the coal pile, and started to fill the wheelbarrow. I dug into the pile and got into a pleasing rhythm, listening to the coal clunking into the metal bottom with a rich and satisfying thud. But after just a dozen shovels-ful, my hands and arms began to ache. With the barrow only half full, a blister formed on my right palm, just below the thumb. By the time it was full, my hands were throbbing in pain. I tipped the wheelbarrow up to move it toward the furnace, but I had taken just two steps when the barrow teetered and tipped over, spilling all of the coal.

"Not so easy, huh?" Koplek laughed. "Make sure you sweep up the dust pile."

Then he went back inside his room and shut the door. I cursed myself and reloaded the barrow. By the time I made it to the furnace, coal dust was coating my clothes and skin. I carefully opened the grated door of the iron furnace, a monstrous wheezing thing, with thick metal pipes sticking out of the top like gigantic arms punching through different points in the ceiling.

My shirt was filthy and soaked with sweat, so I decided to take it off to cool down and spare it further damage. The heat of the furnace stung my hands as I brought the shovel into its mouth and back. I felt a sharp wet pain on my palm as one of the blisters on my hand opened with a rip. I had to keep adjusting the shovel to find an undamaged patch of skin to rest the handle. I was nearly finished when I heard a girl's voice from behind me.

"Well, if it isn't Vulcan at his forge."

I turned to discover Greta Hauser, the greatest object of my desire, standing at the entrance to the basement, watching me with a bemused grin. I immediately felt self-conscious and could only imagine how ridiculous I looked with sweat and soot dripping down my skinny chest. I grabbed my shirt and put it back on, struggling to get my sticky arms into the sleeves.

"It's not polite to sneak up on someone like that."

"I wasn't sneaking, Vulcan. I just walked in."

"Vulcan?" I said.

"The god of fire. Don't they teach you anything at that school of yours?"

Greta and her family lived just downstairs from our apartment on the third floor. She was a year older than I was and had long platinum blond hair that she wore in a thick braid snaking down the center of her back. A small patch of freckles over her nose made her look younger. But her body was just the opposite. In just one year she had gone from being completely flat-chested to sprouting the most miraculous pair of breasts I had ever set eyes on. She wore a plain blue skirt and a white blouse, and a simple silver necklace hung from her neck with a four-leaf-clover charm.

I was never comfortable speaking with girls my own age, but with Greta I was absolutely hopeless. There was something mysterious and intelligent about her. Her eyes and expressions made it look like she was always thinking something clever, making silent judgments or observations. As much as I ogled her body, I also longed just to talk to her, to unravel some of her mystery. I imagined that if I could have her as my girlfriend, life would be perfect. She had come to the basement to retrieve a box of clothes from a storage bin opposite the furnace.

"I . . . uh . . . no. We haven't really covered the Greeks yet," I stammered.

"Vulcan was a Roman god. Wow, you really are dense. Hephaestus was the Greek god of fire."

"Right," I lied. "I know about Hephaestus, but we haven't

gotten to the Romans yet."

"They barely wore any clothes, you know," she said.

"Who?"

"The Greeks. In most of the statues you see of them, they're half naked. Isn't that funny?"

"Uh . . . yeah. I guess."

"I mean, didn't they get cold in the winter?"

"I don't know. Do they even have winter in Greece?" I said.

"Even I don't know that one, Vulcan," she replied.

Images of Greek gods and goddesses dancing naked in the snow played in my mind. I hoped she would ask me why I was shoveling the coal, so it would give me the opportunity to brag about Max Schmeling and my new life as a boxer. But she didn't ask.

"Well, see you later," she said.

And she turned and walked away; her long braid bounced against her back, swishing back and forth like a clock pendulum. I stared at that braid until she glided up the stairs out of view.

Principal Munter

FOR THE REST OF THE SUMMER, I DEVOURED THE PAPER for any scrap of information about Max. In June he traveled to Barcelona and fought Paulino "The Basque Woodchopper" Uzcudun to a draw. I hoped Max would return to Berlin after that bout, but instead he traveled to America to train and fight there.

Despite Max's absence, I continued my training regimen while on break from school. At first Herr Koplek would stand and watch me shovel the coal as he smoked his morning pipe. He smirked whenever I struggled and laughed if I dropped a shovelful. Yet as time passed, the shoveling got easier, and I felt new muscles forming on my arms, back, and shoulders. Herr Koplek soon lost interest.

Each day I nervously expected Greta Hauser to appear

behind me to retrieve something from her family's storage bin, so I would flex and extend my small arm muscles with each shovelful to make sure the biceps were accentuated as best I could, given what little I had to work with, just in case she walked in. The whole process took on the feeling of a performance. Yet she never showed up, and I performed my act for no audience at all.

I also started to chip away at the 300. The sit-ups were the easiest, probably because I was so light. Push-ups were harder, but I developed a pattern in which I added to my total every three days, and my numbers steadily grew. The hardest part of the 300 was the chin-ups. Within two weeks I could still do only 3 or 4, but then I had a breakthrough and was able to get to 10, which had felt like an impossible number when I started. Once I reached 10, my strength seemed to level off again, and it was a few days before I could push it to 11, 12, 13. By the time school started again, I still had not heard from Max, but I had raised my total from 143 to 225—still well shy of the 300, but good progress.

Hildy sometimes woke up early when she heard me at my morning routine and asked if she could come in and help count with me. Generally I said no, but if she persisted, I would let her record my results in my journal. She would sit on my bed with her stuffed rabbit, Herr Karotte, and count my reps. It was one thing to have my little sister as my training assistant, but I felt downright foolish every time I glanced up and saw Herr Karotte perched up next to her, staring at me. One day as I struggled to finish my push-ups, Hildy manipulated Herr Karotte's hand, as if he were counting along. My arms eventually gave way, and I collapsed onto my belly.

"Could you please put that stupid rabbit away?"

"He's not stupid," she replied. "He helps me count."

"Well, I'm going to use him as a punching bag if you don't get him out of my sight."

"Fine," she said, moving to the door. "Are you sure Max Schmeling is going to give you lessons?"

"Of course he is," I snapped back too defensively. "He and Papa made a deal."

"Then why hasn't he called?"

"He's in America," I replied. "He said he'd call when he was in Berlin."

In truth, I was starting to have my doubts about Max, but I would never admit them to Hildy.

Despite my newfound strength, I dreaded my return to school. On the first morning of the new term, I stood outside the entrance door near the stairwell where I had been attacked and hesitated. Would the Wolf Pack be waiting for me? Other kids streamed inside. My friend Kurt Seidler approached.

"Hey, Karl, you look like you're about as excited as I am to be back in there."

"Uh, yeah," I said.

"Well, let's go," he said. "Might as well, right?"

He pushed open the door, and I tentatively followed him inside. I exhaled as I saw no sign of the Wolf Pack and followed him upstairs.

That morning all the boys gathered for an address in the school auditorium. As I shuffled into my seat, I caught a glimpse of Gertz Diener entering one of the back rows, with Franz Hellendorf and Julius Austerlitz close behind him.

They wore small swastika pins on their sweaters. As I scanned the crowd, I saw many boys wearing some sort of Nazi or Hitler Youth insignia, from buttons to belt buckles, or kerchiefs around their necks. It seemed like overnight most German boys were decked out in some form of Nazi regalia. The Hitler Youth uniforms filled me with envy rather than fear. What boy wouldn't want to wear a military uniform?

When all the boys had settled into their seats, a huge man with a round red face capped by a full head of prematurely white hair strode onstage. He wore small, round spectacles, which sat over his eyes like tiny coins, accentuating his fat head, and a green Bavarian jacket with a small enamel swastika pin on his lapel.

Instead of saying, "Good morning, children," or "Welcome back," he raised his arm in the Nazi salute and shouted, "Heil Hitler." On cue, most of the boys in the auditorium raised their arms and returned the greeting. Not wanting to draw attention to myself for not doing it, I also returned the salute. The echo of the unified voices sent a chill down my back.

I sat next to Kurt and our other friend, Hans Karl-
weiss. Neither of them had joined the Hitler Youth, and they
seemed to be oblivious to all the changes that surrounded
us. Kurt yawned and Hans took a peek at a folded-up piece
of the sports page of the newspaper that he had tucked into
the sleeve of his shirt.

"Good." The huge man continued. "It's nice to hear your
strong German voices greet me this morning. Some of you
may have already heard that Principal Dietrich has been dismissed, because he did not agree with some of our school's
new policies. I am your new principal, Herr Munter. This
will be a glorious year for our school and our country. I
believe in high standards, hard work, and discipline. Our
Führer has challenged us to purify our nation from corrupting influences, and that goes for this school as well. I have
meticulously gone through our curriculum, and you will be
pleased to know the works of left-wing radicals and Jews
have already been removed from the library shelves."

He said the word "Jews" very casually, yet to my ears, it
felt as if he had screamed it at the top of his lungs.

"Also, I have been challenged to make sure every boy in
our school joins the Hitler Youth, and I am determined that
we meet this challenge. In your daily life I would also cau-
tion you to avoid corrupting influences, particularly Jews,
who are the greatest threat to our fatherland."

There it was. He hadn't just said the word "Jews" in
passing; he had warned every single boy in the school to
specifically avoid us. For a moment I wondered if he even

knew there were Jewish boys at the school. But then he let his eyes scan the crowd until they came to rest one by one on the few Jewish boys in the room: Benjamin Rosenberg, Mordecai Isaacson, Jonah Goldenberg, and Josef Katz. I prayed he would not include me with them, but finally his beady little spectacled eyes found me too and held my gaze.

I glanced at Kurt and Hans, sitting beside me, but they were tuned out, as if it were just another boring school address.

"Now, let us close by all singing our national anthem, '*Deutschland über Alles*,' followed by the 'Horst Wessel Song.'" As every boy began singing, I moved my lips, but I could barely make any sound come out. The Nazis had recently added the "Horst Wessel Song" as an official part of the country's anthem, and everyone was required to raise his hand in a Hitler salute during the first and fourth verses. I raised my arm and held it high with the others, but I could feel it begin to shake. Despite how much stronger I had become, I could barely get my arm to hold the salute. It ached and shook until finally the song ended and I could bring it back down to my lap.

The Return of Piss Boy

LUCKILY, HERR BOCH WAS AGAIN MY TEACHER, AND HE did not go out of his way to integrate Nazi ideals into his teaching. While other classes studied biology and received long lectures on the purity of Aryan blood versus Jewish, African, or Gypsy blood, Herr Boch stuck to traditional scientific knowledge. He taught us about Nobel Prize–winning scientist Karl Landsteiner's discovery of the ABO blood group system, which divided blood types into three basic categories, A, B, and O.

"Landsteiner later added a fourth type, AB," Herr Boch explained.

Hermann Reinhardt, a boy sitting near me, raised his hand.

"Excuse me, Herr Boch, but did Herr Landsteiner

experiment on Aryan blood or did he use other kinds too?"

"I have no idea whose blood he used."

"I just read in an article in *Der Stürmer* that a scientist has proved that Gypsies and Jews have rat blood in their veins. So wouldn't they fall into a different type?"

"Any scientist *Der Stürmer* would write about probably has a brain the size of a rat," Herr Boch replied. "All human blood is basically the same."

Despite Herr Boch's deft handling of the question, blood was very much on my mind. *Der Stürmer* frequently ran pseudoscientific articles about blood researchers who were proving Hitler's theories of racial superiority, along with medieval myths about Jews' kidnapping Christian children and drinking their blood in strange religious rituals. There was so much talk about blood, I wondered if my own blood *was* different in some way. Jews, Africans, and Gypsies were darker than Aryans, so perhaps they did have some darker element in their blood.

Hans and Kurt knew I was Jewish but didn't seem to care, because like most boys, they took their cues from their fathers, who had not yet joined the Nazi Party. Most of the other boys at school were indifferent to me. My non-Jewish looks still helped to insulate me from the daily hazing that started following Benjamin, Jonah, Mordecai, and Josef. The Wolf Pack, however, had me squarely in their sights. Their ranks had grown significantly, and I carefully avoided them on the schoolyard and tried to stick as close to Kurt and Hans as possible. But many days I came to my locker to discover folded-up pieces of paper stuck inside with anti-Semitic passages from *Mein Kampf,* like vicious little valentines.

One afternoon in between classes I had to go to the bathroom. As I pushed my hand against the door to enter, I felt a shove from behind. I stumbled and fell onto the hard bathroom floor. The black-and-white tiles formed a checkerboard pattern, and I followed the small squares to a row of shoes forming a circle around me.

"You've done a good job of avoiding us," Gertz said, stepping into the room and standing over me.

I looked up and saw that Julius, Franz, and at least four other boys from various grades surrounded me. I lunged toward the door, but Julius and Gertz grabbed me by the arms and pulled me back, pinning my arms behind me.

"Halt!" Franz snapped.

"We have so many new members who have yet to meet you," Gertz added, gesturing to the other boys in the room. "Take a good look, boys. On the outside, he appears like us, but his blood and his cock are pure Jew."

I scanned the faces around me, all of them eager with anticipation at what might happen next.

"Let me go," I said, twisting in their grasp. I flexed my muscles against their grips and shocked them and myself by actually pulling my arms free. I didn't fully realize until that moment how much stronger I was than the last time they had confronted me.

"Grab him!"

"Don't let him get away!"

I stepped back and put up my fists and assumed what I hoped looked like a convincing defensive pose. Before I could throw a punch, Julius, Franz, and Gertz grabbed me again and held my arms more firmly.

"No fighting today, Piss Boy," Gertz hissed in my ear. "We've devised a new method of initiation for our little group. Each member has to baptize a Jew."

He signaled to the new boys, and one by one they entered one of the stalls and urinated into the bowl. I heard their streams filling the bowl. When all four had emptied themselves into the same toilet, they maneuvered me toward the stall.

"Time for your baptism."

Again, I twisted and tried to pull free, kicking wildly with my legs.

"Grab him!" Gertz commanded.

Two of the new boys grabbed my legs and hoisted me up, so I was fully horizontal, like they were carrying a rolled-up carpet. They moved my head toward the toilet, which was now nearly full. The other boys laughed as they bent my head down. I quickly held my breath as I felt my hair and top of my face plunge into the water. I clamped my eyes shut, tightening every muscle and pore in my head to block anything from penetrating the skin. I heard them counting to ten above me. *"Eins! Zwei! Drei! Vier! . . ."*

When they reached ten, the toilet flushed, and I felt an enormous whirling sensation as fresh water poured down into the bowl and in and around my face and the old water was sucked out. My hair twisted down into the porcelain mouth at the bottom of the bowl and then back up as the suction of the flushing subsided. They pulled my body up and dumped me back on the floor in the middle of the room. Urine and water ran off my hair and into my eyes and down my face. I coughed and spat, and they laughed. I felt like vomiting, but choked back the urge, not wanting to give them the satisfaction. Anger rose up inside me, but not as much toward the Wolf Pack as toward Max Schmeling. If he had honored his bargain, I would've been able to defend myself. Just like Gertz and the others, he had probably decided my father and I were dirty Jews.

"Welcome to the club," Gertz said to the four new boys. "Thanks, Piss Boy," he said to me as they all filed out.

That was the last time I ever used a bathroom at school.

Barely Floating

By December it had been six months since the barter. From stories in the newspaper I knew Max had been back in Berlin for several weeks. When I saw yet another gossip-page photo of Max and Anny emerging from a movie theater just a few blocks from our apartment, I realized he was never coming for me. And my hero worship turned to pure bitterness. I continued my training regimen, but now I was motivated by anger. That morning, as I dug into the coal pile, I imagined flinging each shovelful right at him. I resolved to find another teacher and become a great fighter despite Max. In my most exaggerated fantasy, I imagined myself becoming a heavyweight contender and defeating Schmeling himself, with my long arms snapping off a series of rapid-fire punches. "Remember me, Max?" I'd say, standing over his prone bloody body. "Next time, maybe you'll honor your bargains." And I'd strip his European Champion's belt from around his waist and hoist it high over my head to thunderous applause. Of course, to make the fantasy complete, Greta Hauser would be sitting ringside in a tight sweater, waiting to press her body against mine.

In late February we could no longer afford to pay Frau Kressel. The news of her departure sent Hildy into a fit of crying. My mother took the news even harder. On the day she was leaving, my mother retreated to the bathroom to soak in a hot tub and would not come out.

My father was at the gallery when Frau Kressel came to say good-bye to me and my sister. She wore her big overcoat and a kerchief tied over her head. Hildy clung to her as if she wouldn't let go.

"Listen to me," Frau Kressel said. "You both need to be good children for me. *Ja?* Karl, you are a man now, so you must look after your sister and your mother."

I nodded, but in truth at that moment I felt like a little baby. I envied Hildy that she was able to curl up in Frau Kressel's arms and cry.

"Be patient with your mother. She has a hard time, but she loves you. You are both good children. You will be fine."

Neither of us replied. Both of us were thinking: No. We will not be fine! How will we get along? Who will cook for us? Who will bandage our cuts and scrapes? Who will run the house?

She gave Hildy one final hug, and then she hugged me

and kissed me on both of my cheeks and on my forehead. Then she picked up her small suitcase and walked out of our apartment. Hildy and I stood in the silence for a moment as if hoping Frau Kressel would walk back in, but she didn't.

Whenever my mother retreated to the bath, my father instructed us to carefully monitor her to make sure she didn't fall asleep. So every ten minutes or so one of us would knock on the door to make sure she was still awake, and she'd reply with a faint *ja*.

On the stove Frau Kressel had left a large platter of *Knödel* covered with a white dish towel, along with a small bowl of thick brown gravy. She knew the potato dumplings were our favorite of her Bavarian recipes. She mixed just a touch of grated hard cheese with the mashed potatoes before shaping them into the dumplings and dropping them into the boiling water. The cheese added a little sharpness to the smooth, buttery potato. Hildy and I helped ourselves to plates and ate in silence. The dumplings were so smooth and creamy, you barely needed to chew them. But that night the flavor seemed dull and flat, and we both ate without any pleasure.

After finishing dinner, I cleared the dishes while Hildy went to check on our mother again. She knocked on the bathroom door, but there was no reply.

"Mama! Mama!" she called, but there was still no answer.

"Karl!" she shouted.

I ran down the hall and knocked again.

"Mama!" I called.

Hildy's eyes met mine, and I reached for the doorknob. Steam filled the bathroom, and as Hildy and I stepped inside the damp, warm space, we saw our mother lying in the tub, her face just barely floating above the waterline with her eyes closed. It shocked me to see her small, round breasts floating up and breaking the surface of the water, her light brown hair gently swirling around her neck and chest in slow motion like sea plants at the bottom of the ocean.

"Mama!" Hildy cried, and ran over to shake her.

Under the weight of Hildy's touch, our mother's face submerged under the water for just a moment, and she choked and gasped as water went up her nose. Her eyes fluttered open. I ran over and pushed her into a sitting position.

"Mama, wake up!" I said.

She mumbled an inaudible reply.

"Come on, let's get her out of there," I said.

I took her by the hands and was surprised at their cold whiteness. Trying my best to avoid looking at her naked body, I hoisted her out of the tub.

"Get a towel," I commanded Hildy.

Hildy wrapped the towel around Mama's shoulders, the water dripping all over the floor and onto us both as we struggled to dry her off and get her into her robe. As we led her back toward her room, Mama was half awake and swayed from side to side down the hall like a sleepwalker. It was all I could do to keep her balanced on my shoulder. We finally got her into bed and tucked her under the covers. The skin of her hands was swollen and pruned and reminded me of the frogs preserved in formaldehyde we used in science class.

Once she was in bed, her eyes closed, and she seemed to drift off to sleep. Just as we were finishing tucking her beneath the blankets, I heard our father enter the apartment's entryway.

"*Hallo?*" he called.

Hildy and I came out to meet him, both of us dripping wet.

"What is this? You're getting water all over the floor."

Hildy started crying.

"What is it?"

"Mama fell asleep in the bathtub, and we had to get her out," I said.

"*Verdammt,*" he cursed under his breath.

He strode down the hall and entered their bedroom and closed the door. He emerged a few minutes later and returned to the kitchen.

"Hildegard, make your mother some tea. Karl, come with me."

He walked to his small office off the living room and opened his briefcase. He unzipped its hidden compartment and removed a package wrapped in brown paper tied with twine. He placed them on the table.

"I have a delivery to make tonight. And since I have to look after your mother, you're going to have to make it for me."

The Countess

I HAD NEVER MADE A DELIVERY FOR MY FATHER BEFORE. Every week he and my mother printed material for private clients on the old press at the gallery; I knew these pages didn't have anything to do with gallery business. They always kept the contents secret from Hildy and me. They'd wrap the pages in brown paper and deliver them around the city at odd hours. I never knew who any of their customers were. And they were always careful to conceal their deliveries beneath other things in case the police stopped them. Papa's briefcase had a secret zippered compartment along one of the sidewalls, and my mother hid her deliveries in a grocery bag under some pieces of fruit and a box or two of dry crackers. As the deliveries became more frequent and more secretive, my curiosity intensified. Now I would finally get a peek inside this secret world.

No matter who they were, I knew we were lucky to have the printing customers, because business at the gallery had all but dried up. My father had not staged an opening since Hartzel's and had only been dealing with private clients looking to buy and sell specific pieces. Most of his customers were Jews looking to liquidate their art collections to raise money to leave the country and bargain-hunting collectors looking to take advantage of that desperate market.

My father handed me the package, which appeared to be a simple sheaf of papers, maybe a hundred sheets at most. I measured the weight in my hands as if it might give me a clue as to what was printed on them. My father helped me load the package into my rucksack, concealing it beneath a stack of schoolbooks and papers.

"Go to Fourteen Budapesterstrasse," my father instructed. "Ring apartment number three and ask for the Countess."

My mind came alive at the memory of the torn flyer with the suggestive message I had found in the gallery basement. Would I actually get to meet this mystery woman?

"The countess of what?"

"Just the Countess."

"What if she's not there?"

"Walk around the block a couple of times and try again. But she'll be there. The Countess rarely goes out. And she's expecting the delivery."

"What if I get stopped? What if the police want to see what's in the bag?"

"They won't."

"But what if they do?"

"Tell them you're making a delivery for someone who approached you at the train station. He just gave you a few marks to make the delivery."

"What's in the package?"

"It's better that you don't know. If you get stopped, you'll not have to lie as much."

"But what if—"

"Karl." He cut me off. "Just do as I say. Now, when you get there, don't ask questions or stare at anybody for too long. Just drop off the package and go."

I hefted the rucksack onto my back and headed out. Once out on the streets, I carefully glanced about to make sure no one watched or followed me. A strange electric feeling coursed through me at being part of a covert mission. Most of the people out at that hour were commuters coming home, newsboys selling the evening editions of the paper, and a few fruit vendors trying to unload their last few apples and pears. I stiffened as I passed a pair of police officers, but they didn't give me a glance.

As I walked toward the Budapesterstrasse, the sky turned from the dull yellow of the winter sunset to the gray-blue of early evening. The air was cold, and I tried to blow rings with the steam that huffed out of my mouth as if I were smoking a cigarette in a spy movie.

The package wasn't heavy, but it weighed on my back as if I were carrying a living, breathing organism that was calling out to me, "Just open me up and take a look. I won't bite." My mind danced with possibilities. Perhaps my father was working with a monarchist resistance movement led by a rich countess, and he was supplying them with arms and ammunition and this was a catalog of his latest line of weapons. Or maybe the Countess was an underworld figure like a character from a Jimmy Cagney gangster movie, and the papers were some sort of numbers racket or a price list of illegal narcotics.

Most likely the Countess was just another art collector and the papers contained images of banned paintings or sculptures my father was trying to sell. Even that scenario had an air of danger and excitement to it. My father was a black marketeer, living outside the law, and now I was to be a cog in his underworld operation. But why would the Countess not come to the gallery or the house like other collectors?

The package continued to squirm and call out to me until the temptation became too great. I furtively ducked into an alley behind some garbage cans and ripped open the rucksack. My fingers twitched as I slowly peeled open the tape that sealed the brown paper wrapping, careful not to cause any rips and keep the tape unfolded and flat, so I could reseal it. The first couple of pages were blank, but when I lifted them off, I caught an image that took me completely by surprise. It was a simple illustration of two people dancing. What made the image so strange was that both of the people were men with slicked-back hair, wearing tuxedos. The caption above the image read:

THE COUNTESS PRESENTS ANOTHER PRIVATE
WINTER BALL FOR THE BEAUTIFUL BOYS OF BERLIN

Printed beneath the image of the men dancing were a date, a time, and an address, with instructions to "Knock three times, pause, and then knock four more to gain entry to paradise. If you forget the knock, you can forget the ball, boys!"

My throat went dry, and a deep knot of nausea formed in my stomach. My father was not running guns or in league with exciting criminals like in a Jimmy Cagney movie. He was somehow in league with homosexuals. It was risky enough being Jewish, but associating with homosexuals would put us at an even greater risk. Even Jews didn't like homosexuals. It was the one thing everyone seemed to agree on.

I felt the strongest urge to throw the pages into the trash and walk away and let my father and the homosexuals deal with the consequences. But I knew we needed money. I carefully resealed the package and returned it to my rucksack and made my way to the Countess's apartment building.

When I rang the bell, a strange voice called from inside: "Just a minute, love."

A few minutes later the door opened to reveal the Countess, a tall woman approximately my mother's age, with striking blue eyes and platinum blond hair tucked under a fancy turban. She wore a long dressing gown made of white fabric with a strange blue and black geometric pattern running up and down the front that looked vaguely

Egyptian. I followed the pattern down to the bottoms of her legs, which were sheathed in fishnet stockings. Her rather large feet were sandwiched into gold high-heeled sandals.

"*Ja?*" she said.

"I have a delivery for the Countess."

"I am she. Come in, come in."

She beckoned me inside, and I stepped into the dimly lit hallway. A strange smell—heavy, sweet, and smoky—caught my nose..

"Oh, how lovely, Sig finally sent a delivery *boy*," she purred. That's when I saw the Adam's apple bobbing in her throat and the faintest outline of five-o'clock shadow beneath a layer of makeup. Then I noticed a few stray chest hairs on the otherwise smooth skin.

I did my best to conceal my shock and quickly removed the package from my school bag and handed it to the Countess. He reached inside the top of his dressing gown and pulled out a roll of bills that was somehow tucked inside. I accepted the bills, which to my distress were warm and slightly moist. I turned to exit, wanting to flee as fast as possible.

"Wait a minute," the Countess said. I considered ignoring him—or her? What were you supposed to call those people? But then he placed a hand on my shoulder.

"Are you Karl?"

I froze. How did this person know my name? He turned me around.

"Yes!" he said. "You must be."

"How do you know my name?"

"The Countess knows all, *mein Liebster*."

He touched the bottom of my chin, assessing my face. His manner had lost all pretense of flirtation, and he seemed to be examining me with sincere interest, almost affection.

"You don't look much like your father, but I can see a little bit of his expression in your face."

I subtly jerked my head aside.

"How do you know my father?" I asked impulsively. Part of me dreaded hearing the answer.

"Ah, Sig and I go way back, dear. He's never mentioned me?"

"No."

"Well, he is a secretive man in many ways, I suppose. And a great man, but don't tell him I said that. Wouldn't want to swell his head. You *can* tell him I said that his son was a very impressive young man."

He touched my cheek again, and I instinctively jerked away from the caress. I had no intention of telling my father any such thing.

"I have to go," I said.

A young man with short blond hair appeared at the other end of the hall. He wore a knee-length bathrobe and appeared to have nothing on underneath. He held up a plate of food and called: "*Komm*, Baby! Your food is getting cold."

"All right, Fritz! I'll be there in a minute," the Countess called over his shoulder. He reached into the top of his dressing gown and pulled out another couple of bills. "Here, something extra for you."

He pressed the money into my hands.

"Be safe out there," he said.

I walked out of the apartment and stumbled back out onto the street, feeling dazed and sick to my stomach. How did my father know this person? Was Papa a homosexual himself? My most disturbing private fears about my father came crashing into my head. He did have a flamboyant way about him. I had always thought that the blue silk scarf he loved to wear was a very girlish affectation. He had represented artists who did male nudes. If my father was a homosexual, what did that mean for me? Did I have homosexual blood in my veins too? And what about my poor mother? Did she have to suffer through the humiliation of having a homosexual husband? Perhaps that was the reason for her "moods." My skin crawled under the places where the Countess had touched me, and anger rose up in me against my father for exposing me to that world.

When I arrived back home, the front of the apartment was dark. I decided just to give my father the money and go straight to bed. I heard muffled voices from the kitchen, which lifted my spirits slightly because it meant my mother had probably emerged. I took the money out, careful to withhold the tip the Countess had given me, and walked toward the kitchen to present it to my father.

Then I heard a familiar voice, though I couldn't place it at first. I paused and listened. The voice was low and manly and boomed with a hearty laugh at something my father said. I slowly wound my way down the hall. The voice grew louder, clearer, and more familiar, and my heartbeat quickened. I entered the kitchen and saw my father sitting with Max Schmeling at our table over cups of tea. I was so shocked to see him, I was literally struck dumb, unable to move or speak for a moment.

"Ah, there he is," my father said. "Out making mischief again, Karl?"

Max stood up, and his height and the sheer physical force of his presence awed me. He extended a hand.

"Karl, good to see you again."

I was so dazed, I reached out the hand carrying the folded money. Max chuckled.

"You are already trying to pay me! That's good. A trainer should be well paid."

My father laughed and reached over and plucked the bills from my hand.

"Karl was just picking up some cash for me that I had left at the gallery."

"Hello, Herr Schmeling," I said, finally shaking his hand.

"I owe you an apology," he said. "I got so caught up in preparing for the Uzcudun fight and other things, I forgot all about our deal. Anny reminded me because just this very week we finally hung the portrait of me by Grosz in our country house. Are you still interested in the lessons?"

PART II
1935-1937

"To truly succeed in the ring, a boxer must live for the sport. You must train yourself to eat, sleep, and breathe boxing, no matter what else is going on in your life."

Helmut Müller, *Boxing Basics for German Boys*

The Berlin Boxing Club

Mist rose off the cobblestone streets as I made my way by a row of tall industrial buildings along the Spree River. As I walked, I anxiously fingered a piece of paper with the Berlin Boxing Club's address written on it, although I had long ago committed it to memory. Something about the piece of paper anchored me, as if it were some sort of magical pass. It was a rough neighborhood. Garbage, horse manure, and broken glass filled the gutters, and rats scurried in and around the alleyways. Despite my being intimidated by the environment, it also thrilled me, and filled me with excited anticipation about the type of fearless man I would become through my boxing training.

I finally arrived at an old brick factory that took up half a city block. The Berlin Boxing Club occupied the top floor.

Frosted glass laced with steel wire covered the windows, so I could see only vague shadows of activity inside. A textile company that manufactured wool blankets filled the bottom three floors, and as I climbed the wide iron staircase, I heard the loud whir of weaving machines and the deep thumps of pounding mechanisms smoothing rough-hewn cloth into fine fabric. I reached the top floor and paused outside the door, which featured faded gold letters:

THE BERLIN BOXING & HEALTH CLUB
ESTABLISHED 1906
MEMBERS ONLY

I tried to hear what was going on inside, but any noise was drowned out by the sounds of the machines on the other floors. The mechanical pounding seemed to match my heartbeat as I took a deep breath and opened the door.

Inside was a hive of activity. Two full-size boxing rings dominated the center of the main room. In each, pairs of men sparred with each other under the watchful eyes of trainers. In one corner stood a row of heavy bags and speed bags, and on the other side were weight-lifting apparatuses and barbells with men training in all areas. Posters and photographs of fighters of the past and present lined the walls. Some of the posters dated back to the early part of the century and featured fighters with strange mustaches standing with their bare fists cocked, while others depicted recent champions, including Jack Dempsey, Gene Tunney,

Max Dieckmann, and, of course, Max Schmeling.

The sounds of men hitting speed bags and jumping rope mingled with the guttural grunts of exertion and blended into a strange primitive symphony. The place also had a very distinct animal smell that was warm and damp like a butcher shop on a summer day.

I wandered inside unaware of the short, bald man sitting behind a counter near the door, chewing on the stub of a cigar. Beside him, a huge, thick-headed man with small eyes folded towels. A large fighter covered in sweat leaned against the counter drinking from a water jug. He looked as if he had just finished a training session. The short man with the cigar called out to me with a heavy Polish accent: "Where do you think you're going?"

"I'm here to box."

"You a member?"

"No, but—"

"Didn't think so. Look, you're too young for this club. We don't have a youth program here. This gym is for real fighters."

"I could use this kid to pick my teeth, right, Worjyk?" the fighter said to the bald man with a laugh.

"Yeah," Worjyk added, "or you could fold him up and use him to wipe your ass."

"Nah, he's too thin for toilet paper."

Worjyk and the fighter laughed harder. The third man folding towels shook his head with a small smile. My face burned. I had hoped that my training had added enough bulk to my frame to pass for "normal," but I was still skinny as a rail.

"I'm supposed to meet—"

"*Verschwinde!*" Worjyk gestured with his cigar toward the door. "I don't have time for this."

Worjyk turned away to continue his conversation with the fighter. The big thick-headed man folding towels finally spoke. Despite his bulk, he had a soft voice and spoke with a stutter.

"Thh-there are youth clubs that have b-b-b-boxing around. You should be able to find wawawa-one."

I scanned the gym to see if I could find Max, but he wasn't there. I couldn't believe he had let me down again. I turned to exit, and just as I reached for the door, Max entered, carrying a small gym bag. When the fighter slouching against the counter saw Max, he immediately straightened as if coming to military attention, and Worjyk's face opened up into a smile.

"Max, welcome back."

"Good to see you, Worjyk."

The two men shook hands. The other fighter offered a hand to Max, and they shook too.

"Herr Schmeling, it's an honor."

"Are you going to be training with us again, Max?"

"Training and teaching," Max replied. "I see you've met my protégé, Karl. He's going to be the next German Youth Champion."

He placed a hand on my shoulder, and I felt myself puff

up as if my body were being hoisted by a pulley.

"We were just welcoming him to the club," Worjyk lied.

"Good," Max said. "I need to get him signed up for a membership right away. He'll be training here."

"Not a problem, Max."

Max turned to the big man folding towels.

"Neblig, help get Karl set up with a locker and some gear."

"Sh-sh-sh-sh-sure, Max."

Neblig came around and walked me back to the locker room to the left of the entryway. He led me to my own small locker and gave me a key, a towel, and some tape that I assumed I would use to wrap my hands. At the end of the lockers stood a rusted metal bin, filled with discarded white towels spilling over the top. Some of the towels were smudged with light pink bloodstains, and I thought: This is where real men challenge themselves. Real men aren't afraid to bleed.

"Excuse me," I said. "Am I supposed to have gloves?"

"Th-th-they don't allow bare-knuckle f-f-f-fighting," Neblig replied with a laugh. Now even the janitor was laughing at me. I cursed myself for not thinking of gloves. I guess I had assumed there would be a supply of them on hand. I certainly didn't want to have to ask Max for anything; he was already being so generous by just showing up.

"Is there a place here I can buy—"

"N-n-n-n-not here. You've got to go to an athletic s-s-s-supply store."

Neblig read my disappointment and walked over to a small janitor's closet nearby, filled with brooms, mops, buckets, and other cleaning supplies. He moved aside some boxes of powdered soap on the top shelf and extracted an old pair of boxing gloves.

"H-h-h-here," he said, tossing them to me. I caught the gloves and felt the cracked brown leather, soft yet hard at the same time. These were not toys but fighting instruments.

"Th-th-those are my old ones," he said.

"How much do you want for them?"

"You can b-b-b-borrow them. J-j-j-just remember me when you're a champion, *ja*?"

"Thanks," I said, meeting his eyes with a serious nod. "I will. I'm Karl," I said, extending my hand.

"You can call me Neblig," he replied as we shook.

Neblig returned to the closet, grabbed a broom, and went to work sweeping the floor by the toilets. Nervous and excited, I tucked the gloves under my arm and walked out to the main room, wondering what I would learn first. Maybe Max would demonstrate how to properly use the speed bag. Perhaps he would show me how to work out with the weights. Or maybe he'd start by testing me on my mastery of the three hundred. This thought filled me with anxiety, as I was still well shy of that number. I found Max standing beside one of the boxing rings, where two men sparred. Max cheered encouragement and comments as the men circled each other, trading punches.

"Good, Johann, give him that jab." Max noticed me

approaching. "Ah, Karl, come take a look. See how Johann circles his man. That's good footwork. Too many people go to the fights just to see the punches, when the real action is happening with the legs. Just watch his feet for a while."

I watched the two fighters and found it hard not to concentrate on the punches being thrown and blocked. Their muscled arms snapped back and forth, looking for an opening and then coming back to defend the body. But when I turned my attention down, I saw their feet were engaged in a battle of their own, circling and dodging with surprising deliberateness, almost as if it were some sort of dance.

"How many fights have you been in?" Max asked me.

"Boxing matches? None."

"No. I mean real fights. With other boys in the school-yard."

I considered the question. I had not really been in any fights. Max knew I had been beaten up from the way I had looked on the night he first met me. But that was nothing I would consider a fight, because I had not fought back.

"None really."

"Then we've got to get you fighting right away," Max said.

He rang the bell attached to the side of the ring, and both men stopped sparring.

"Hey, Johann," he called to the shorter man. "Would you mind letting Karl step into the ring with you for a couple of minutes?"

Johann was a lean fighter with dirty blond hair and a

large nose that was bent to one side and looked as if it had been broken more than once.

"Sure, Max," he said as the other man stepped out of the ring.

"You're kidding, right?" I said.

"No," Max replied. "I want to see what kind of instincts you have. Here, get your gloves on and I'll get you a mouthpiece."

Max walked away toward the locker room.

Instincts! My only instinct was to run and hide or cry. I couldn't believe he was putting me in the ring. And this guy Johann wasn't another kid; he was a grown man and a real fighter. I had been certain we would start my training by my demonstrating my mastery of the three hundred, or maybe jumping rope and learning how to hit the punching bags, not actually fighting. My body went cold. It was all I could do to stop my teeth from chattering and my knees from clacking together like a frightened cartoon character's.

I watched the muscles ripple on Johann's back as he raised a bottle and took a drink and spat into a metal bucket in one corner of the ring. I looked closely at his face, and in addition to the broken nose, he had a couple of visible scars, one on his chin, the other on his forehead. I was a couple of inches taller than he was, but I felt like he would destroy me with one punch.

Max came back and handed me a small mouthpiece made of black rubber.

"Here, put this in and step into the ring."

"But I don't know how to box," I whispered.

"There is an art to boxing and plenty of skills to learn, but at the end of the day, boxing is just fighting, plain and simple. Right, Johann?" Max winked at the fighter, who nodded back to him.

Several of the men in the gym stopped what they were doing and gathered around the ring to watch.

I pushed the mouthpiece into my mouth. It tasted bitter.

"Bite down on that, but not too hard or you'll give yourself a headache," Max advised me. I tried to loosen my grip on the mouthpiece, but my jaw kept tightening in a nervous pulse, as if I could bite away the tension.

I pulled myself up to the outer rim of the ring and tried to navigate my lanky frame between the ropes. It was not as easy as it looked. I ducked my head under the top rope and pulled myself through to the other side. Yet my foot caught on the bottom rope as I was coming through. I lost my balance and tripped into the ring, falling face-first onto the mat. I tried to break my fall with my gloved hands but wound up knocking over the spit bucket, which spilled everywhere. The men laughed.

"Well, Max, he knocked out the spit bucket with no problem," one of them said.

"Let's call him Kick the Bucket Karl!" Worjyk called over from the counter.

"Or how about the Spit Bucket Kid'" another fighter quipped. More laughter.

I almost gagged from the humiliation. After being

dubbed Piss Boy by the Wolf Pack, I couldn't bear another demeaning nickname. Neblig appeared with his mop and cleaned the small mess and set the spit bucket right. He saw the fear in my face.

"D-d-d-don't worry," he whispered. "You'll be o-o-okay."

He stepped back out of the ring, and I was alone, facing Johann, who waited for me at the center of the ring, looking serious. He nodded and gestured for me to come forward.

"Get in there and keep your hands up," Max said. "Just try to hit him without allowing him to hit you. That's really all there is to it."

I walked to the center of the ring like a prisoner approaching the gallows. I tried to tell myself that we would only be sparring and that he wouldn't really try to knock me out. But I was deathly afraid of being hurt. The last time I had been punched, it had taken weeks for the bruises to completely heal.

I finally came to meet Johann at the center of the ring. Max rang the bell, and Johann assumed a fighting stance.

"Get your hands up!" Max shouted.

I put my hands up, and Johann started to move around me. What was I supposed to do? My body froze in the same way it had when I'd squared off against Franz.

"Now, try to attack!" Max said.

Johann circled me, watching me closely from behind his raised gloves, waiting for me to make a move. The men surrounding the ring shouted catcalls and encourage-ments: "Come on!" "Let's see some action." "Come on, *Spit*

Bucket—fight!" "Mix it up." "We want a refund!"

My heart raced in my chest, and sweat beads sprouted on my forehead. Somehow my body lurched forward, and mustering all of my will, I threw a right-handed punch at Johann. I aimed the punch directly at his chest, but he was moving, so it barely touched the side of his arm. The crowd roared.

"Good!" Max said. "Attack!"

I moved back toward him. This time my punch was better timed and landed near the center of his body. Johann was easily able to knock the punch away, but at least I had gotten closer to the target.

Before I could think, Johann moved toward me, and in a flash he threw two quick punches, one that landed on my left arm and the other on the side of my stomach. I could tell he was not punching at full strength, but the punches had enough force to send me stumbling back, tripping over my feet. I desperately balanced myself and managed to stay upright. I felt small, tingly stings where the punches had landed, but my adrenaline was pumping so fast, I didn't register any pain. The crowd whooped and hollered.

"Keep your hands up!" Max shouted.

I threw my hands back up just in time. Johann came back at me with another combination of punches. The first punch came at my head, but I managed to block it. The next two punches were jabs to the center of my belly that sucked all the wind out of me. I audibly gasped, and the men around the ring laughed as I struggled to suck in more breath. My gut ached, and it felt as if someone were sitting on my chest and stomach. I scanned the laughing faces around the ring.

Then something happened. Instead of getting more scared, I got angry. The feeling built inside me like a quick-boiling pot until it shot me forward at Johann like a jet of hot steam.

Johann's smirk melted into a look of surprise as I moved in and started throwing wild punches. None of the punches really landed, but he still had to constantly move his hands to defend himself. He danced away from me and quickly counterpunched with a couple of blows that landed on my body, though I barely felt them. I punched at him again, and this time I felt one of my fists penetrate his defenses and actually land on his body. I'll never forget the feeling of that punch, when my fist actually connected on his exposed flesh and it yielded just a bit. I had often heard people talk about a punch "connecting," and I finally understood what that really meant. The punch had mass and weight, and a wonderful electric thrill ran down my hand and across my body as I sensed his muscles tighten. He even gave a small grunt.

The crowd gave a loud WHOA and laughed.

Johann instantly moved forward and landed a couple of quick punches, including one to the side of my face. Up until that moment he hadn't really been aiming for above my neck, and the punch sent my head snapping back. I stumbled backward but again was somehow able to stay on my feet. I saw him moving toward me, and I knew my hands were down and I was totally exposed. But then I noticed something wonderful. I wasn't afraid. I was thinking: Get your hands up and move. Just as Johann was about to move in for some more, Max rang the bell, and Johann lowered his hands.

The crowd let up a groan of disappointment.

My heart beat so fast, I thought it might pop out of my chest.

Johann came forward and put a glove on my shoulder.

"Not bad, kid. You actually landed a punch on me."

"Good," Max said as I approached. "You've got a nice natural jab. Some people never learn that. How do you feel?"

"Fine," I said, so out of breath I had difficulty getting any words out.

"Do you know how long you were in there with him?"

I had no idea, so I guessed. "Three minutes?"

"Three minutes?" Max laughed. "It was about fifty seconds."

I couldn't believe that. It had felt like I had been in there for an eternity.

"Every second in the ring feels like a minute, and every minute can feel like an hour. That's why conditioning is so important to a fighter," he explained. "It's an endurance test. Today you had a very important lesson on taking punches. A lot of people will tell you that the first thing you have to learn is how to take a punch. But I believe the first thing you should know is that you can take one and survive. A punch won't kill you. Conquering your fear is the first step to becoming a powerful fighter."

He took a small red book out of his back pocket and

handed it to me. It was *Boxing Basics for German Boys* by Helmut Müller.

"This book should help you. But remember, you can't learn the fight game from a book. Experience is the best teacher. Read the book for some basics, and the next time we'll learn some skills."

Pandora's Box

I FLOATED HOME FROM THE GYM THAT NIGHT. NOT ONLY had I not run away or wet my pants like a coward, I had taken punches and landed one of my own. I had entered a new world, a world of men and warriors. I was Max Schmeling's protégé. And a dream of becoming German Youth Champion began to crystallize in my mind.

When I got home, I went right to the basement to shovel the evening coal into the furnace. I enthusiastically dug into the coal pile and got into an easy shoveling rhythm, replaying all the events of the day in my head.

"Back at work again, Vulcan?" Greta's voice called from behind me.

I turned to discover her holding a large cardboard box that she had retrieved from her family's storage locker. She wore a tight gray sweater and had her beautiful blond braid draped over one shoulder. While typically the sight of Greta left me a blabbering mess, that night I felt calm and confident. Since our last meeting I had studied up on ancient mythology.

"I prefer to be called Hephaestus," I said. "The Greeks are better than the Romans any day."

"Oh, really?" she said.

My adrenaline and testosterone were at a full boil, so I boldly walked toward her.

"Yeah, you know that Hephaestus created the first woman, right?"

"Hera?" she asked, unsure of herself.

"Hera was a goddess—Zeus's wife. What do they teach you at that school of yours? I'm talking about Pandora."

"Oh, that's right," she said, recovering her composure.

"Zeus ordered Hephaestus to create Pandora to punish mankind for stealing the secret of fire. So if I'm Hephaestus, I guess that makes you Pandora. She had a box too," I said, gesturing to the cardboard box she carried. "Her box released all the evils of mankind—vanity, greed, envy, lust. . . ."

I stared into her eyes.

"Well?" I said.

"Well what?"

"What's in the box?"

"My dad's winter pants."

"That's not quite all the evils of mankind."

"Well, some of his pants are really ugly," she said. "So I think they're evil."

We both laughed.

"What are you doing down here anyway?" she asked.

"Training."

"Training to shovel coal?"

"No, it's strength training. Max Schmeling is teaching me how to box, and this is part of the training to get my upper body in shape."

At last. I had been hoping for an opportunity to brag about my new life as a fighter. Surely this would impress her.

"Boxing?" she said. "Why would you want to do that?"

Her response caught me so off guard that I couldn't come up with a quick reply and just stood there staring at her for a moment.

"Lots of men are into boxing," I finally managed to say.

"Lots of dumb men," she said.

"Excuse me?"

"Running around a ring, trying to hit each other—seems pretty dumb to me."

"Boxing's a noble sport."

"What's so noble about it?"

"Boxers fight with honor, skill, courage."

"Organized fighting doesn't make sense to me," she said. "Why would you want to let yourself get hurt if you didn't have to? And why would you want to hurt an innocent person who you're not even mad at, who you don't even know?"

Again I couldn't come up with a response. Somehow

I had lost control of the conversation. I started to feel the strange self-consciousness I always felt around her.

"I wouldn't expect a girl to understand."

"I understand more than you think, Karl."

"Oh, yeah?"

"Yeah," she said.

"Like what?" I said, trying hard to maintain my composure.

"Like I understand how much you really want to kiss me," she said, with a sly look in her eye.

Did she really just say that? I felt the heat of the furnace on my back spreading out across my whole body. She stared at me with an amused little grin, and sweat formed along the back of my shirt. Before I could think of anything to say, she stepped forward and gave me a small kiss on the mouth.

CLANG!

We jumped apart as the shovel I had been holding fell to the floor. We both laughed, and then Greta put down the box she was carrying and leaned in and we kissed again. It was a warm, wet kiss, and just like the punch I had landed on Johann earlier in the day, it sent an electric thrill through my body.

She wrapped her arms around me, rubbing the back of my neck. Goose bumps spread down my spine, and our kisses became more intense as she pressed her body against mine, so close that I could feel the pulse of my heart beating against hers.

We both breathed heavily. Then I heard her breathing

become even heavier, and the sound struck my ears strangely. For a moment I thought she might be wheezing, but then I realized that it was the sound of someone *else* breathing. Greta must have heard the same thing, because we both stopped kissing and listened. And there it was: the distinct sound of heavy breathing.

We both turned to see Herr Koplek, standing in the shadows at the entry to the boiler room.

"Don't stop on my account," he said with a sickening grin.

A look of panic swept across Greta's face.

"I'm enjoying the show," he continued.

Greta quickly grabbed the box at her feet and ran past Herr Koplek and back up the stairs. He watched her ascend the stairs, his eyes firmly planted on her backside. He let out a hoarse chuckle.

"Nice. Very nice."

After Greta had disappeared up the stairs, he turned back to me and said: "Hope she tasted good, Stern. I've had my eye on that for a long time."

I felt the strongest desire to punch Herr Koplek in his fat red face. I took a step toward him, but something held me back. A warning went off in my head. I knew he could get me in big trouble. Or was it my old cowardly instincts kicking back in? Before I could deliberate much more, he slipped back into his room and closed the door, like a snake slithering back into a hole in the muddy soil of the garden.

• • •

Greta and I didn't run into each other for another week. Because we attended different schools, our opportunities to see each other were limited to chance meetings at the apartment building, and I figured she wouldn't dare venture down to the basement again. We both knew I could not publicly court her. Even before the Nazis, gentiles rarely dated Jewish boys. And now the Nazi propaganda rags constantly published supposedly true stories about perverted Jewish men taking advantage of pure Aryan girls. What if she regretted kissing me and would never talk to me again?

I considered slipping a note under her apartment door but worried it would be intercepted. The day after the kiss, I passed her coming into our building with her mother as I came down the stairs. My heart rose up in my chest, but she just looked down at her feet and wouldn't meet my eyes.

A few days later I stood waiting around the corner from our apartment building near Greenberg's Art Supplies for her to walk home from school. When she finally approached, she was with another girl. Her eyes went wide when she saw me, but though I tried to signal her with my eyes, she just looked down and walked right by. A sour rumble formed in the pit of my stomach as I watched her move off down the street. I wanted to call out her name, but the words caught in my throat. I already had my answer: She wanted nothing to do with me. But then I heard: "I forgot. I've got to pick up some pen nibs. I'll see you tomorrow, Liesel."

"Okay, Greta. *Auf Wiedersehen.*"

Her friend continued on, and Greta turned and walked back toward me. She silently signaled me to follow her into Greenberg's.

Inside the store, old Herr Greenberg stood behind the counter, arranging a new display of paintbrushes. A religious Jew, Herr Greenberg always wore the same shabby black suit and a yarmulke. His body curved in a permanent stoop, and he had a long gray beard and tired but kindly eyes. I was a regular customer, and he waved hello to me as I walked in.

"*Guten Tag*, Herr Stern. Help you find anything?"

"Just looking around."

Greta pretended to browse through a display of sketchpads toward the back of the store. As casually as possible I joined her. We walked together to the end of the row, where the high shelves blocked us from Herr Greenberg's view. Anger still boiled inside me from the way she had been ignoring me. It was one thing if she didn't want to be my girlfriend, but she could at least have the decency to treat me like a human being. As I tried to find the words to express my outrage, she leaned in and quickly kissed me on the lips.

"I'm sorry I haven't been able to talk to you," she said.

"You used to at least say hello to me."

"I know. But I'm afraid. My father is very strict, and Herr Koplek might've said something to him about us."

"What do you mean?"

"Out of the blue the day after we kissed, my father asked if I had been talking to boys. I said no, but then he said that he doesn't want me talking to strange boys."

"I'm not strange."

"Well, maybe a little bit," she joked.

"Is it because he knows my family is Jewish?"

"I didn't even know that."

My mind suddenly froze. I couldn't believe I had just let it slip out that I was Jewish, because I typically tried so hard to guard that fact. I already felt an ease and openness with Greta that I had never experienced with anyone else. Now I might have ruined it.

"You didn't know we were Jewish?"

"No." She shook her head.

I attempted to read her expression but couldn't tell what she was thinking.

"Does it matter?" I said, holding my breath.

"Not to me," she said, with a small smile. "But it would to my parents. Look, I don't know if my father knows anything about you. I'm not even sure he knows anything happened. But Herr Koplek has been looking at me funny ever since he caught us in the basement, and my father said something to me the very next day. The timing seems too strange to be a coincidence. Any boy is strange to my father. We're Catholic, so he doesn't want me talking to Lutheran boys either."

"So that's it?" My voice rose. "We never get to see each other anymore?"

"Keep your voice down!" she whispered.

"You need help finding anything back there?" Herr Greenberg called from the front of the store.

"No, that's okay," I said.

"We just have to be careful." She continued. "I take piano lessons on Tuesday afternoons at a lady's house near my school. You could meet me at the park across the street. No one would see us there."

My heartbeat quickened at the fact that she wanted to see me again and at the prospect of secret meetings. She leaned in and kissed me again, but before I could get too swept up, she broke away.

"I've got to go now. Meet me on Tuesday at four in the park across from my school."

She grabbed a small packet of pen nibs and paid for them on the way out.

I moved to the window and watched her walk away down the street, feeling a rush of both satisfaction and a powerful longing to be with her more. When she was finally out of sight, I turned and saw Herr Greenberg staring at me with an arched eyebrow.

"Found a muse, Herr Stern?"

"Uh . . . she's just my neighbor."

"Quite a beautiful one at that."

I blushed. *"Guten Tag,* Herr Greenberg," I said, quickly exiting the store.

Learning to Stand, Breathe, and Eat

FOR THE NEXT SEVERAL MONTHS, MAX TRAINED AT THE Berlin Boxing Club and lived at the Excelsior Hotel on Stresemannstrasse in preparation for a rematch with Paulino Uzcudun in Berlin. I had my lessons with him once a week, on Wednesday afternoons. On other days I trained at the club just like the other fighters. Being the only "junior" member under eighteen years old, at first I was a novelty. Whenever I walked in, the others would laugh and make comments, mostly about my skinny physique. Worjyk had taken to calling me *Knochen*, or Bones, not the most flattering nickname but a step up from Piss Boy or Spit Bucket. Many of them would watch me train, chuckling and picking apart my poor technique. I wrongly assumed that they might have shown more restraint in front of Max or that he would say something to shoo them away, but he never did.

"Name-calling is a part of fighting," he said. "The weak-est punches are thrown with the tongue. You've got to thicken your skin against that kind of attack just the same way you thicken your muscles to throw hard punches."

After a couple of weeks most of the fighters lost interest in me, partly because the novelty had worn off. And also because once I had mastered the basic skills, there wasn't as much to laugh at.

Max taught me the fundamentals of boxing, from how to make a fist to how to stand to how to throw all the basic punches: the jab, the straight right, the uppercut. Some of this came naturally. Max said that from the moment I was first in the ring with Johann, he could tell I had a natural jab and the makings of a decent hook. And once I was exposed to other fighters, I could tell I did indeed have good reach, just as Max had told me all those months ago.

Yet some of the most difficult things to master seemed to be the simplest. It took me several days just to learn the right way to make a fist. I had an instinctual tendency to position my thumb over the top of my knuckles, as opposed to tucking it below, which left the thumb exposed to impact. Max was a physical guy and always reinforced his teachings with an active demonstration.

"You hold your hand like that and you're just as likely to break your thumb as break your opponent's nose," Max said. "Here. Punch my hand with your fist like that."

I punched his hand, and sure enough, I felt a sting along

the top of my thumb.

"It hurt a little," I said.

"You see, you're feeling it after only one punch. I barely felt anything. Imagine what your thumb would feel like after dozens of punches. You'd snap it right off your hand. You've always got to tuck your thumb like this."

He showed me the proper way to make a fist, with the knuckles in a straight line and the thumb parallel and protected behind the fingers and then had me punch his hand again, several times.

"You see, this time no pain, *ja*? Your fist is your weapon, so you've got to keep it tight and strong like the head of a hammer. It's got to be able to give a lot of pounding and not show any weakness."

Each night in my journal I drew sketches of the things I had learned; they helped me to both process and memorize each bit of new knowledge. I drew my own fist in both the proper and improper positions, posing with the left hand while I sketched with the right. I used thick lines to make my hands look rough and manly, like the hammer Max had described. I also made quick illustrations of the basic punches, trying to capture the proper motion as well as hand and arm position.

In addition to making a fist, I had trouble learning how to stand properly. I couldn't believe even this turned out to be such a challenge.

"Your feet are way too far apart. You're making yourself too easy to knock down," he said. "Here, put your feet even wider apart and try to stay on your feet when I push you."

RIGHT   WRONG

THE LEFT JAB

RIGHT TO THE JAW

RIGHT UPPERCUT

COUNTER PUNCH

I spread my legs wide, and Max gave me a hard shove. I fell onto the floor, bruising my tailbone. I was surprised at how much force he had used, and my backside stung. A twitch of anger rose up in me until he reached out a hand and pulled me up.

"Okay, now stand with your feet all the way together, like you're standing at military attention."

I placed my feet together, and Max pushed me again. I tried to brace myself but again lost my balance and fell down hard, letting out a small groan.

"See, that's no good either. Now position your feet somewhere in the middle, with your left foot in front about fifteen or twenty inches from the right."

I did as he instructed, careful to position my feet just the right way. This time when he shoved me, I was able to able to resist the force and stay standing.

"Good," he said. "Now keep making adjustments an inch or two one way or the other until you find your greatest point of balance. Think of your body like a building. The other fighter is trying to knock down the building, and you have to position your body so it has the best chance of staying up. When you're in the ring, always look for your opponent to be off-balance, because that's when a fighter is most vulnerable. Practice your perfect stance in front of a mirror, and then remember to always fall back to that position. If your body is a building, your stance is your foundation. A good building needs a strong foundation, *ja*?

"There's a science to boxing, and so figuring out the equations is important. I know lots of bruisers who could punch a lot harder than I could but never went anywhere because they had lousy balance and footwork. You've got long, skinny legs, so you've to be careful not to make your movements in the ring too wide. Short, quick steps. Just a few inches each time. And always make sure your feet are planted when you throw a punch; that's where the power comes from."

I also dutifully continued my training regimen, increasing my limits on the three hundred.

"I'm going to teach you skills, but you've got to keep up your training," he said. "Jumping rope, running, push-ups, all that stuff you do on your own is just as important as the technical skills you'll learn. All the calisthenics are meant to improve your breathing. Remember how winded you got fighting Johann? That was nothing. Imagine going twelve rounds like that. Always try to breathe through your nose when you're doing your workout. You have to have your mouth closed when you fight because you'll be wearing a mouthpiece."

When we were together, Max was a font of information, and I ate up his words like they were my personal gospel and he was my savior. Beyond just the physical training, boxing provided me an entire system of living that I was more than happy to adopt.

"A boxer must lead a disciplined life," Max counseled me. "No late nights. No tobacco. No coffee or tea. No booze— none of the fun stuff. You've got to structure your day so it builds up your strength for battle. That means you've got to eat differently from other boys, think differently from other boys, sleep differently from other boys. No fatty foods or too many sweets. You should avoid unripe fruit or anything with too much spice in it. Boxers eat like animals, simple stuff, whole grains and lots of vegetables. Chicken is good, and red meat, but try to get lean cuts. Too much fatty meat gets in your blood and slows you down. I eat at least two eggs every morning. Eggs are good for strength and energy. You need to put some weight on, so eat lots of cheese and drink milk. Milk, milk, and more milk. Cows are a fighter's best friend. Most fighters I know drink up to two quarts a day, especially when they're trying to gain weight."

We never talked about anything besides fighting, but that was okay with me. In fact I noticed that all Max ever talked about at the club was boxing. He never revealed anything about his personal life or his opinions. If politics ever came up, he diplomatically dodged voicing any point of view. One day in the locker room, Johann and Willy, one of the club members I knew to be a Nazi supporter, were discussing Hitler's diet as Max and I were getting ready for a training session.

"I'm trying to cut down on my red meat," Willy said. "Hitler is a vegetarian, you know."

"I don't think Hitler would make a very good boxer," Johann replied. "I've never met a fighter who didn't love steak."

"You should watch you say about the Führer, Johann."

"All I'm saying is—I don't think he's going to challenge anyone for the welterweight title, right, Max?"

Max lifted an eyebrow and paused before replying: "I think Hitler would probably compete in the light heavy-weight division."

"But he would make a great fighter, right?" Willy asked.

"Well, if he were to box against the other world leaders, he'd probably do quite well. Roosevelt is old, and Mussolini is horribly overweight. Must be eating too much of that nice fatty Italian salami, right?"

The two men laughed, and Max guided me out into the gym.

Several months went by, and I tried my best to follow every word of Max's advice to the letter. Every day I worked out, ate, drank, and slept according to Max's teachings. And sure enough, I started to notice changes in my body. My upper chest and shoulders broadened out, and my forearms and biceps had more definition and mass. I spent hours studying myself in front of the mirror in the bathroom, practicing my stance and punches and flexing different parts of my body, try-ing to discern any muscle growth. I weighed myself every day and recorded my weight in my journal, along with an exact accounting of what I had eaten and my daily workout statistics.

Sometimes I enlisted Hildy to help me measure my biceps and chest with a tape measure, and then recorded those results too. One day she caught me staring at myself in the mirror and said: "You're definitely getting bigger, Spatz."

"Do you really think so?"

"Well, your head is getting bigger. You want me to mea-sure that too?"

I grabbed a hand towel off the rack and threw it at her, as she ran away giggling.

Neblig and Joe Palooka

As the months progressed, I spent less time with with my classmates and more and more time training. Besides Max, my only real friend at the club was Neblig. Despite his speech impediment, he turned out to be much brighter than most of the other fighters. While Max was my teacher, Neblig was my confidant, friend, and cheerleader. He kept an eye out for me and always seemed to be there with a word of encouragement when I needed it most. Some of the other members of the club reveled in cutting me down and played little pranks on me, particularly Willy, who seemed to thrive on pointing out my weaknesses.

One day, as I suited up in the locker room, I saw Willy and another fighter watching me from a distance. When I put on my boxing glove, my hand slid into something cool and mushy, and I discovered the glove had been filled with shaving cream. Willy and the other fighter doubled over with laughter as I removed my cream-covered hand. Just then Neblig entered the locker room.

"You should tell your little friend that you're not allowed to play with yourself in the locker room," Willy said to Neblig as he and the other fighter exited.

Neblig shook his head and threw me a towel to wipe it off.

"Why is he always picking on me?"

"He's only g-g-g-giving you what he got h-h-h-himself when he first joined the club. Here, I'll help you rinse th-th-those out."

In addition to boxing, Neblig and I shared a passion for comic strips and cartoons. He had a big collection of boxing magazines that he kept at the gym along with a vast stash of comic strips he had cut out of newspapers and pasted into notebooks. Neblig had a cousin in America who would cut out and mail him all the latest comic strips along with the most up-to-date boxing magazines. He particularly liked American strips such as *Mutt and Jeff* and *The Katzenjammer Kids*, and we both loved Ham Fisher's *Joe Palooka*, about the adventures of a big, kindhearted heavyweight champion. Something about the Joe Palooka character reminded me of Neblig. They were both big, strong men who were also sensitive and kind.

I developed and drew dozens of my own ideas for comic strips, which I shared with Neblig, including *Fritz the*

Flying Fox and *Herr Dunkelheit: Gentleman Spy.* My personal favorite, though, was *Danny Dooks: Boy Boxer*, about the adventures of a plucky orphan boxer who rises from nothing to become a champion. I used the *Danny Dooks* strip to mirror my own fantasies about my personal evolution and transformation, giving him not just success in the ring but a beautiful girlfriend, a loyal manager, and lots of friends and supporters as well.

I had never really shared any of my original comics with anyone besides Hildy, and I was nervous the first time I showed them to Neblig. One afternoon we went to the corner store and each had a vanilla shake at the lunch counter as he read over several *Danny Dooks* strips. He nodded with approval.

"He's a g-g-g-good character. And I like your line w-w-w-work. It's like a cross b-b-b-between *Joe Palooka* and *Little Orphan Annie.*"

"Oh, it's not very original, I guess," I said, dejected.

"No. It is. All the best s-s-s-stuff in comics b-b-b-builds on what came before. *The Katzenjammer K-k-k-kids* is just a c-c-c-copy of *Max und Moritz*, right? It's really good stuff, Karl. Honest."

"Thanks, Neblig," I said, feeling a deep sense of satisfaction. It meant a lot to me to have Neblig praise my stuff, as I knew there were very few people as expert in the field as he was.

But our passion for comics was second to our passion for boxing. We spent most of our time comparing and contrasting the leading boxers of the day. Through over-heard conversations at the club, I learned Neblig had been a promising fighter as a teenager but had given up boxing years ago and no one really knew why. He was in good shape, and sometimes he worked out on the fitness equipment, but I never saw him sparring with anyone. Some of the fight-ers made fun of him behind his back, but he was so large and powerful looking that they rarely openly taunted him. It hurt to hear them joke about him and imitate his stutter. One day we walked out together, and I finally asked him.

"How come you don't fight anymore?"

"It's a l-l-l-long story."

"You're the biggest guy in the whole gym, probably the strongest too."

"I'd get clobbered by anyone."

"No, you wouldn't."

"I c-c-c-can't fight," he said. "I'm b-b-b-blind in one eye."

"I'm sorry. I didn't know."

"That's okay. I always t-t-t-t-talked like this. So my father taught me how to b-b-b-box, so I could defend myself against the other k-k-k-kids. Boys from my school d-d-d-didn't like me. I was not the most p-p-p-popular k-k-k-kid."

"Me neither," I confessed.

"A group of them cornered me one day. F-f-f-f-four or f-f-f-f-five of them. They had s-s-s-sticks. I just had my fists. I held th-th-them off good. But then one of them hit me in the eye, and it almost p-p-p-popped right out. The boys got scared and just l-l-l-l-left me th-th-th-there, passed out and

HERR DUNKELHEIT
~ GENTLEMAN SPY ~
BY
KARL STERN

FRITZ
THE
FLYING FOX
BY
KARL STERN

bleeding. S-s-s-s-someone found me, and the doctors got my eye b-back in. But I c-c-c-can't see anything out of it, just blurs. It's okay not to t-t-t-talk in the ring. But you have to be able to see. P-p-p-people think I'm slow because of the way I t-t-t-talk, so it was hard to get w-w-w-work. Worjyk w-w-w-was one of the only people who w-w-w-would hire me. I know he acts like a b-b-b-b-bastard sometimes. But he's got a good heart."

"He sure is hard on me," I said. "Always picking apart my technique, calling me names."

"That's because he's p-p-p-paying attention to you. He thinks you have potential. If he didn't, he'd l-l-l-leave you alone."

I doubted Neblig's comment but hoped that it might be at least partially true.

As my training progressed, I volunteered myself whenever someone in my weight class was looking for a sparring partner. Most of the fighters I sparred with were full-grown men who were aspiring professional fighters, so I not only absorbed a tremendous amount of blows but also gained invaluable experience each time I stepped into the ring. In my ever-evolving series of nicknames at the club, I started to become known as the Punching Bag. But unlike my other nicknames, this one was said with a certain amount of respect and even affection.

At first I *was* little more than a punching bag, defensively holding up my hands and barely able to move or put up any sort of fight. But over time I learned how to navigate around the ring and evade punches with dexterity rather than by just covering up. Eventually I even started to make some offensive moves and try out my different punches, even a combination here and there. My skills evolved, and I gained a reputation for being tough and wiry.

I sparred most frequently with Johann. Although he always controlled the action, I was able to score punches on him with increasing regularity. Even Worjyk complimented me after I landed a solid right hook to Johann's solar plexus. As I came out of the ring that day, he and Max approached me.

"Not bad, Knochen," Worjyk said.

"I think you're ready," Max said, nodding with a pleased expression.

"Ready for what?"

"A real fight," Max explained. "Sparring is one thing, but you need to get in the ring with someone who really wants to hurt you."

"There's a Youth Boxing Tournament next week that I signed you up for," Worjyk said. "You'll be representing the Berlin Boxing Club in the tournament, so you'd better not embarrass us, Knochen."

A Prayer

"I STILL DON'T UNDERSTAND," GRETA SAID.

"What?"

"Why you want to fight in the first place."

Greta and I met every Tuesday afternoon at the park near her school, where we could walk and talk together without much risk of being seen by anyone we knew. Although our meetings lasted only twenty minutes, they were the highlight of my week. We always met at the same bench and then walked around in the twilight. Sometime during the stroll, I'd take her hand and we would steal away behind some trees off the path for several minutes of heavy kissing.

I opened up to Greta about everything that was going on in my life, and she did the same with me. Her father was an accomplished violinist who played in one of the city's traveling orchestras. He brought her small gifts whenever he traveled, including the clover charm she wore, which he had picked up when his group had an engagement in Dublin. She longed to study music in Paris. As much as I had become fixated on the United States and its endless parade of boxers and comic strips, Greta dreamed of France, a place she imagined was filled with music, art, and fine food.

We were sitting together on our bench when I told her about my upcoming fight. She was the person with whom I most wanted to share the news, but as I talked excitedly about the upcoming bout, her face grew dark.

"It seems so stupid to risk getting hurt for nothing," she said.

"It's not for nothing."

"Then what's it for?"

"To prove something."

"What?"

"I don't know. To prove I'm stronger, smarter, better than the other guy."

"But why does that matter?"

"To prove to myself that I'm not afraid."

"Afraid of what?"

"Anything. Look, growing up, I used to be scared of getting pushed around by other kids at school, so I did whatever I could to avoid any kind of fight, always trying to stay back and not get in anyone's way. And I don't want to be like that anymore. Can you understand that?"

She stared at me for a long moment and then nodded. "I guess I do."

"You're going to think this is crazy," I continued. "But in some ways I feel safer in the ring than I do at school."

"Safer?"

"In boxing there are rules. You wear padded gloves. It's always a one-on-one fight. You can't hit below the belt or use a weapon. I may get beat, but at least I'll always have a fair chance of winning. The rest of the world isn't always like that."

"You really won't back out?"

"Of course not."

"Well then, I'll have to say a special prayer for you on Sunday."

"I thought you weren't sure if you believed in any of that."

"Well, it couldn't hurt. And I'll be in church anyway. So I might as well make use of the time, right?"

Greta's parents were devout Catholics, and one of her most daring confessions to me had been that she was not sure she believed in God at all, which I didn't find too shocking, coming as I did from my own nonreligious household. The Nazis didn't approve of the hierarchy of the Catholic church, which threatened their own ideas about being in charge of everything and everybody. Greta explained that their priest had forbidden his congregants to join the Nazi Party. Her father agreed with their priest, although many in the congregation did not.

"Just promise me you'll be careful," she said, her eyes suddenly serious.

"I promise."

She touched the side of my face with her hand, and then we slipped off the bench. As we stepped back onto the main path through the park, I saw Kurt and Hans coming toward us in the distance. Greta and I were holding hands, and I quickly released my grip as they came nearer. I hadn't told them or anyone about Greta for fear of exposure. Had they seen us holding hands?

"Karl?" Kurt said as they approached.

"Hi," I said.

"What's going on?" Hans asked.

"Nothing. Just walking home."

They both stared at Greta for an awkward beat.

"This is Greta; she lives in my building."

"Hans Karlweis," Hans said, with a silly bow.

"Kurt Seidler," Kurt said.

"We were both on our way home," I said too defensively, "when we bumped into each other."

"Bumped?" Kurt giggled.

"I've got to get home," Greta said.

"Me too," I said. "I'll see you guys tomorrow."

Greta and I hurried off as they watched us with suspicious amusement.

"Gute Nacht," I heard them sarcastically singsong after us.

Uniform Shirts and Rotten Apples

BETWEEN THE COMBINED DISTRACTIONS OF MY BOXING lessons, training, and Greta, I barely had time to worry, even as the rest of my life seemed to be crumbling around me. My father's "legitimate" art-dealing business at the gallery had slowed to the barest trickle and then finally stopped. He now spent most of his time arranging surreptitious deals with private collectors. Some of these transactions took place at the gallery, but most happened in our apartment at odd hours. Typically a Jewish seller would arrive with his paintings or etchings concealed in a bag or some sort of wrapping, looking desperate, scared, or angry.

Late one night a finely dressed man came with several etchings to sell. He stood very erect and had a haughty air as he presented them to my father, who studied the works carefully and praised their quality, condition, and beauty. Yet when my father made an offer, the man reacted furiously.

"Are you kidding?" he yelled, pounding his fist on the table. "These are original Rembrandt etchings!"

"I know what they are," my father responded calmly.

"You couldn't buy a cheap wall calendar with what you're offering."

"I'm offering what I can offer. I only mark up fifty percent. Most other dealers would give you less and mark up seventy-five or eighty percent. And I am assuming all the risk."

"I won't be robbed right in front of my face!"

"Suit yourself."

The man collected his etchings and indignantly stormed out of the apartment. However, just a few days later, the same man returned with the same pieces. When my father opened the front door to let him in, the man only said: "My family has to eat."

My father nodded, and almost no other words were exchanged between them as the man accepted the amount my father had originally offered.

My father's buyers were almost all gentiles, mostly from Berlin, although some hailed from Switzerland, France, the Netherlands, and even England. I overheard my father speaking snippets of various languages as he conducted these deals. With buyers, he always managed to maintain an air of jollity and excitement about the art, charming and convincing them of the works' merits and value. As soon as the client left, his beaming expression melted into a hard scowl, and he'd complain bitterly to my mother about the vultures coming to pick at our bones.

Life at school continued to be difficult, but for the most part I had learned to avoid the Wolf Pack. Also, word of my boxing training and my association with Max Schmeling had spread and earned me a certain measure of respect. Principal Munter continued to encourage all the boys in school to sign up for the Hitler Youth. It seemed as though with each weekly assembly, more and more uniform shirts appeared, spreading out like a beige rash.

Finally even Kurt and Hans showed up at school wearing brand-new Hitler Youth belt buckles made of polished chrome. Although I was not surprised, I did feel a sharp pinch of betrayal. They didn't talk to me about joining, and I didn't ask questions. Kurt noticed me staring at the belt buckle, and he confused my envy with anger. Now I would be one of the only students at school who didn't belong. Kurt tried to defend their joining up.

"It's just like the Scouts, really," he said. "It's not a big deal."

He had no idea that I just wished I could have a belt buckle of my own and wear the uniform like everyone else.

One night I came home from my afternoon workout at the gym to find my parents out.

"*Hallo?*" I called, but no one answered.

I heard the sound of muffled sniffling. I walked down the hall and opened the door to Hildy's room and discovered her crying, staring at the ceiling, clutching her stuffed rabbit,

Herr Karotte. She immediately turned away from the door.

"Get out!" she said.

"What is it?"

"Nothing."

She buried her head in her pillow. I sat beside her.

"Just go away, Spatz!"

"Come on, you can tell me."

"You wouldn't understand."

"Try me, Winzig," I said.

Finally she rolled over. Her nose was red, and her eyes were puffy from crying.

"The girls at school . . . they call me a rotten apple."

"A rotten apple?"

"Yes. It's because of that dumb book that we all have to read."

"What book?"

She handed me an illustrated children's book titled *The Rotten Apples.* The front cover featured an image of a cherubic-looking young Aryan girl standing beside an apple tree. The tree was filled with beautiful apples, except some of the apples had strange human faces with large noses and droopy eyes. I flipped open the book and read.

The Rotten Apples
by Norbert Aufklitenburg

One day little Elsa and her mother decided to make an apple strudel.

So they traveled to the fruit market in their village and purchased a small basket of bright red apples.

On the way home they passed a dirty old Jew who tried to get them to come into his shop.

The Jew dressed in shabby black clothes and had a hooked nose and wet red lips that he kept licking like an animal.

"Come to my store, little girl," the Jew said. "I have toys for you. Good prices."

Elsa's mother quickly threw an arm around Elsa and pulled her daughter along.

When Elsa and her mother arrived back home, they set to preparing the apples in the kitchen.

"Mama, why couldn't we go into that man's store?" Elsa asked innocently.

"That man was a Jew," her mother explained patiently. "And you should never trust a Jew. They will cheat and rob you, and they do terrible things to girls and boys."

Elsa looked confused. So, seizing the basket of apples, her mother decided to teach her an important lesson.

"Think of this basket of apples as Germany. There are so many beautiful, firm, strong apples. Those are the Aryans, like you, Papa, and me. But every so often you find a rotten apple, like this one."

She pulled out an apple from the bottom of the basket. "See how it is brown and soft here. The flesh is putrid inside. You wouldn't want one of these apples in your strudel, would you?

"Well, Jews are like rotten apples. Just like a bruised apple, they have marks on them, like their hooked noses, red lips, and curly dark hair. You should always be on the lookout and avoid them."

"But what if the apple . . . I mean, the Jew looks the same as us on the outside?"

"Those are the worst kind of Jews," her mother answered. "It is like an apple with a worm that has crawled in through a tiny hole that you can't even see from the outside."

"What can we do about it?" Elsa asked, frightened.

"Well, what do you do if you find a worm in your apple?" her mother asked patiently.

"Cut it out with a knife?"

"Exactly," said her mother. "And that is exactly what the Führer is doing with the Jews, cutting them out of Germany so we can all be pure and free."

Elsa smiled.

"Now, let's bake that strudel."

THE END

I looked at some of the illustrations, and a sinking feeling washed over me as I recognized an undeniable similarity between Hildy and the hideous Jewish apples.

"I'm an ugly rotten apple just like the book. Look at my nose and my eyes and my hair."

"There's nothing wrong with the way you look."

"You're lying. I look like a Jew. Everyone says so."

She was right, of course. I was lying. As much as it pained me to admit it to myself, I hated how Jewish Hildy and my father looked. My mother and I could both easily pass for gentiles, and our daily lives were easier for it. At school I had to avoid the Wolf Pack, but almost anywhere else I could walk the streets without the risk of being harassed. Except for Max, no one at the Berlin Boxing Club knew or suspected I was Jewish. But with Hildy and my father there was no doubt, and when they walked the streets, they were subject to taunts and catcalls nearly every day now. I worried that they were exposing us all.

"Look at me, Hildy."

I lifted her chin so she looked directly in my eyes.

"You have beautiful eyes, a beautiful nose, and beautiful hair. I told you before, you're starting to look like Louise Brooks."

"Stop lying, Spatz! Louise Brooks doesn't have an ugly nose and glasses."

"Winzig . . ."

"Go away. All you care about is boxing anyway. Ever since you started that stupid training, you never have time for me."

"That's not true."

"Get out of my room!"

She buried her face in her pillow again. I touched her shoulder, but she flinched and pulled away.

"Go away!"

I couldn't think of anything to say. I had always possessed the magical power to make her feel better, but now I felt stymied and angry. I was mad at myself because I knew so much of what she said was right. I had become completely swept up in my own life and hadn't been spending any time with her.

All my rage focused on the book. I ripped open the cover and pulled out all the pages from the spine with one powerful jerk. Hildy gasped. Books were sacred objects in our home, and we were both shocked by what I had done.

"Come on," I said.

I took the pieces of the book, grabbed her hand, and led her out of the apartment. She wasn't wearing her shoes, but I pulled her down the stairs until we got all the way to the basement. I led her to the furnace, whose burning coals cast a red glow across the room, and carefully opened the metal door with the tongs and handed her the book.

"Throw it in," I commanded.

She hesitated.

"Go on. They burn books. So can we. Throw it in."

She cautiously stepped forward and tentatively tossed the cover into the open mouth of the furnace. It landed just inside the door, and I had to poke it with the tongs so it slid back toward the burning coal. We both silently watched as the book cover caught fire and blue, green, and yellow flames turned the cover illustration of the apple tree into black ash.

Hildy stepped forward and threw in the two remaining

pieces of the book. The paper instantly burst into flame. Yellow fire danced in her eyes, which were misted over with tears. She turned away from the furnace and fell into my arms, sobbing. Anger rose inside me as I watched the flames devour the book. I hated Norbert Aufklitenburg for writing such an awful piece of filth and causing the girls to taunt my sister. I hated Hitler and the Nazis for turning our entire country against us. Most of all, I hated myself for being blind to Hildy's suffering.

That night I let her do her homework in my room, and for the first time in a long time drew her a Winzig und Spatz cartoon to try to cheer her up. It wasn't my best work, but at least it got her to smile again.

ONE DAY FEFELFARVE THROWS A ROTTEN APPLE AT WINZIG!

TAKE THAT YOU STUPID RODENT!

OUCH!

LUCKILY SPATZ HAS TO GO TO THE BATHROOM

AND HAS GOOD AIM

PLOP

URG. THE COFFEE IS BITTER TODAY

The Secret History of Jewish Boxers

THE VERY NEXT DAY, AS I MADE MY WAY TO THE CLUB TO train for my first real fight, I came across two young Nazi brownshirts standing in front of Herr Greenberg's art supply store. Little more than teenagers, they wore sharp uniforms and polished jackboots. One of the boys held a large can of paste while the other dipped a thick paintbrush into the can and slathered a sticky layer across Herr Greenberg's window.

Through the glass, I could see Herr Greenberg's panicked expression become obscured behind the milky white paste, then blocked altogether as one of the boys slapped a poster onto the sticky spot. The sign simply read DON'T BUY FROM JEWS!

A moment later Herr Greenberg emerged from his store. "Stop!"

The boys simply ignored him.

"Stop that now!" Herr Greenberg repeated.

"What are you going to do about it, Jew?" asked one of the boys.

"I'll call the police," Herr Greenberg replied.

"Yes, go to the police." One of them laughed.

"The chief of the local precinct is also the head of our SA division," the other added.

He was a tall blond kid with bad acne scars along the sides of his cheeks. Herr Greenberg studied the boy with a slow-dawning expression.

"I know you," he said. "You're Gertrude Schmidt's boy."

The boy stiffened at the mention of his mother.

"Do you know she has been a customer of mine since before you were born? And so was your grandmother. You live just a few blocks from here. I know who you are."

The boy looked shocked. The other boy elbowed him in the ribs. "Are you going to let a Jew talk to you like that?"

The first boy continued to stare at Herr Greenberg. I couldn't read his expression, which could have been indignation, embarrassment, or rage. Finally the boy straightened his posture, took a deep breath, approached the old man, and spat directly in his face.

"Don't you ever mention my mother's name again."

Then he turned and threw his paintbrush into the can, and both boys walked away.

I approached Herr Greenberg as he wiped the spittle off the side of his cheek.

"Are you okay?" I asked.

"The world is going crazy, Karl. And when the world is crazy, a sane man is never okay."

He turned to his big plate glass window. The poster had already started to dry.

"He used to play with modeling clay," he muttered to himself.

"Huh?" I said.

"Modeling clay. That's what his mother would buy, so he could make little zoo animals. I never forget my customers."

"Can I help?" I offered.

"No," he said with a sigh as he tried to rip the poster off the window. Only a small corner came off in his hand.

"I'm going to have to use a razor to get rid of it."

He balled up the small piece of paper he had been able to rip off, threw it in the gutter, and went inside to retrieve the razor.

Once I got to the gym, I unloaded all my shame and rage onto the heavy bag. Jab, jab, uppercut. Jab, jab, uppercut. Jab, jab, uppercut. I let out small grunts of release with each hit, so I could hear as well as feel the primitive cadence echoing in my chest and throat. I punched until my shoulders ached and my wrists felt like they were on the verge of snapping, venting my frustrations and anxieties onto the thick leather skin of the bag. Uppercuts gave me the most visceral satisfaction, as I used more of my entire body to pound my fist into the body of the bag, pivoting my legs just right so that the power came from my thighs and torso just like Max had taught me.

After finishing my workout, I was toweling off in the locker room when something on a small table beside Neblig's supply closet caught my eye. The table held a neat pile of clean towels and a large stack of sports magazines, including Germany's leading boxing magazine, *Boxsport*, as well as the American magazine *The Ring*. An illustration on the cover of an old copy of *The Ring* depicted two men squaring off, both wearing boxing trunks with Stars of David stitched on them.

I had been studying English at school for several years, so I was able to read the headline: "The Battle of the Hebrew Light Heavyweights." I eagerly flipped open the magazine and read the cover story about the light heavyweight championship fight between Bob Olin and "Slapsie" Maxie Rosenbloom. The fight went fifteen long rounds before Olin was handed the decision and the world title. Not only was it a startling revelation for me that both of the fighters were Jews, but one paragraph of the article shocked me even more: "This was the first time that two Jewish brawlers have squared off for a world title in five years, since Maxie defeated Abie Bain with a KO in the 11th round of another classic bout. There have been ten 'Jew on Jew' championship bouts since the dawn of this century, and with Maxie, Olin, Barney Ross, Ben Jeby, and Solly Krieger all fighting at the top of their game, there might be plenty more where that came from."

Not only were there other Jewish boxers out there in the

world—but Jewish world champions? America seemed to be teeming with Jewish fighters. I stared at the photographs of Bob Olin and "Slapsie" Maxie Rosenbloom. They each had tightly muscled physiques along with dark hair and prominent noses. These were tough Jews, so different from the sniveling caricatures that I was seeing in the Nazi press all around me and the religious Jews, like Herr Greenberg, who I had been exposed to in my life. I saw in these men exactly who I longed to be, role models I hadn't even known existed.

Neblig entered the locker room, and I quickly shut the magazine before he could see what I was reading. I still did not want anyone to know I was Jewish, not even Neblig.

"Hi, K-k-k-k-karl," he said.

"Oh, hi, Neblig," I replied as casually as possible. "Could I borrow some of these copies of *The Ring*? I'm trying to work on my English, and it's good practice."

"S-s-s-s-sure," he said. "Just make sure to bring them back."

I grabbed a stack of magazines, and that night in bed I flipped through every issue, looking for more stories on Jewish fighters. Four minority groups—Italians, Irishmen, blacks, and Jews—dominated American boxing. Sure enough, I turned up several articles along with photographs of more chiseled Jewish warriors.

The story that most captured my attention was a huge profile of Barney Ross, whose father had been an Orthodox rabbi. As a boy Ross had aspired to follow in his pacifist father's footsteps and become a great Talmudic scholar. Yet Ross's world turned upside down when his father was killed during an armed robbery and Ross and his brothers and sisters were sent to live with relatives or in orphanages. Ross transformed and hardened himself into a street thug and a fighter, vowing to reunite his family through his success in the ring.

He became one of the few fighters in history to hold three championship belts: lightweight, junior welterweight, *and* welterweight. The story of Ross's almost magical transformation from a meek rabbi's son to a muscle-bound champion hit me with a stunning force. The magazine featured a full-page photograph of Ross in a fighter's stance, his bare hands curled into fists, glaring at the camera with his dark hair neatly combed against his head. I carefully ripped out the page and pasted it up on my wall for inspiration. I figured Neblig would never notice one missing page.

I immediately set about drawing a caricature of my new hero. His face was angular and handsome, and there was a tough, determined set to his eyes that I had never tried to capture before in any of my other drawings. As I explored his face, it took on so many virtues to me: pride, confidence, rage. He had none of Max's easygoing smile lines. Fighting wasn't just a sport to this guy; he fought to survive and for his family. After finishing the caricature, I started to sketch out the beginnings of a comic strip about Barney Ross too. Unlike Joe Palooka or my own Danny Dooks, Barney Ross was a real person whose very existence seemed to defend Jews all around the world. If Barney Ross could do it, so could I.

The profile I read was written in anticipation of an upcoming fight against one of Ross's greatest rivals, Jimmy

BARNEY ROSS

KID BERG

MUSHY CALLAHAN

BOB OLIN

MAXIE ROSENBLOOM

BARNEY ROSS

AL SINGER

GREAT JEWISH BOXERS

FROM OUT OF THE JEWISH GHETTO
THERE AROSE A WARRIOR . . .
BARNEY ROSS!

McClarnin, set for May of 1935. I realized that the fight had already happened, but none of the magazines I had reported the results. I had to find out who had won. The next day I went back to the club and hunted through the recent magazines and newspapers in the locker room but didn't turn up anything. What if Ross had lost the championship? Would that be a bad omen for Jews everywhere?

I didn't want to risk asking anyone, for fear my interest in Ross would expose my Jewishness. Luckily the guys in the gym were always talking about the other fighters, and I overheard Worjyk, Willy, and Johann discussing a new fighter on the scene named Joe Louis.

"I'm telling you, he's the one who's going to take Jimmy Braddock's heavyweight belt before Max even has the chance," Worjyk said.

"A Negro champion?" Willy said. "It won't happen."

"What do you mean? It already happened," Johann said. "Remember Jack Johnson?"

"A fluke," Willy countered. "Negroes don't have the brainpower to be champions."

"I'm telling you, this kid Louis has the brainpower and punching power to beat anyone. I'd rather Max fight Braddock any day."

"I watched a film of a Louis fight," Willy said. "He was all brawn. No strategy. I'm telling you, Negroes are just like animals. Put him in the ring with a thinking fighter like Max, and he wouldn't stand a chance."

"What about Henry Johnson?" Worjyk said. "He's a

Negro, and he's all about technique. Everyone says he's got the best shot at taking Barney Ross's crown."

My ears perked up at the mention of my hero.

"Ross is a pushover," Willy said.

"After what he did to McClarnin?" Johann said.

"McClarnin's a pushover too."

"You think everyone's a pushover."

"What happened in the Ross-McClarnin fight?" I said, not able to hold myself back. Worjyk frowned at me for interrupting.

"Ross kicked his ass," Worjyk said, relighting the stub of his cigar.

"They're both pushovers," Willy said.

"Pound for pound Ross is probably the best fighter in the world," Johann said.

"My mother could compete in his weight class," Willy countered.

"She's too heavy," Worjyk replied. "She's at least a middle-weight."

"Hey, watch what you say about my mother."

"You brought her up."

"Well, it's none of your goddamn business," Willy said.

"And she isn't more than a welterweight anyway," Johann added.

"I said shut up about my mother," Willy snapped.

I walked away satisfied and relieved. Ross had defeated McClarnin and was still champion. If a rabbi's son held a world boxing title, how bad could things really get for the Jews?

Stern vs. Strasser

ON THE EVE OF MY FIRST FIGHT, I HAD TO MAKE A LATE delivery for my father and didn't return to our building until after dark. As I made my way up our darkened staircase, a figure emerged from the shadows of the hallway and grabbed my arm. I instinctively jerked back and cocked my fists.

"What the—"

"Shhhhh . . . ," Greta whispered into my ear as she pulled me into a dark corner on the landing of the third floor. Since our first kiss in the basement we had been strict about not talking to or approaching each other in our own building. Standing in the shadows of our hallway with her set my heart racing.

"What are you doing?" I said.

"I wanted to wish you luck tomorrow." She kissed me quickly.

"I thought you didn't believe in boxing."

"I don't, but if you're going to do it, I don't want you to get hurt."

"I won't."

"Here, take this."

She pressed something into my palm. I felt it in the darkness and realized it was the four-leaf clover charm that she usually wore around her neck.

"Slip it into your sock. It'll bring you luck."

"*Danke.*"

"And don't let him hit your lips."

"Greta?" a voice called from inside.

She playfully touched my lips with her index finger and gave me another deep kiss. Then she broke away and slipped back into her apartment.

The next morning, as I got dressed, I slipped the charm into the top of my sock. Feeling it pressing against the side of my ankle gave me a strange feeling of confidence and purpose, like she would be standing beside me in some way.

Max traveled frequently, mostly to America, the center of the boxing universe. "Everyone wants to fight in the U.S.," he explained. "Over there I can earn ten times what I make for a fight staged in Europe." As a result, he was away in New York during the week of my first real fight.

"Don't worry," he'd said on the afternoon of our final lesson before his departure. "Remember the basics, and you'll be fine. So just concentrate on your balance and breathing, and then attack."

Ever since I had first met Max and he had praised my reach, I had dreamed of one day becoming German Youth Champion. This would be the first official step toward that goal. Neblig offered to serve as my cornerman. I was grateful to have someone in my corner, but I felt self-conscious about the possibility that the other kids might make fun of him because of his stutter. The last thing I wanted was to become more of a target because of my cornerman. But I needed someone, and I didn't want to hurt Neblig's feelings by refusing his offer.

Most of the boys were accompanied by their fathers, but my father claimed he was too busy with his business. I most wanted Greta to attend, to impress her with my manliness in the ring. Yet we both knew that her attendance might expose our relationship.

And of course I was also partially relieved that she couldn't go because of my very real fear that she would see me get pummeled.

I *would* have one very important person cheering me on. My uncle Jakob was thrilled when he heard about the fight and promised he would be there. "Are you kidding? I wouldn't miss this for anything, buckaroo," he said. "In fact I'm going to bring some of my friends, so you'll have a whole cheering section."

Dozens of young fighters gathered at the Schutz Youth Center on the west side, which was housed in a decaying white brick building stained with black soot. The building had a large outdoor courtyard in the center where a ring surrounded by portable bleachers had been erected for the tournament. The whole place probably held no more than five hundred people, but to my eye it looked like a football stadium packed with hostile fans.

Groups of boys from various clubs gathered among one another dressed in their clubs' uniforms, including several Hitler Youth groups, who wore swastikas on their boxing trunks and warm-up jackets. At least a hundred uniformed Hitler Youth members sat in the bleachers, cheering for various clubs, along with many grown men in Nazi uniforms, who were the fathers of some of the fighters. The presence of the Nazi regalia didn't disturb me as much as my own lack of any sort of official uniform or gear. I wore a plain white T-shirt and blue trunks. I even became self-conscious of Neblig's moldy old boxing gloves, which in comparison to the other boys' gloves seemed like oversize antiques, something a circus clown would wear.

I scanned the crowd to find Uncle Jakob and his "cheering section" but didn't see him, though I did find Neblig waiting for me at the registration desk. He waved me over.

"How d-d-d-do you f-f-f-feel?" he asked as I approached.

"Like I'm going to puke."

"G-g-g-good. That's exactly how you're supposed to feel."

He turned to the registration desk, where an older boy checked in the fighters.

"Yes?" the boy said.

"He's K-k-k-karl S-s-s-s-stern," Neblig said, nodding

toward me. "The B-b-b-b-berlin Boxing Club."

"K-k-k-karl?" the boy echoed mockingly. "I don't see anyone named K-k-k-karl down here."

"It's Karl," I corrected.

"Ah, yes. There it is. You're fighting at ten thirty against Wilhelm Strasser," he said, and made a crisp check mark beside my name.

Neblig and I went up to the bleachers to watch the other fights while we waited for my turn in the ring. Steel gray clouds hung low in the sky. I silently prayed for a downpour that would postpone my fight, but for the moment the weather held. The day was structured as an elimination tournament. I tried to figure out who in the crowd might be Wilhelm Strasser, and each face I landed on looked more confident and menacing than the next. I also kept waiting for Uncle Jakob to arrive. I had told him the fights started at nine-thirty, but he still hadn't arrived by the time I was called down to the ring at ten twenty-five.

The boy who had checked us in waited by the ring with his clipboard. A large boy with curly blond hair and a thick flat nose, who I assumed was Wilhelm Strasser, waited beside him. He stood beside his coach and another boy from his club. Both wore Hitler Youth insignias on their shorts. While we waited for the preceding fight to end, Strasser looked me up and down with smug confidence. I could feel his eyes measuring my too-thin limbs, my moldy old gloves, my plain shorts and T-shirt. Worst of all, when his gaze met mine, he saw the terrified look in my eyes. My stomach lurched, and I turned back to the ring, pretending to take an interest in the other fight.

Suddenly Worjyk appeared at my side carrying a brand-new pair of brown leather boxing gloves under his arm.

"There you are," he said, thrusting the gloves toward me. "I can't have you representing my club with those ratty old mitts."

"These are for me?"

"Consider it payment for all the sparring rounds you've given my fighters. Here, Neblig, help him get these on."

Strasser and his friend snickered as they watched Neblig help me change gloves.

"Look, baby's getting a diaper change," Strasser said. The others laughed.

"Does the retard wipe your ass too?" the other joked. Strasser snickered.

"Just remember," Worjyk said, ignoring them, "if he's going down, he's going down. You don't have to hurt him too badly like you did last time if the fight is already won."

"Right," I managed to stammer.

"If you see his nose bone sticking out of the skin again, tell the ref." Worjyk continued. "You don't want to risk causing brain damage. This guy already looks brain damaged enough."

Strasser scoffed and looked away, as if he knew Worjyk was just trying to make him nervous. Still, after that, he didn't look at me again until we were in the ring.

Neblig's gloves had been fourteen ounces, the type most

commonly used for training. The new gloves were ten ounces and felt light on my hands. Neblig finished tying them on just as the bell rang, ending the other fight. I looked up at the clouds, hoping for divine intervention that would halt everything and allow me to walk away with dignity. But nothing happened.

The next thing I knew, I was standing face-to-face with Strasser in the middle of the ring. The ref ran through the rules, but I didn't hear a thing. My head throbbed with the noise of the crowd; each voice and clap was a tribal prelude to my certain death. The bell rang, we touched gloves, and my fighting career officially commenced.

Almost as soon as the bell clanged, my mind went completely blank. All the basics instantly escaped me, like a helium balloon that a child accidentally lets go. Poof—it was all gone into the ether. Strasser advanced toward me, and I couldn't even assume my stance. My arms just hung at my sides, and my legs didn't budge. Strasser landed a light punch on my left upper arm, and I almost fell over. Laughter rose up from the crowd. He punched me again, and I tumbled backward, all the way back to the ropes.

Worjyk screamed from the corner, "Get your goddamn hands up!"

I tried to lift my hands, but Strasser came at me with a quick combination of punches that landed on my stomach and chest. Then he hit me in the jaw with a quick upper-cut that sent my head snapping back, and I fell against the ropes. Loud jeers rang out as the audience smelled blood. I heard shouts of "Put him away" and "Knock out this skinny clown" and "Kill the bum!" I managed to get my hands up and spent the rest of the round blocking punches, ducking, and retreating.

Finally the bell rang again, bringing a chorus of boos aimed at me.

I found my way to the corner, where Workyk and Neblig waited.

"What the hell are you doing in there?" Worjyk barked at me. "You're twice the fighter that kid is."

I was so winded and dazed, I could barely speak. My stomach churned, and I felt the bile rising in my throat.

"I . . . don't know," I said. "I can't remember anything."

Then my stomach lurched, and I grabbed the spit bucket and vomited, a violent heave that made my head shake and throat rasp.

"*Mein Gott,*" Worjyk said to Neblig. "He's falling apart."

I coughed and heaved more vomit into the bucket.

"M-m-m-maybe we should throw in the towel," Neblig said.

"No," I said, regaining my composure. "I feel better now."

Vomiting had released some of the tension and cleared my head.

"J-j-j-just find your balance," Neblig said. "K-k-k-keep your hands up and find your balance. This guy c-c-c-can't hurt you. Are you in pain?"

I thought about it. Despite being hit many times and not landing any punches of my own, I barely felt any pain at all.

"No," I said.

"He's got no punching power," Worjyk said. "You've stood in the ring with guys ten times stronger than this bum."

"F-f-f-find your breath and find your balance," Neblig said.

Neblig gave me a quick sip of water that I spat back into the bucket. Then the bell rang, and they pushed me back toward the center of the ring. This time I focused all my mental energy on finding my balance. I heard Max's voice in my head, and suddenly my stance came back to me, and I felt my feet fall into the right place, setting the foundation of my building. Strasser came out punching, hoping to put me away quickly, but I absorbed the first few blows easily and this time was conscious of how softly he punched compared with the men I sparred with at the club.

My body started to move with a natural rhythm as I ducked and maneuvered away from his attack. More boos and catcalls rose up from the crowd. "Come on! Let's see a fight." Finally I saw an opening and attacked with a series of jabs that sent Strasser backward. I could feel the shift in his body as I moved forward. He instantly switched to a defensive posture. My eyes met his, and I saw what he had seen in mine before the fight: fear. I knew he was a fighter who was afraid to get hurt.

Then it happened. I landed a perfectly placed punch to his chest. Max had instructed me to aim for the solar plexus. "People think you get knockouts with lots of head punches.

But the solar plexus is the best target. If you can hurt someone there, you'll take away his breath, and the fight will
be in your control." That's exactly what happened with
Strasser. As soon as the punch landed, I heard him take in a
sharp breath, and his body posture crumbled. His hands fell,
and I instantly landed more punches, trying to pound away
at the same spot. In my new gloves, my hands felt like tight
little hammers. Another hard jab landed on the bull's-eye on
his chest, stealing more of his breath and bending him over.
His building was collapsing in front of me.

All it took was one right uppercut to the jaw and he fell
to the mat. The crowd let out a gasp as Strasser struggled
to get onto all fours. I heard him wheezing, desperately trying to catch his breath, as the ref started the count. Strasser
stayed on his hands and knees, trying to breathe, and I heard
the ref finish the count, *". . . sieben . . . acht . . . neun . . . zehn!"*

A surprised cheer rose up from the crowd, and Neblig
and Worjyk rushed into the ring and lifted my right arm
above my head in victory.

At that moment a loud clap of thunder drowned out the
crowd, and the clouds finally burst, as if slit open with a
razor blade. Thick sheets of rain poured down, causing the
crowd to instantly scatter. Neblig and Worjyk ran for cover,
and I was alone in the ring. I let the rain fall on me, cooling
my heated body, and looked around the empty ring with a
deep feeling of satisfaction.

I had won my first fight.

Concentration

Neblig, Worjyk, and I waited under cover for two hours, but the rain didn't stop, and the fights never resumed that day. Most people on the street huddled under umbrellas or half-folded newspapers, rushing to get out of the storm, but I ran with my head up, the cool drops running off my hair and down my face. I sprinted all the way home, anxious to tell Greta, Hildy, my parents, someone of my triumph. My feet slapped the slick gray sidewalks with a steady satisfying rhythm; and I smugly gazed at all those ordinary people afraid to get a little wet. I was a warrior, impervious to everything. I burst into our apartment, soaking wet and feeling like a conquering hero, but only Hildy was there to greet me.

"Did you win?" she asked, greeting me at the door.

"A second-round knockout."

"Wunderbar!" she squealed. "Wait here. I made you something."

She ran back to her room and retrieved a drawing she had made, depicting Spatz, the bird, my alter ego in her storybook world, wearing boxing gloves on his wings with the words KNOCK 'EM OUT, SPATZ! painted along the top.

"Tada!" she said, handing me the drawing.

"Thanks, Winzig."

"Will you hang it in your room?"

I didn't want to hang the babyish picture on my wall next to my other boxing photos, but I also didn't want to hurt her feelings.

"Of course, Winzig."

I had hoped to bump into Greta on the way into the building, so she could run into my arms, like I imagined Anny Ondra did after Max came home with a victory. I had also been looking forward to telling my father and having him be impressed with me about something for a change.

"Where's Uncle Jakob?" Hildy asked. "I thought he was going to come home with you after the fight."

In all the excitement of the fight, I had forgotten all about Uncle Jakob and his cheering section.

"He never showed up," I said. "Where's Mama?"

"I don't know. She got a phone call that made her very upset, but she wouldn't tell me what it was about. Then she went to find Papa and told me to wait here for you."

"Who was the phone call from?"

"Mama wouldn't say."

Hildy and I spent the rest of the day waiting for our mother or father to return. Hours passed. Hildy perched at our front window, looking out at the rainy street and hoping that they'd come around the corner. At seven P.M. I made dinner by frying some bratwurst in a cast-iron pan and scrounging up some leftover potato salad with green onions and sharp vinegar. We both ate silently at the table. Papa often worked odd hours and missed meals, but it wasn't like our mother to leave us for so long with no word.

Finally, at nearly eleven P.M., we heard keys jingling outside our door and they both entered, in the midst of an argument.

"We need to hire a lawyer."

"Who has money for a lawyer?" my father replied.

"We do," she said.

"But then how will we pay rent? You want us to be on the street?"

"Sig, he needs us. He needs a lawyer."

"A lawyer's not going to help him. You know what goes on in the courts these days. It'll be like throwing money into the toilet."

"He's my brother," my mother said.

"He's a fool. He's always been a complete fool."

"What happened?" I said.

"It's your uncle Jakob . . . ," my mother began.

"It's nothing," my father interrupted.

"What do you mean, nothing?" my mother shouted at him.

"The less they know, the better," my father replied.

"The less we know about what?" Hildy said.

"Nothing, Hildegard. Go to bed."

"What happened?"

"Your uncle Jakob's been arrested," my mother said flatly.

Hildy gasped. I froze, not quite believing what I'd heard.

"Oh, great, Rebecca. That's just great. You want all their friends to know? You want the SS knocking on our door now?"

"Why was he arrested?" Hildy asked.

"He was arrested because his political group doesn't agree with the Nazis."

"You can be arrested for that?" Hildy said, her voice rising nervously.

"You can be arrested for almost anything these days," our mother replied.

"Will we be arrested too?" Hildy said, on the verge of tears.

"That's really smart, Rebecca," my father said. "Why don't you just scare her half to death over nothing?"

"It's not nothing!" my mother said. "They need to know what's going on. They took him to a concentration camp in a place called Dachau," she said.

"What's a concentration camp?" I asked.

"It's a kind of jail that the Nazis built for anyone who

doesn't agree with them," my mother said.

"Look," my father said, "your uncle brought this on himself. He and his group were taking too many risks."

"At least they're trying to do something," my mother countered. "You don't do anything."

"What is there to do?" my father snapped back. "You're so smart. You have all the answers? What is there to do?"

"Something! Anything! At least my brother stands up for what he believes in."

My mother turned away and walked down the hall toward the kitchen. My father pursued her.

"And look where that got him," my father said. "You want me to be rotting in some prison camp in Bavaria?"

"The way things are going, we'll be heading there anyway."

Hildy started to cry and ran to my mother, throwing her arms around her waist. My mother rested her arm over Hildy's shoulder.

"You're upsetting the children," my father said.

"They should be upset!" she said.

"We shouldn't discuss this now." He turned his attention to Hildy and me. "Listen, don't mention what happened to your uncle to anyone. Not even your best friends. We all could be arrested too if they think we're involved with his group. We've all got to be more careful now, thanks to Uncle Jakob."

"We can't go on like this," my mother said.

"We don't have a choice," he shot back.

"We could leave," she said.

"We've been over this a million times."

"Other people are doing it. The Schwartzes left last week for Geneva. And the Bergs are going to Amsterdam."

"They have family there."

"So we could just pick a place."

"Pick a place? And where would we go, Rebecca? Have you thought that one through?"

"Anywhere."

"Oh, great. Anywhere. That's helpful. Pack your bags, kids! We're moving to anywhere."

New fears took root in the pit of my stomach. My parents had never openly discussed the idea of leaving Germany. Things were worse than I had realized.

"What about the United States? You have cousins—"

"You know we can't do that."

"Why not?"

"First of all, it's halfway across the world and I haven't been in contact with any of them since before the war. Second of all, we don't speak any English. And most important, we haven't got anywhere near the kind of money it would take to get us all over there. And we'd need thousands of marks just for the sponsor payments. I don't know why you keep bringing this up."

"Because things keep getting worse and worse."

"It's just politics. It will pass."

"It won't," she said. "You can't just stand around doing nothing."

"Okay, you want to go, then go!" He ran into their bedroom and pulled one of their suitcases out of the closet and tossed it at her feet. "Here! Pack up and go wherever the hell you want."

He kicked the suitcase so it slid into my mother's leg with a dull thud. She grabbed her shin in pain where the suitcase had struck her.

"Goddamn you!" she screamed.

She picked up the suitcase and hurled it toward my father. He ducked out of the way, but it struck him on the shoulder and then bounced against the wall.

"Coward!" she spat.

The word stopped him short. He stared at her for a long moment. His neck reddened, and his face seethed with anger.

"I'm getting out of here," my father finally said.

He turned and awkwardly stepped over the suitcase, which blocked his path in the hall, and stormed out of the apartment.

After the front door slammed shut, my mother picked up the suitcase and returned it to her closet. Then her face crumpled into her hands, and she started bawling. Hildy and I had seen our parents fight before, but never like this. Hildy cried too.

"Will Uncle Jakob be okay?" Hildy asked.

"I don't know," she said. "I just don't know. You two should go to bed now."

She kissed us both on the forehead and then entered her room and shut the door. We could hear her crying from inside, her sobs muffled in her pillow. Hildy and I both went to our rooms. I dreaded hearing the sound of her running the bath, but for the moment my mother stayed in her room.

I tried to block out all the dark thoughts that were swimming through my head by focusing on my victory in the ring. I faithfully recorded the results of my fight with Strasser in my journal, trying to remember the exact sequence of punches, what had worked, what hadn't worked. Max had taught me that good fighters always tried to gather as much information as possible about their opponents to understand their strengths and weaknesses. "Think of yourself like the general of your own army, trying to find out as much intelligence as possible about the other army before battle." I also sketched a small caricature of Strasser so I would remember what he looked like in case we ever fought again.

WILHELM
STRASSER

WEAK RIGHT
AFRAID OF HEAD
PUNCHES

Then I lay in bed and flipped through my old boxing magazines, trying to lose myself in the world of Barney Ross, Max Schmeling, Tony Canzoneri, Jimmy Braddock, Henry Armstrong. Race and religion didn't seem to matter in the ring, or if they mattered, they were points of pride or distinction. Jews were described as "Hebrew Hammers" and "Sons of Solomon." Negro fighters were "Black Bruisers" and "Brown Bombers." I wished Germany could be as accepting as the boxing world seemed to be.

My mind kept straying to Uncle Jakob sitting in prison. I wondered why they called them "concentration" camps. What did concentrating have to do with anything? I could still hear my mother's low sobs as I finally drifted off to sleep.

A Real Fighter

MY FATHER RETURNED THE NEXT MORNING, LOOKING drawn and smelling of cigars and the peppermint-flavored liquor he favored. He and my mother barely exchanged a word when they saw each other. He poured himself a cup of coffee and sat heavily at the kitchen table. As soon as he settled into the chair, she stood up and walked out.

There was no way to communicate with prisoners in Dachau, and my mother's mood turned very dark. We heard rumors of torture and murder in the camps, and in the absence of any concrete information, my mother assumed the worst. She retreated to her bedroom and to the bath for longer and longer stretches, until it seemed as if she spent the majority of her days in either room with the door shut.

I focused all my energy on my life outside our apartment.

The first day I returned to the club after the Strasser fight, I walked in, and Worjyk sat at the front desk. Because of the rain, we had not had a chance to talk after the fight, and I expected him to congratulate me or at least give me some pointers about how I performed in the ring. But he just grunted a half greeting at me, as if nothing special had happened. Neblig approached, carrying a bundle of towels. Surely he would say something.

"Worjyk, where do you want me to s-s-s-stow these new towels?"

"Just put 'em in the supply closet back there."

"Okay. Oh, hey, Karl." He waved at me absently and walked off toward the closet.

I stood there, dumbfounded. I didn't expect my parents to care about my boxing, but I'd thought a victory would at least get me some respect at the club. I had been mistaken. I looked around at the men training, completely oblivious of me, and started to move slowly toward the locker room.

Suddenly I felt something strike the back of my head.

"Ow!"

I turned to see Neblig staring at me with a big grin; a boxing glove lay at my feet.

"What the—"

The men in the gym fell silent and turned toward me.

"Congratulations, Knochen," Worjyk said.

All the other fighters removed their gloves and threw them at me. I tried to duck and dodge them, but the gloves just kept coming, as the men moved toward me, chanting my name. "Karl, Karl, Karl, Karl."

Neblig, Johann, and most of the other fighters converged on me and hoisted me onto their shoulders as they continued chanting my name, slapping me on the back, and congratulating me. I looked around at the faces of the men surrounding me, men I had sparred with, trained with, argued and laughed with. I had never felt so much a part of something, so at the center of things. I swelled with pride. It was one of the happiest moments of my life.

I trained as often as I could at the Berlin Boxing Club, despite the fact that Max came by the club less and less. After beating Paulino Uzcudun in a rematch in June, he had traveled to America to lobby for a chance at a title fight against Jimmy Braddock, who was known as the Cinderella Man because before he became champ, he had been so poor that he had to live on government relief. The other leading contender was the young Negro fighter Joe Louis, and people were already speculating about the possibility of a Louis/Schmeling fight on the horizon.

My totals for the 300 rose to 375, 400, and eventually 450. My body was still skinny, but where the flesh used to be soft and formless, taut muscles now lined every limb.

Worjyk helped me enter more youth boxing tournaments around the city. After my shaky first fight, I settled down and gained a sense of inner confidence. My months of training and sparring with grown men had given me a distinct advantage over opponents my own age. I boxed regularly throughout the summer of 1935. I easily won my next

several fights and started to gain a reputation as someone to
be respected and even feared in the ring.

My tenth fight proved to be the most challenging. I
battled back and forth with a good strong puncher named
Heinz Budd. In the second round he surprised me with a
combination and landed a crushing right cross to the side
of my head that nearly sent me down. My mouthpiece got
knocked out of place, and I bit the inside of my lip. A warm
trickle of blood ran down my throat.

"Get back!" Worjyk yelled from my corner.

I couldn't retreat fast enough, and Budd landed another
series of punches on me. I lost my footing and fell back
against the ropes. Budd moved in for the kill, but I was able
to duck out of the way of an uppercut and land a quick jab
of my own. Two more jabs and I was able work my way out
of the corner. We traded punches until the bell rang, ending
the fight.

Budd met me at the center of the ring.

"Good fight," he said.

"You too," I replied. We exchanged pats on the shoulder
with our gloved hands.

I returned to my corner, and Neblig handed me a towel
that I used to wipe off my sweat-streaked face. I took a long
drink from my water bottle as the referee retrieved a small
slip of paper from the judges and moved to the center of the
ring.

"The winner by unanimous decision," he said, "is Karl
Stern."

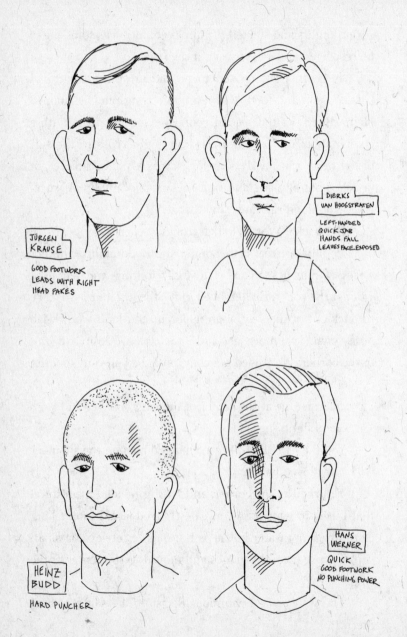

JÜRGEN
KRAUSE

GOOD FOOTWORK
LEADS WITH RIGHT
HEAD FAKES

DIERKS
VAN HOOGSTRATEN

LEFT-HANDED
QUICK JAB
HANDS FALL
LEAVES FACE EXPOSED

HEINZ
BUDD

HARD PUNCHER

HANS
WERNER

QUICK
GOOD FOOTWORK
NO PUNCHING POWER

Neblig clapped me on the back.

"Nice job, Knochen," Worjyk said. "Most of your other fights have been against pushovers, but this kid could really box. You actually showed some skills out there. You may yet become a real fighter someday."

A real fighter. No two words had ever meant more to me, because I knew he really meant them.

Early Dismissal

WHEN SCHOOL RESUMED THAT FALL, HERR BOCH WAS no longer a member of the faculty. There were several new teachers, including my main instructor, Herr Kellner, a thin-lipped man with a small toothbrush mustache, which I was sure he'd grown to resemble Hitler. Many men in Germany shaved their facial hair to look like Hitler, and it became much more rare to see the bushy mustaches that Kaiser Wilhelm had popularized.

A few weeks into the new term, Herr Kellner announced that there would be a special assembly that morning for the entire school in the auditorium. My friend Kurt raised his hand and asked what the assembly was about. Herr Kellner just smiled and said that we would find out. He seemed to look directly at me as he said it.

We all shuffled into the auditorium, and I took my usual place toward the back with Kurt and Hans. Once all the students had gathered, Principal Munter took the stage. He raised his flabby arm in a salute and cried, "HEIL HITLER." And the entire auditorium answered back as one, "HEIL HITLER." Principal Munter put on his little round spectacles and produced a piece of paper from the inside of his jacket pocket.

"I have some very important news to announce this morning," he said. "Our government has just passed some new laws that it is my honor and duty to tell you about. They are called the Nuremberg Laws, and they have been carefully designed to protect and secure the purity of German blood against the insidious influence of the Jews. I will summarize them for you now."

My throat went dry, and I felt my spine collapse into my seat.

"Henceforth anyone who is born of three or four Jewish grandparents shall be officially considered a Jew. Jews will no longer be allowed to marry those of true German blood. Extramarital intercourse between Jews and true German citizens is forbidden."

At the mention of intercourse a chorus of chuckles rippled through the crowd. I heard Kurt and Hans laughing next to me. Didn't they realize what Munter was saying? This was nothing to laugh at. I immediately thought of Greta. What would happen now that our relationship was officially illegal?

"All right, quiet down!" Munter instructed. "Jews may not employ female citizens under the age of forty-five as domestic workers. And Jews are hereby forbidden to display the national or Reich flag. Any violation of these laws is punishable by hard labor. I will post the new laws and this chart of racial classification on the school bulletin board for your inspection."

He folded the piece of paper and returned it to his jacket pocket.

"In keeping with the new direction of our government"—Munter continued—"our school will also be ridding ourselves of the corrupting influence of the Jewish race defilers. Would the following students please come forward? Mordecai Isaacson."

A burst of catcalls erupted from around where Mordecai sat in one of the front rows. He stood and was pushed out of the row and down to the front of the auditorium.

"Jonah Goldenberg and Josef Katz, come forward," Principal Munter continued. Jonah and Josef too were pushed out of their rows toward the front of the stage.

"Benjamin Rosenberg . . ."

I realized he was listing the Jewish students in alphabetical order and that I was next. Unless by some miracle the new laws exempted me. I did have one non-Jewish grandfather. Did that mean I was spared? I couldn't remember what he had said. If you had three grandparents, did that mean you were a Jew according the law? Then he read my name.

"Karl Stern. Come forward."

I hesitated for a moment, dreading joining the line of Jews at the front of the room. None of them had been my friends. I didn't belong there. Some of the boys sitting behind me grabbed my collar, lifted me out of my seat, and pushed me down the aisle. Kurt and Hans looked down at their feet as I went by. As I made my way up toward the stage, all the boys started chanting, *"Juden! Juden! Juden!"*

I stood beside Benjamin and looked out at the happy chanting faces of my schoolmates, as if it were all a game to them. Gertz Diener, Franz Hellendorf, and Julius Austerlitz stood and cheered the loudest. Principal Munter raised his hands to quiet the crowd.

"You four students are officially expelled. You may retrieve your books and leave the building at once. You are dismissed."

A loud cheer went up from the audience as the four of us turned and walked out of the auditorium, and again the chant: *"Juden, Juden, Juden."*

Benjamin Rosenberg and I had our lockers near each other, and we both walked down the empty hallway together, looking pale and bug-eyed, as if in a trance. We stopped at our lockers, and my hands were shaking as I gathered my books, wondering where we would go to school or if we would go at all.

After a few moments the doors of the auditorium flew open, and Gertz Diener and the Wolf Pack emerged at the front of the stream of exiting students.

Gertz saw Benjamin and me from a distance, pointed,

and said, "There they are!"

Suddenly he ran toward us, leading a huge group of boys.

"Karl, what do we do?" Benjamin said as they came toward us.

"Run!"

We dropped our books and took off toward the exit stairwell at the far end of the hall. I flew down the stairs, jumping three and four steps at a time, with Benjamin close behind me.

"Wait! Karl!" he gasped, as if proximity to me might protect him.

We heard the muffled chant of *"Juden, Juden, Juden."* And then the door to the stairwell exploded open behind us, and at least two dozen boys snaked down the stairs in hot pursuit. I made it to the bottom and out the side door that led into our school's courtyard and sprinted across the courtyard and out the main gate into the street. Benjamin fell behind.

"Karl!" he screamed. "Wait!"

"Juden, Juden, Juden!"

My months of roadwork had given me superior speed and endurance, so I kept pulling farther ahead. I glanced back over my shoulder just as the Wolf Pack caught up to Benjamin. Gertz Diener grabbed him by the back of his jacket and swung him to the ground. Benjamin fell to his knees, and then the other boys swarmed on top of him like ants on a discarded sweet until he was completely covered by the kicking and punching bodies of the other boys.

I felt a twitch of shame at not going back to help him, but I kept running, knowing there was nothing I could do but take a beating myself. I had become a good fighter, but I'd be helpless against a dozen boys. My strength had increased, but had my bravery? As I ran on, I wondered if this act of self-preservation was just my old cowardice chasing me down.

I turned a corner and saw a police officer down the street. For a brief moment my mind seized on the idea of telling the policeman about what was going on. I even started to move toward him, but then I remembered the new laws. Jews were not even citizens anymore, so it was no longer the job of the police to protect us. For all I knew, he might join in on the beating or arrest me. Desperation swept over me as I realized how vulnerable my Jewish blood made me, and I ran on toward our apartment. Along the way, I passed several advertising pillars that had huge sheets with the Nuremberg Laws printed on them for everyone to see.

Bertram Heigel

"YOU WERE WHAT?" MY FATHER GASPED.

"Expelled," I said. "Not just me. All the Jewish kids were kicked out."

My mother, my father, Hildy, and I were just sitting down to a meager dinner of boiled potatoes, carrots, and brown bread when I broke the news.

"It'll only be a matter of time before Hildy's school follows suit." My mother sighed.

"I don't want to go to school anymore anyway," Hildy said. "It's awful there."

"What'll we do, Sig?" my mother said.

"I don't have to go to school," I said. "I can find a job."

"There are no jobs," she said.

"Then I can work for Papa."

"Me too," Hildy added quickly.

My father cocked his head, intrigued.

"No. You both must go to school," my mother said. "I'll not allow them to turn our children into ignorant savages."

"But only if we can find a school to take them," my father interjected.

"We'll send them to a Jewish school," my mother said.

"A Jewish school?" I said.

"I don't want my son turned into a rabbi," my father said.

It felt good for my father and me to be on the same side of an argument for a change.

"Nonsense," my mother said. "He certainly won't be harmed by being exposed to the Torah. You went to a Jewish school and survived it."

"Barely," he muttered.

"We've always taught you children to have open minds," my mother said. "I'm confident a little Jewish education won't close them."

Soon after, Hildy and I were both enrolled in separate Jewish schools not too far from our apartment. My old classmate Benjamin Rosenberg started going to the same school, but we avoided each other. I was ashamed that I had not stopped to help him when he had been overrun by the Wolf Pack. And he was probably either mad at me or just embarrassed for taking the beating.

On the first day in my new classroom, my teacher, Herr Haas, a large man with a thick red beard, called me up to the front of the room. He wore a heavy black suit, and long curls of hair dangled beside his ears.

"Herr Stern, you seem to be missing something."

"Sir?"

"A yarmulke," he said, pointing to the small skullcap on his own head.

"I don't have one," I admitted.

Several boys gasped, while others chuckled.

"Well, I suggest you get one to wear in school as soon as possible. It is required. For now wear this."

He reached into his desk drawer and produced a yarmulke made of folded white paper.

"Now, go sit down."

I returned to my desk, and the boy sitting behind me leaned close and whispered: "How come you don't wear a yarmulke?"

"Why should I?"

"Why? Because God commands it," he said.

"I don't understand why God would care about me wearing a hat. Besides, these days it's like wearing a target on your head."

The boy shook his head and leaned back.

Everyone was required to learn Hebrew and study Torah and the Talmud. As one of the only students with absolutely no Jewish observance at home, I was a hopeless Hebrew student, so far behind my contemporaries that I didn't even try to catch up. In general there were two types of students at the school: the old students who came from more observant families and we new ones who were forced to attend because we had been kicked out of our secular schools.

I felt no connection to the religious Jews and didn't believe in any of their traditions. Why should God or anyone else care if I ate a pork sausage or walked around without a hat? I reasoned that if everyone could have just been secular, none of this would have happened. The religious Jews didn't think too highly of the nonobservant kids, including me, either. To them, we were just as strange for being born Jewish but not believing or practicing in any way. I avoided most of the other kids, new and old, focusing all of my social life around the Berlin Boxing Club, Greta Hauser, and my cartooning.

After dinner one night I sat in our living room working on a new comic strip about Barney Ross based on a story I had read in *The Ring* magazine in which Ross went back to his old neighborhood and defended his rabbi against a group of thugs. As I made the story come to life as a cartoon, it struck me that Ross never wore a yarmulke and yet he considered himself an observant Jew. He was able to balance being a boxer and a proud Jew in a way that was utterly impossible in Germany. I was just finishing the last panel when my father burst into the room, carrying a package.

"There you are. I've been looking for you."

"I was just drawing."

My father approached, and I instinctively tried to cover what I was working on, but too late. My father frowned as he saw it.

"Comics," he said with disdain. "I don't know why you

waste so much of your time on something so trivial."

"It's not trivial to me."

"Well, I need you to make a delivery."

He handed me the package.

"Where?"

"The Countess," he said. "And make sure you get the cash."

My heart sank. I dreaded making deliveries to the Countess, as he and his boyfriend, Fritz, always made a fuss about how big and strong I was getting and tried to tempt me inside with a cup of tea. Of course, since I'd begun training, I longed for people to notice the changes in my physique. But not those kinds of people.

And I was happy that my parents continued to do a brisk business with the printing press, although the pickups and deliveries became even more shrouded in secrecy than before. Sometimes I anonymously dropped packages outside apartment doors and left without collecting the payment, while with other clients I would just go to collect money. My father didn't want to risk the same person's being seen too frequently at the same address. My regular clients included the Countess as well as other members of the Berlin underworld—homosexuals, Gypsies, Jews, Communists, anyone whose lifestyle or beliefs forced him or her to live in secret.

Reluctantly I made my way to the Countess's apartment building, determined to leave as quickly as possible.

When I rang the bell, a man's voice that I didn't recognize called from inside. It didn't sound like Fritz, who sometimes answered the door.

"Who is it?"

"Karl Stern."

A moment later the door opened to reveal a tall middle-aged man with a balding head ringed by a thin wreath of brown hair.

"Uh . . . is the Countess here?"

"Come in," he said.

Ordinarily, I would have just dropped the package and left, but I needed to collect the money. My father was very clear about needing to collect on the spot these days whenever possible. The man who answered the door turned and moved toward the sitting room. Suddenly I was seized by the fear that the Countess and Fritz had moved or been arrested and that this was the new occupant of the apartment. The weight of the flyers in my bag felt very heavy, and I knew I couldn't leave them with a stranger or risk getting everyone in big trouble. I hesitated by the door. Should I run?

"Does the Countess still live here?" I ventured.

The man did not turn.

"Yes, Karl. The Countess is still lurking around here somewhere. She's just not feeling like herself today."

He knew my name, so I followed him into the small sitting room near the front door. He sat heavily beside a petite rolltop desk.

"Would you like a cup of tea?" he offered.

"No, thank you." I replied. I was still afraid of offering up the package to a stranger. "Is Fritz around?"

"Fritz? No, Fritz doesn't live here anymore," the man

said. "Fritz decided to become a different person because the government doesn't like the person he really is."

The man's voice caught in his throat as if he were on the verge of tears, and I realized whom I was talking to, despite the lack of wig and expert layers of makeup.

"Countess?" I said.

"Yes," he replied. "Although most people call me Bertram when I look like this. Bertram Heigel—good to meet you," he said, comically extending his hand. We shook hands.

"I have the package for you."

"Yes, well, I'm sorry for your trouble coming over here, but I won't need it this week. In fact I probably won't be needing them at all anymore with the way things are. My parties have gone dreadfully out of style."

My mind froze. The Countess was one of our only remaining reliable customers. I had no idea what we'd do if we didn't have this small but steady flow of income.

"But these have already been printed," I said, removing the packet from my rucksack.

"Of course I'll pay for these, but it looks as though I won't be having any balls anymore, so this will be the last delivery."

He removed a roll of marks from the desk and handed it over to me, noticing the look of unease on my face as I accepted the money.

"How is the rest of your father's business?"

I wondered how I should answer that question. My father's business didn't really exist anymore. The gallery was forced to officially close after the passing of the Nuremberg Laws, and his private clients seemed to be drying up with each passing week, as more and more of his old associates either were jailed or fled the country. The Countess acknowledged my silence with a nod.

"I see," he said. "Do you know how I met your father?"

"No," I said. In fact I really did not want to know. My mind had danced around the edges of the idea that my father had some secret life as a homosexual or cross-dresser or both, but I had tried to bury those thoughts as quickly as they'd come into my head.

"Come over here. I want to show you something."

He removed a worn leather photo album from a shelf in the desk and opened to a page that featured several photos of young men, boys really, in war uniforms. He pointed to a group photo of six soldiers each holding a rifle in one hand, their free arms slung around one another's shoulders.

"That's me on the end. And that's your father there in the middle. The short one."

I examined the image of my father from twenty years earlier, looking young and thin. It was hard to conceive that the people in the photograph were really my father and the Countess.

"That photograph was taken just a few days after we completed basic training. I was a terrible soldier. But your father was a born warrior."

"What?"

"Oh, yes. A natural leader. A great marksman. Always

kept cool under fire. Has he not told you anything about the war?"

"Nothing."

"Do you know that he was awarded an Iron Cross?"

"He would never discuss his experience in the war."

"Well, there are some things that should be told. It was late 1916 in northern France. Your father had already been promoted to corporal by then. We were dug in for days during the Battle of the Somme. Tens of thousands perished during that battle. The enemy was making a big push, and we were retreating under heavy fire. Two of us, me and Habermaas, who is the tallest one in that picture, got tangled in some barbed wire as we ran back toward another trench. Your father had already made it and was returning fire to give us cover when a mustard gas cloud swept over us. Habermaas and I were goners, trapped in the wire with the mustard cloud blowing into our faces. We had lost our masks during the retreat, and I started gagging as the gas hit the back of my throat. I fell to my knees and tried to hold my breath until the cloud passed. Habermaas got hit in the back with a bullet, and I saw him go down. I couldn't hold my breath any longer. I took a short breath through my nose and immediately started coughing, and I knew I was a dead man. I fell forward, the skin on my legs ripping on the barbed wire. I still have the scars running down my legs."

He lifted his right pant leg and revealed a long, rutted scar running up the side of his calf. "Thankfully you can't see them when I wear stockings," he quipped.

"So I was just lying there, waiting to die, when your father appeared out of nowhere, wearing a gas mask and carrying two others. He didn't even have his weapon. He just charged across the battlefield under heavy fire. Somehow he got the masks over our faces, freed us from the wire, and carried us both back to safety. I have no idea how he found the strength, but he did. It was the bravest act I've ever witnessed. I owe him my life.

"Habermaas died a few weeks later from an infection. Two of the other boys in that photo died as well. So many friends literally torn apart before our eyes. After the war, your father became a pacifist and refused to accept his Iron Cross. They say that war breeds hawks and doves, and your father became a wonderful dove, as did I. Only I became a dove with much brighter plumage."

He let go a halfhearted chuckle. Then he turned the page in the album, and there was another photograph of my father holding his gun, looking much harder and world-weary than on the previous page.

"This one was taken just a few days before the end of the war."

He carefully removed the photograph and held it up to closely examine it.

"We were just children really," he said. "Here, I want you to have this. But don't tell your father I gave it to you."

"I won't," I said. And I tucked the photograph into my rucksack along with the cash he had given me.

I stood, thinking that this might be the last time I would

be in that apartment, as he walked me to the door.

"So—I will see you next week. Same time," he said.

"But I thought you said—"

"The Countess's famous balls may return sooner rather than later. You never know. And even if they don't, I can afford to pay for the printing for quite a while now that I don't have Fritz to blow my money on. But don't tell your father. He's a proud man."

"Thank you," I said.

When I arrived back home, I found my father in his office, his head bent low over some papers. He rubbed the side of his forehead as if massaging away a headache, and he looked broken and tired, quite a contrast to the photograph of the tough young soldier I had in my rucksack.

I approached and placed the money I had collected on the desk. He didn't look up. He examined a balance sheet, and he kept shaking his head, as if the numbers didn't make sense.

"Papa?"

"Huh?" he grunted, eyes still glued to the papers on the desk.

I wanted to ask about the war and why he had refused the Iron Cross. I wanted to know what it was like to shoot a gun at another man and what it felt like to kill. I wanted to be able to tell him that I was proud of him for saving those men. I was about to speak, but the words got stuck in my throat. In that instant I decided that if he wanted to keep that part of his life a secret, it wouldn't be appropriate for me to bring it up. So I resolved to keep the photograph to myself. Something about that decision made me feel older, as if it were the most mature thing I had ever done. And the fact that I was now the keeper of my father's secret made me feel closer to him than I ever had.

"Good night, Papa," I said.

"Good night, Karl," he said absently.

I retreated to my room and took out the photo of my father and compared it with the images of my boxing hero, Barney Ross, I had ripped out of *The Ring* magazine. Whereas before I had perceived my father as the complete opposite of Ross, I now saw similarities in their expressions: hard looks of determination, as if they both were fighting for their lives.

The Brown Bomber

After a long trip to America to lobby for a shot at a heavyweight title fight against Jimmy "the Cinderella Man" Braddock, Max returned to Berlin, and our lessons resumed as before. Despite the fact that he had trained me for almost two years, he remained an enigmatic figure. More and more, he was being pictured in the press with Hitler, Goebbels, and the other Nazi leaders and described as proof of the supremacy of German blood. Yet this didn't make sense to me, given how many Jewish friends and associates he seemed to have. Even his manager, the legendary Joe Jacobs, was an American Jew. Because the fight world was centered in the United States, some European fighters had American managers, and many of those managers were Jewish.

When Max brought Jacobs to Germany for his fight against Steve Hamas in May of 1935, it caused a huge scandal. The fight was staged in Hamburg, and first the hotel where Max had booked rooms wouldn't even let Jacobs check in. The hotel management relented only when Max threatened to expose the hotel in the American press.

Max pummeled Hamas so badly, the fight had to be stopped in the ninth round. The hometown crowd went wild and spontaneously sang *"Deutschland über Alles."* Jacobs was standing beside Max when the entire crowd rose and gave the Nazi salute, and he was even photographed giving the salute along with everyone else, holding his ubiquitous cigar in his hand. The photograph of Jacobs and Schmeling saluting together appeared in newspapers all around the world. In America Jacobs was accused of being a traitor to his country and his religion. And in Germany Max was accused of the same kind of disloyalty because the Nazis thought that Jacobs's salute was an insult, particularly because of the cigar he held in his raised hand.

Although he was considered old at thirty, Max had emerged as one of the top contenders to take the heavyweight crown. The other most exciting contender was Joe Louis, who had never been defeated, and the boxing press seemed to think his ascent to the championship was inevitable. The grandson of slaves from Alabama, Louis had many nicknames in the press: the Dark Destroyer, the Mocha Mauler, the Mahogany Maimer, and the Chocolate Chopper, but he was best known as the Brown Bomber.

Max knew that if he wanted a shot at a title fight against Jimmy Braddock, he would have to fight Louis first, so a bout was scheduled to be held in Yankee Stadium in New York on June 19, 1936. In the months leading up to the fight, Max became obsessed with Louis, studying films of his fights with a scientist's eye and building a strategy to defeat the man who most boxing writers considered unbeatable.

Most of his training tips for me at that time were put into the context of his upcoming fight with Louis.

"You've got to work on your jab," he said one afternoon as he watched me pound the heavy bag. "The more power and speed you can pack into your jab, the less you'll need to rely on bigger punches that sap your energy and leave you open to counterattacks. They say Joe Louis has such a strong jab, he doesn't even need any of his other punches. That's why he never gets knocked out."

I stopped pounding the bag and asked the question that had been on my mind, along with everyone else's in the gym: "Are you afraid to fight him?"

"I'm never frightened of getting in the ring," he said with a small grin.

"Why not?"

"I've been hurt before. I understand pain. But there are rules and codes of honor in boxing that I've lived my whole life by. A loss is a loss. Everyone has them. It's the world outside the ring that's getting more and more complicated and making losing more challenging."

"What do you mean?"

"These days it seems the whole government has taken an interest in whom I fight. Reich Minister Goebbels has made it very clear that he doesn't want me to take on Louis."

"Why not?"

"He's afraid I might lose. A German losing to a Negro would hurt their theories of German superiority."

"What do you think?"

"I think I can beat him," he said. "I saw a flaw in his technique."

"No, I meant, what do you think about their theories?"

I had never really asked Max's opinion about any-thing outside my boxing training. And it felt like I had crossed a line when I asked this question, but it had just slipped out. No one really discussed politics in the gym, particularly around Max. He paused a moment before responding.

"I've fought dozens of men of all backgrounds, and you see every type of human emotion in the ring: heroism, cow-ardice, rage, fear, doesn't matter the skin color. Everyone bleeds the same."

"Do you hate Louis like the papers say?"

"I don't even know him. That's just sportswriters trying to stir things up. Sport is sport," he said. "Hate has nothing to do with it."

"How are you going to beat him?"

"Ah, you want to know the biggest secret in boxing,

huh? If I tell you, you must swear to never tell a soul. If word ever got out, Louis would destroy me."

"I swear," I said.

For weeks Max had been hinting at the flaw he had discovered in Louis's technique, and the sportswriters had been trying to guess at the secret, but nobody had. He claimed that he hadn't shared the information with anyone, not even his wife.

Max glanced over his shoulder to make sure no one was nearby or listening; then he led me aside to a corner of the gym to hide us from view and positioned me as if I were Joe Louis and he were squared off in the ring against me. My pulse quickened as Max lowered his voice.

"When Louis delivers his jab, he drops his left," he said.

He demonstrated by moving my left arm in a jab and then freezing it in the lowered position.

"You see?" he continued. "That leaves him vulnerable to attack by my right-hand counterpunch."

He punched me in slow motion with his meaty right hand.

"Your straight right is your best punch!" I said.

"Exactly," he said. "All I have to do is to be patient and wait for my openings, and I know I can beat him. If I can survive enough of those jabs." Max looked me in the eye. "Don't tell anyone, Karl. My fate rests with you now."

That night I drew a sketch of Joe Louis into my journal. It was the first time I had ever drawn a Negro. At first his facial features seemed so different, but as I stared

THE BROWN BOMBER

at his photograph and drew the face, I noticed how young he looked. It made me realize that he was closer to my age than either Max or Barney Ross. He looked young and hungry, as if he wanted to prove something to the world, just like me.

Sour Sixteen

IN THE WEEKS LEADING UP TO THE LOUIS FIGHT, MAX went to train in America. I continued working out at the club and entering local youth tournaments, always with an eye toward the goal of one day becoming the German Youth Champion. My only true distraction was Greta.

Just a few days before the fight, Greta was due to turn sixteen. I made her a hand-drawn card depicting the Eiffel Tower. At first I just created the card using black ink on paper, but it didn't look nice enough. Unlike the comic strips and caricatures I created, this needed color. So I started over. I carefully drew the picture in pencil and then colored it with watercolors. I let the paint dry and then filled in the details in pen and ink.

With some of the meager money I had saved, I also bought her a small silver charm shaped like the Notre Dame Cathedral to replace the clover charm she had given me. I had the new charm wrapped in a small box and tucked in my back pocket as I approached the park at our usual meeting time.

The sun hung low in the sky and gave off a flaming yellow glow behind darkening clouds. As I walked, I squeezed the small rubber ball that Max had given me. In addition to being a tool to strengthen my grip, the ball provided a good tension release, as I always felt a nice little knot of anticipation before seeing Greta. I arrived at our meeting place by the bench and was surprised not to find her already there.

She typically beat me by about a minute or two. I sat on the bench and waited, scanning the near darkness for her approach.

Then I heard some rustling in the bushes nearby and the distinct sound of Greta crying out, "No." I moved toward the noise. I heard her gasp. I moved behind the first row of shrubs to discover Greta pressed up against a tree by Herr Koplek.

"Please stop," she pleaded, straining against his grasp.

"Come on, open up for me," he growled, leaning his face forward and sniffing her neck. His tongue darted out and touched the skin of her throat.

"Hey!" I shouted.

"Karl!" she gasped.

I approached, but Herr Koplek did not release her.

"Get away, boy," he said. "If you know what's good for you. *Schnell!*"

"Get your hands off her," I said.

"I know what you've been up to," he said. "You both could be in deep trouble. Now if you want me to keep my mouth shut, you'd better get out of here, Jew."

"Karl, please," Greta said. "Don't go."

"I said take your hands off her now."

I grabbed him by the shoulder and spun him toward me. I balled up my fists and assumed a fighting stance.

"Don't do anything stupid," he said. "If you don't get out of here this minute, you and your family will be out in the street tomorrow. I swear it."

I stood there with my fists cocked, feeling the blood pulse through my fingers, wanting more than anything to unleash a torrent of punches at him. He was flabby and slow, and I had been doing all the coal shoveling for the past two years, so I was certain that his shoulders and arms had weakened. I knew I could beat him. I wanted to hurt him badly, to defend Greta and myself. But my mind quickly calculated the risk, and I knew that if I punched him, there would be dire consequences.

So I lunged forward and gave him a quick shove, which sent him tumbling to the ground. Then I grabbed Gteta by the hand and shouted, "Come on!" We both took off out of the bushes and through the park.

Koplek called after us: "You'll regret that, Stern!"

We ran without speaking for several blocks, feeling eyes following us that weren't there, certain that Koplek was hot on our heels. When we were just a few blocks from our apartment building, Greta started to slow. I glanced around to make sure no one was watching and pulled her into a dark alley.

"What do we do now?" she said, out of breath.

"I don't know," I replied. "I have to think."

"He knows we've been meeting. He'll tell my father."

"We haven't done anything wrong. He did. He attacked you. We should turn him in. It's our word against his."

"No one will believe us," she said. "We're kids. And you're a Jew. Who knows what he'll say we've been doing?"

"He never saw us do anything."

"He saw us kiss in the basement that first time."

"But that was two years ago."

"That doesn't matter. It's enough."

"Enough to what?" I said. "Get me arrested?"

"I don't know. Maybe."

"I should've hit him anyway," I said.

"Then you'd really be in trouble. Look, I've got to get home."

"What if Koplek says something?"

"I don't know," she said. "We've got to come up with a story."

"I'm not going to tell a story," I said. "I'm going to tell the truth."

"We can't tell the truth." Her eyes welled up with tears. "Please, Karl. Just don't say anything. Maybe Koplek won't say anything either."

"Even if he doesn't, what if he comes after you again? What'll you do then?"

"I don't know. Just please don't say anything."

"Greta . . ."

"Please, Karl, I've got to go." She backed away from me.

"Wait," I said. I was desperate for her to stay, to hold and protect her.

"I'm sorry. I've really gotta go," she said.

And she turned and ran back out of the alley toward our apartment building.

I watched her dash away. It was only after she disappeared from sight that I realized that I still had her card and the small box in my back pocket.

The Reopening of Galerie Stern

I DIDN'T SAY ANYTHING TO MY PARENTS THAT NIGHT. AS the hours passed, the weight of guilt built up inside me, coupled with the raw fear of exposure, so I could feel each tick of the clock pass like the Sword of Damocles swinging over my head. Greta's desperate voice echoed in my head. I had recurring visions of her pressed against the tree in Herr Koplek's grasp. Her expression, which was typically so confident and in control, looked vulnerable, horrified, and scared. All of this made my feelings for Greta more pronounced than ever, and my desire to see her rose up like a fast-escalating fever.

In the morning I stayed away from the basement and did my best to avoid Herr Koplek. I hoped to see Greta in the hallway and lingered by the front door on my way to and from school to increase my chances of seeing her, but I didn't. I still carried her birthday gift and card in my back pocket, planning to furtively pass them to her if I got the opportunity. I wanted more than anything to speak with her, to know she was okay and to find out if she had confessed anything or if Koplek had approached her father.

A full day passed without incident, and I started to relax. That night we dined as a family, which had become a relatively rare occurrence because of my father's odd schedule and my mother and me running deliveries for him. My mother had prepared a simple meal of noodles with mashed turnips and gravy flavored with just the slightest amount of shredded meat. Meat had become a rarity, and the quality was generally poor. Hildy called the dish "shoelace stew" because the strands of meat reminded her of thin strips of leather. We had just sat down when there was a loud knock at the door. Everyone froze at the noise. Since Uncle Jakob's arrest, we had heard more and more stories of the Gestapo's coming to arrest people at night with no warning or explanation. My father shot my mother a glance.

"You expecting anyone?"

"No," she answered quietly.

As soon as I heard the knock, my body tensed as I assumed it was Herr Koplek finally coming for revenge. My father did not reply, perhaps hoping whoever it was would just go away. But after a moment the knocking resumed.

"Herr Stern?" A voice called from behind the door. "It's Fritz Dirks."

My father registered surprise and rose to answer the door.

Fritz Dirks worked for the large real estate company that managed several buildings in the neighborhood, including ours. He was also an art lover. And although they were not friends, he and my father got along well. He had attended several openings at the gallery and even purchased a painting from my father years earlier. From the kitchen I could see down the hall as my father opened the door and Herr Dirks stepped inside, holding his bowler hat in his hands, wearing a grave expression. An extremely tall, gaunt older man, he had just a few strands of gray hair that he combed over his bald head.

"I'm sorry to disturb you, Herr Stern."

"Not at all, Herr Dirks, please come in. May I offer you something?"

"No, thank you."

"What can I do for you?"

"I'm afraid I'm here to perform an unpleasant task."

"Oh?"

"There's been, well, an accusation against your son."

"Karl?"

"Yes. And it is quite serious. Apparently he's been making sexual advances on the Hauser girl."

"What?" my father gasped.

"That's not true," I said, rising and joining them in the front hall. My mother and Hildy followed.

"Hildegard, go to your room," my father said.

"But, Papa—"

"Come, Hildy," my mother said.

"Mama," she whined.

"Come," my mother repeated, leading her down the hall and into Hildy's room. My mother went inside with her and shut the door, leaving me and my father alone to face Herr Dirks.

"Herr Koplek caught them in the basement in a compromising situation."

"Koplek's a liar!" I spat.

"Karl." My father held up his hand to silence me and then turned back to Herr Dirks. "What exactly is my son accused of?"

"I don't have specific details. Suffice it to say there was apparently inappropriate physical contact."

"We weren't doing anything wrong," I said. "Koplek is the one who—"

"Karl." My father cut me off again. "What is going on with you and the Hauser girl?"

"We're friends. Good friends. She would never say I did anything *inappropriate.*"

"She has said nothing," Herr Dirks said. "And she will say nothing. Her parents don't want her to be involved in this. As a result, they refuse to deny or acknowledge anything. They just want it to go away."

"But Koplek is lying," I said.

"Jürgen Koplek has worked for my company for seventeen years. He is not the most agreeable man, but he has an unblemished work record. I'm afraid that given the circumstances, I'm going to have to ask you to move out."

"Move out!" my father gasped. "You must be joking."

"I'm afraid not," he replied.

"But this is nothing. Two sixteen-year-olds holding hands—"

"Herr Koplek said they were doing more than holding hands."

"He's a liar, Papa. He is the one who was inappropriate. He was jealous."

"I didn't come here to arbitrate anything between you and Herr Koplek," Dirks interrupted. "But I must say it would be hard for anyone to believe that a forty-two-year-old Aryan would be jealous of a sixteen-year-old Jew. You must be rational about this."

"Rational?" my father said. "We've lived here for ten years. Ten years. Even in the leanest times I've always paid my rent on time, haven't I?"

"Yes, but this is not about that."

"We have rights as tenants too," my father said.

"Unfortunately for you, that contention is now open to interpretation. Everyone in the building has heard about this. True or not, there is a scandal. There are party members living in this building. I don't want any trouble. No one wants any trouble." He lowered his voice. "Look, I'm not saying I don't believe your son. I'm terribly sorry. I really am. This is not how I want things to be. But I can't overlook this, given the way things are. I have to ask you to leave."

"The way things are . . . ," my father muttered. "What if we refuse to go?"

"When I said I was *asking* you to leave, it was merely a polite turn of phrase. You are being evicted, Herr Stern. Please don't make any trouble. You have nothing to gain and even more to lose."

"Where will we go?" my father said, as much to himself as to anyone in the room.

"I wish I could help you. I really do. But I'm afraid there's a new policy in our company to conform to the new laws that we are not allowed to rent vacant apartments to Jews. I can give you to the end of the week. Again, I am sorry."

With that, he put his bowler hat back on and walked out. My father and I stood in silence for a moment. I waited for him to confront me. Here I had just caused our family to be evicted from our apartment with nowhere to go. I watched him rub his eyes, anticipating the explosion. After a moment he took a deep breath and said: "Well, now I've got to find a way to break this to your mother."

He started to move down the hall.

"Papa, I—"

"You don't need to explain anything to me, Karl. I trust that you were a gentleman." And then he added, "Or at least I trust that you were a gentleman to as high a degree as she wanted you to be." He gave a small grin. "I was a boy once too. No matter who is in power, I never want you thinking it's wrong to desire a girl's attention. That is life's greatest sweetness. I would never want to deny you that joy. Come on. We've got to start packing."

I watched my father retreat down the hall and was filled with a strong mix of emotions toward him. For the first time it hit me that he understood me more than I ever gave him credit for. Despite our troubles, he walked straight and tall with his head slightly lifted, a posture I used to think conveyed arrogance or aloofness, but now communicated strength and resolve. It was as if I could see the shadow of the soldier he used to be coming into focus and following him close behind.

My father and I spent the next two days trying to find us a place to live. I went with him from building to building, always with the same results. None of the gentile buildings would accept Jewish tenants anymore. We ventured into the Jewish neighborhoods too, but most of the Jewish-owned apartment buildings were overcrowded because Jews were being forced out of the gentile neighborhoods.

We finally found a small apartment that was available in the Jewish quarter. It was a two-bedroom in a shabby tenement building, less than half the size of our old apartment. My father and I walked through the filthy hallway with the landlord close behind and entered the kitchen.

"You're charging twice as much as I pay now for a place half the size and half as clean," my father said, running his finger along the countertop. He lifted his finger, which was now covered with a visible layer of gray dust.

"It's supply and demand," the landlord said. "All you need is a little bit of dusting and mopping, and this place will be as good as new."

My father opened one of the kitchen cabinets, and a dozen roaches scurried out on the counter and quickly disappeared into cracks in the wall.

"What's a few bugs?" the landlord said.

"Come on, Karl. We're leaving."

"Suit yourself," the landlord called after us. "But you won't find anything better for the price. You'll see."

The landlord turned out to be right. And with no better options, my father decided that we would have to move into the gallery until we could find a better circumstance. The days of art exhibitions were long over, and he had not used the space for anything but storage in well over a year. We owned the small freestanding building. And although it was not made for people to live in, it did have the advantage of having no neighbors who could object to us living there. And the price was right.

My mother was appalled by the idea. I overheard them arguing about the decision late at night through the walls of my bedroom.

"The gallery is only one room!" she said.

"There's the back office," my father countered. "And we can divide the front room."

"Four of us in the front room?"

"Well, there's also the basement. Karl can sleep down there, and we can split the front room with Hildy."

"I do not want my son sleeping in the basement with the rats."

"We don't have rats, Rebecca. And he's too old to share a space with his sister. He's almost a man now. It'll be okay."

"It will not be okay," she said. "Living on top of one another like animals."

"We don't have a choice right now, damn it."

At first I was angry about the prospect of having to live in the basement. But then I realized that given the choices, it was the best option. My father was right that I needed my privacy. And a part of me thrilled at his acknowledgment of my maturity. Something about the gritty environment appealed to me in my boxing training mode, which encouraged the shunning of creature comforts. When Hildy found out the plan, she was excited, as if the whole thing were a big adventure. I knew she had been feeling neglected, and the idea of everyone in closer confines appealed to her, as if it were going to be a big slumber party.

The next day we packed what we could and moved the bare essentials over to the gallery. We had a one-day sale to get rid of the furniture and other things we would not be taking. Several people who lived in our apartment building and the surrounding blocks came to buy. My mother observed bitterly, "One minute they're our neighbors; the next minute they're looting our apartment."

"They're not looting. We need the money," my father reminded her. "And we don't need these things. They're helping us by buying."

"You call it helping, I call it cannibalism."

She couldn't stand to watch her soon-to-be former

neighbors pick over the things that she had carefully accumulated over the life of her marriage, so she went to the gallery to sweep, dust, and set things up. I feared that she might be heading into one of her moods. Our family was already in such terrible circumstances, I didn't know how we'd manage if she did.

Hildy and I each had to get rid of half of our books and toys. I hoped Greta would come by with her family. I still had not seen her since she had run away from me that night. The night before the sale, I had gone to her apartment to deliver the birthday card and present to her. I figured we were already being evicted from the building—what more could happen for merely delivering a gift? But when I knocked, nobody answered. I thought I heard someone quietly approach the door from the other side to look through the peephole and then retreat. But when I tried to stare through the small glass eye, I could see nothing. I knocked again and again, but still no one came. So I left the card and the small box beside the door. I had signed the card, "May all your birthday wishes come true. Fondly, Karl," which I thought was inoffensive enough to risk having her parents find it and read it before it got to Greta. However, neither Greta nor her parents ever showed up at our apartment.

After the sale, a grimy old junk dealer came and gave my father a few hundred marks for the things that had gone unsold. The man loaded everything into a large wooden cart pulled by a donkey. After he left, the three of us took one last look through the empty apartment where I had spent all my life. I walked into my room and looked around. I could just make out the faded outlines of where my boxing posters had once hung on the walls, the only evidence I had ever occupied the room. I stood in the corner where I had done my push-ups and sit-ups every morning and wondered how many of each I must have done in the past couple of years. The sun shone in through the windows and filled the room with warm light. I had never really noticed how bright my room was until that moment. I didn't want to go live in the dark basement of the gallery, which I now realized resembled a prison cell more than a proper room.

"Karl?" I heard my father call.

I joined my father and Hildy in the front hall, where they waited with glum expressions. My father gestured to the door, and we walked out, leaving the front door open as we went. It felt strange not to close and lock our door, but I could see that my father had left it ajar intentionally, as if to announce that those rooms held no value to us anymore. They were just a series of walls and doors, and not a home that needed to be protected. On some level I understood that the open door would also serve as a reminder or even an accusation to the neighbors that we had been kicked out of our home and they had let it happen.

As we emerged from inside the building, I glanced back, hoping to catch a glimpse of Greta through her window. While I was turning, I noticed a hand had been holding aside the drapes in the Hausers' front room. But before I could see who it was, the drapes fell back over the window.

My father called to me to come along.

I reluctantly turned from our building and followed them down the street toward our new home. I half expected Greta to come running out of the front door and into my arms just like in an American movie. I imagined us holding a long embrace and then promising we would wait for each other. I reached into the bottom of my pocket, where I had tucked the clover charm, and held it in my fist, trying to hold on to a piece of her. Yet with each step I took away from our building, I could feel my life with Greta disappearing into the distance.

Word from Dachau

THE ONE POSITIVE ASPECT OF LIVING IN THE GALLERY was that the move seemed to reawaken something in my mother's spirit. She took on the task of converting the gallery into a home with an energy I had feared she no longer possessed. She immediately divided the front room into three sections, using thick white cloth curtains hung from hooks my father screwed into the ceiling. The front half served as the living room and dining room, while the back half was divided into two bedrooms, one for Hildy and one for my parents, with a narrow hallway down the middle and leading to the back. She set up each area to maximize the space, and by the time she was done, she had created the illusion of a home.

Because of its proximity to the bathroom, the only

source of running water, the back office was converted into a makeshift kitchen. Our coal-burning stove was placed by the back window. And my father bought an old freestanding washbasin that he converted into a sink by running a hose from the faucet in the bathroom. A small cupboard from our old kitchen stood in the corner of the living area filled with our good china. We had room for only one set of dishes, and my mother had insisted on getting rid of our everyday dishes and keeping the china, which had been a wedding gift from her parents.

The bathroom was fairly large and had a huge porcelain bathtub that hadn't been used in more than a decade. A thick layer of dust and rust stains scarred its interior. My mother spent the better part of an afternoon scrubbing that tub, and she managed to clean it to the point where there were only a few small stains visible near the drain. She knew she would need her bath more than ever, as it would be one of the few places to achieve any real sense of privacy.

Although a bit cold and damp, the basement provided me with a larger living space than I'd had in our old apartment. The room had a dirt floor and thick stone walls that formed the foundation of the building. The old printing press occupied one section of the room. Most of the art bins had already been cleared away. My mother placed one of our Persian rugs on the floor, covering a good section of the dirt. I set up my bed, chair, and dresser; and I had just enough room left over for a small workout area, where I kept my dumbbells, jump rope, and boxing gloves. I was even

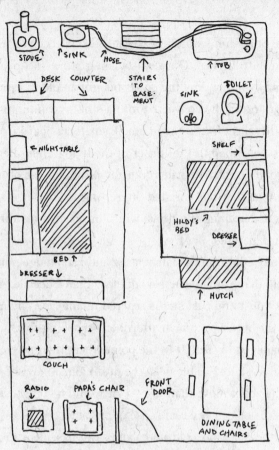

STOVE   ↑ SINK   HOSE   STAIRS TO BASE-MENT   ↑ TUB

DESK   COUNTER   SINK   TOILET

← NIGHTTABLE   SHELF →

HILDY'S BED ↗

DRESSER →

BED ↑

DRESSER ↓   ↑ HUTCH

COUCH

RADIO   PAPA'S CHAIR   FRONT DOOR

DINING TABLE AND CHAIRS

THE NEW GALLERY FLOOR PLAN

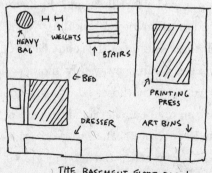

HEAVY BAG ↗   WEIGHTS ↑   ↑ STAIRS

← BED

PRINTING PRESS ↗

DRESSER ↓   ART BINS ↓

THE BASEMENT FLOOR PLAN

able to hang an old heavy bag I had salvaged from the club from one of the thick wooden beams that lined the ceiling.

For a while life seemed fairly normal at the gallery, or as normal as it could be. We were distracted from our diminished circumstances by all the work it took to make the place habitable, and the shared project bonded us. Hildy was right that it also forced us to spend more time together, and despite the close quarters, we managed to find moments of levity. Even my parents appeared to be getting along better. One night over dinner they both shared a laugh when my father suggested that they try to have a gallery reception with the rooms configured this way.

"Yes, we could hang paintings from the pillows on the beds," my mother joked.

"Or better yet," my father suggested, "we should just be like Marcel Duchamp and claim the furniture *is* the art."

Years earlier Duchamp had caused a major stir in the art world when he took an actual urinal, signed it, titled it *Fountain*, and declared it a work of art.

"I wonder how much we could get for our toilet," my mother said.

"Well, that all depends on if it's been flushed or not," my father replied with a grin.

"Oh, Sig, that's disgusting."

But she said it with a laugh, and we all laughed together for the first time in as long as I could remember. From then on, when someone had to go to the bathroom, we would say, "Excuse me, I have to use the sculpture."

After a couple of weeks we found a routine. My mother returned her focus to trying to find out information about Uncle Jakob, who had been in Dachau for well over a year. Originally established to hold political prisoners, the camp also housed "religious prisoners," like dissident priests and preachers, and Jews. At the time of his imprisonment, political prisoners like Uncle Jakob were considered the greatest threats to the Reich and were not allowed to communicate with the outside world. The fact that he was also Jewish would only have made things that much worse for him. Because of their need for secrecy, we never knew the full names of any of Uncle Jakob's political associates, so my mother had no way to track them down to find out if they knew anything.

One day Hildy and I were shopping with our mother at an outdoor market near the gallery. Farmers sold vegetables, meats, and dairy products in rows of stalls lining the street. We walked most quickly by the vendor selling horsemeat, because of the powerful stench of the entrails, which were displayed in buckets beneath the trays of butchered meat.

Because of our non-Jewish looks, my mother and I could walk the streets without incident. But with Hildy with us, we had to always be on guard. As we wandered through the market, I noticed several women sneer in our direction when they caught sight of Hildy. At the cheese stall, my mother picked out a small piece of Brie. When she handed it to the farmer to be weighed, he refused to take it.

"I don't sell to Gypsies," he said.

"We're not Gypsies," my mother said.

"Or Jews," he replied, staring directly at Hildy. "Go find a kosher cow."

My mother placed the piece of Brie back down and pressed her thumb into it, leaving a dent.

"Come on," she said, dragging us both along.

We quickly wound our way back through the market. Suddenly a man grabbed my mother's arm. He wore a tattered coat and a gray wool cap pulled low over his face. My mother quickly stepped back, assuming he was a beggar or a thief. I instinctively moved forward to defend her, positioning my body between the man and my mother. I held up my hand in warning, and he backed off a step.

"Stay back," I said, my voice cracking just enough to remind myself of the fear that still resided inside me, even after years of boxing.

"Wait. You're Jakob Schwartz's sister, *ja?*" he said.

"Yes," she replied, startled to hear the name of her brother.

She looked closer at the face under the hat, and some recognition dawned on her.

"We've met before. You're Stefan—"

"Yes." He cut her off, glancing around nervously as if at any moment he would be arrested. "Your brother and I were comrades."

"Have you any word from—"

"That's why I risked approaching you. I received word through our channels that Jakob is not well."

"What do you mean?"

"He's very sick."

"How sick?"

"I've told you all I know." He started to pull away.

"But—," she said.

"I have to go. You shouldn't be seen talking with me. I've told you all I know."

And with that he disappeared into the crowd.

That night my mother implored my father to let her go see Uncle Jakob at the concentration camp. In our new living conditions there was no place for private conversation, and Hildy and I could easily hear every word of their argument through the the fabric walls of their bedroom.

"Are you insane?" he said. "You want to go to Dachau?"

"My brother is sick. I need to help him."

"What help would it be for you or me to go there? We wouldn't get past the first barbed wire fence. You're talking about suicide."

"We have to do something," she said. "I can't stand this silence anymore. Just sitting and waiting as things get worse and worse."

"If we ask questions, it'll draw attention to us. Do you want to be interrogated by the Gestapo?"

"If that's what it takes."

"Takes to do what? I understand you care about your brother. We all do. But even if we find out more information, there will be nothing we can do. And we'll have risked something just for a small bit of useless knowledge."

"It's not useless knowledge. I need to know he's okay. He's my only relative. I'm all he has."

"I'll tell you one thing. He wouldn't want you going anywhere near Dachau or doing anything that would put you or the kids at risk."

"I'm going to find out what's happening to him."

"Rebecca . . ."

"I don't care if they lock me up. What kind of country is it that they can lock you up for asking a question? I don't care anymore. . . ."

Then she started crying, and my father softened. He lowered his voice into a more soothing tone.

"Look, I know a man on the police force, someone I was in the war with. It's been many years since I've had any contact with him, but I can go to him and see what he can find out. He may not agree to help us, but I trust that he would at least be discreet about the request."

The next day my father reached out to his contact, a man named Lutz, who had been with the Berlin police force for over twenty years. The Berlin civil police had come under the supervision of the Nazis, but they still operated with some autonomy, and a few in their ranks, including Lutz, were not Nazi Party members. My father came back that night and said that Lutz had agreed to find out what he could, but that it might take a couple of days. I was struck by the loyalty my father's army buddies seemed to have toward him. I wondered if Lutz was the other surviving soldier in the photograph the Countess had shown me.

We heard nothing for several days. Finally, late one Friday night, there was a knock at the door. I heard the knock and my parents stirring up above me from my bed in the basement. Through the darkness I glanced at the clock beside my bed. It was one A.M. Any late-night call was cause for alarm. I rushed upstairs and into my parents' bedroom, where Hildy was already huddled between them on their bed. They had not turned on a light. There was another soft knock at the door.

"Don't answer it," my mother whispered. "Pretend we don't hear."

"If they were here to arrest us, they wouldn't be knocking so softly. In fact they wouldn't bother with knocking at all. Just stay here."

My father tied on his bathrobe and went to the door. From inside the bedroom we heard him open it.

"*Guten Abend*, Sigmund," a voice said. "I'm sorry to call so late, but I didn't want to raise suspicions."

"No, no, please come inside, Lutz."

"I suggest we leave the lights off," Lutz said. "I don't want the neighbors to think you're holding a clandestine meeting."

"Of course," my father agreed. "Come inside."

My father led Lutz through the darkness to the kitchen, where he turned on a small desk lamp, the light of which could not be seen from the street. My mother tied on her bathrobe, and the three of us joined our father in the office. Lutz was a tall, big-boned man, with a helmet of graying thick hair. He wore a policeman's uniform.

"*Guten Abend*, Frau Stern," he said. "Dolph Lutz." He formally offered his hand with a slight bow.

"*Guten Abend*," my mother said, shaking his hand.

"I'm sorry to call so late, but as I explained to your husband, I didn't want to arouse any suspicion."

"Of course," she said.

"You have fine-looking children, Sigmund," he said, nodding toward me and Hildy.

"Thank you," my father said.

"Unfortunately I'm not sure you want them to hear what I have to say."

"We now live without walls," my mother said, "so secrets are impossible."

"Yes, I see," he said, taking a deep breath. "I'm afraid I have some terrible news. Your brother passed away last week."

Seeing Red

BEFORE LUTZ HAD EVEN FINISHED THE SENTENCE, MY mother emitted a sharp cry as if she'd been stabbed and fell back against the counter. Papa had to grab her arm to hold her up. I fetched a chair, and my father and I lowered her into it. She buried her face in her hands and sobbed. It was a guttural howl, from deep inside. I was scared that someone might hear her, but I knew we could not attempt to silence her. Lutz awkwardly stared at his feet. Finally her tears subsided.

"How?" my mother asked.

"I could not find out many specifics," Lutz said. "All I know is that the official cause of death was listed as dysentery."

"Dysentery?"

"Yes, I'm terribly sorry."

"How does a healthy young man die of dysentery?" my mother said.

"What's dysentery?" Hildy asked through her tears.

"It's a bad stomachache when you have lots of diarrhea," my father quickly explained.

"I really must be going now," Lutz said.

"Of course," my father said. "I will see you out."

Lutz awkwardly bowed toward my mother, and then my father led him back out to the front door of the gallery. Hildy curled into our mother's lap, sniffling. My father returned from the front room and placed a comforting hand on my mother's shoulder.

"Rebecca . . . I'm sorry."

"He really believed it, you know?"

"Believed what?"

"All of that Communist crap about all men being brothers, that one day there would be a workers' paradise where everyone got an equal share. It wasn't just politics for him. He believed it."

"I know." My father nodded. "Karl, Hildy . . . please go back to bed. It's late."

My mother kissed Hildy on the head, and she slid from my mother's lap and went to her bed. I kissed my mother and returned to the basement, where I lay down and listened.

"We've got to get out, Sig," my mother said.

"I know," he answered softly. "I know."

• • •

Later that night, as I lay in bed in the dark, damp basement, the loss of Uncle Jakob started to sink in. It was hard for me to imagine that I would never hear his open laugh again. We would never see an American western movie together again. No one would ever call me buckaroo like he had. Uncle Jakob had been the one person who had encouraged my boxing, and he had never had the chance to see me fight.

The very next day I was scheduled to box at the Voorman Youth Center on the west side of town. It wasn't an official tournament, but rather a small series of exhibition bouts that the center had set up for its members. Neblig met me at the club to be my cornerman and immediately noticed my sour disposition. We usually kidded around a bit before a fight to keep me loose, but that morning I was in no mood for kidding.

"Y-y-y-you okay?" he said.

"I'm fine," I answered shortly.

"You s-s-s-seem mad about something."

"What would I have to be mad about?" I said, with more than a hint of bitterness.

I had plenty to be mad about. I was a Jew living in Nazi Germany. I had been kicked out of school and lost my girlfriend. My father had been denied any chance at a legitimate livelihood, and our family had been evicted from our home. I was living in a damp basement beneath my parents and sister, who had given up all sense of privacy, living in one room divided by bed sheets. My "hero" Max had disappeared to America to chase fights with Joe Louis and Jimmy

Braddock. And my favorite uncle had just died in a prison camp, simply because he was a Red or a Jew or both.

"It's not g-g-g-good to be too mad before a f-f-f-fight," he said. "A little b-b-b-bit of anger is okay to get you going. But if you're too mad, you can m-m-m-make mistakes and leave yourself open."

"When was the last time you were in the ring?"

"It's been a while," he said.

"Then just let me alone, okay?"

I regretted snapping at Neblig; none of my problems were his doing. But the regret was consumed by the anger inside me. Approximately thirty boys had gathered to fight in the cramped little gym. We stood beside the ring, and I waited for my turn to fight. I couldn't wait to get in there. I made my arm muscles pulse under the skin, taking inventory of each in an agitated roll call.

When I finally stepped into the ring, I coiled my body like a crouching lion, waiting to pounce. I was set to fight a beefy kid named Kliegerman, who had blue eyes and wavy blond hair that almost looked white against the pink hue of his scalp. He was a member of a Hitler Youth Athletic League and wore boxing shorts with a red swastika stitched on the front. In the past I had never cared too much about whom I fought in the ring. But now I felt a deep sense of visceral anticipation because of his Aryan features. He was exactly the type of Nazi I wanted to face to vent my rage.

At the bell, I charged out of my corner and immediately

went on the attack, unleashing a furious barrage of punches. Kliegerman was a strong kid with big arms and hands and was able to block most of the punches in that first burst. He landed a hard left jab and right uppercut to my ribs, which I had left exposed after missing on a right cross. His punch landed hard, and I had some of the wind sucked out of me.

I swallowed the pain and attacked again. A couple of my punches broke through his defenses. I snapped off a series of combinations, jab, jab, uppercut, jab, and then a cross, jab, uppercut. Kliegerman attempted to retreat, backpedaling into the far corner, but I stayed with him, aggressively dancing forward with each step he took back. One of my uppercuts landed on his chin and snapped Kliegerman's head back sharply. He accidentally bit his upper lip, and a small trickle of blood escaped from the side of his mouth. For the first time I understood the expression "seeing red." My heartbeat accelerated at the sight of the red blood, and I wanted to see more. My mind shifted into some primitive mode, as if I had become a jungle animal or a shark aroused by the blood. I charged at him, aiming all my punches at his head, wanting to see his lip split open even more. Or better still, I hoped to bloody his nose too or open a cut over his eye. I needed to see more red.

I paid no attention to defense, and Kliegerman threw several punches that all landed, but I didn't feel them. Rage and adrenaline numbed any feeling, and I just kept punching. Eventually Kliegerman's defenses wore down from exhaustion until his hands dropped and he was no longer defending himself at all. I just kept on punching until his legs collapsed beneath him and he fell hard into a sitting position, his feet comically splayed out wide in front of him. He looked stunned and touched his bleeding lip with his gloved hand. I hovered over him, taunting him so I could continue the beating.

"Get up!" I said, my eyes wild with bloodlust. "Come on! Get off your ass and fight. *Schnell!*"

"Okay, step back," the ref said, pushing me back to my corner.

The ref stood over Kliegerman and counted him out and then came over and raised my hand to signal victory. And for the first time I noticed the small audience cheering and hooting at the lopsided match they had just witnessed. My chest heaved with effort, sucking in great gulps of air. I could feel my body decompress, as if the rage were slowly siphoning out of a small hole in my body, leaving me feeling limp and empty

My eyes found Neblig. He shook his head in disapproval. Neblig's look communicated what I was already thinking: that what I had just done had nothing to do with the sweet science of boxing and everything to do with raw violence.

And then I saw him. Just behind Neblig, standing with a group of boys, was Gertz Diener, my old nemesis from the Wolf Pack. His eyes met mine. I tried to read his expression. Was it confusion? Fear? Clearly I was no longer the Piss Boy he remembered.

As shocked as Gertz was to see me, I was even more

surprised to see him. The sight of him hit me harder than any punches Kliegerman had thrown. Until that moment, no one in my boxing world had had any idea I was a Jew. Now I could be exposed.

I looked away from him and tried to pretend I hadn't seen him at all. I quickly stepped out of the ring and approached Neblig.

"What was th-th-th-that all about?" he said. "You're lucky he wasn't m-m-m-much of a fighter, or you could've gotten hurt in there."

"Come on," I said.

I headed straight for the exit, and Neblig followed. I could feel Gertz Diener's eyes on me as I walked out.

The Fight

WHILE I WAS FIGHTING KLIEGERMAN, MAX WAS IN NEW York preparing for his own fight against Joe Louis at Yankee Stadium. For Max, this would be his last and best shot at regaining the heavyweight crown. Whoever won would become the top-ranked contender and challenge Jimmy Braddock for the title. In the days leading up to the fight, anticipation swept across Germany. Every magazine and newspaper ran daily stories about Max, from biographical profiles to his training regimen to detailed analysis of what he needed to do to beat Louis. Radio advertisements for the fight declared: "It is the obligation of every German citizen to tune in to listen to Max defend the white race against the Negro."

There were even newspaper articles about where prominent Germans would be listening to the fight on the radio.

Max's wife, Anny Ondra, had been invited to listen at the home of Propaganda Minister Goebbels and his wife, Magda. Hitler himself had specifically ordered technicians to make sure his personal radio was in perfect working order so that he could listen in his private railroad car, which would be in transit at the time of the fight. The Nazis allowed bars and restaurants to stay open late so people could listen together and cheer their countryman on. Thirty million Germans tuned in as the fight began at ten P.M. New York time, which was three A.M. in Germany.

As great as the anticipation for the fight was across the country, it was even greater among the members of the Berlin Boxing Club. In a rare showing of generosity, Worjyk hosted a listening party at the club. He and Neblig set up Worjyk's large radio on a stand in the center of one of the boxing rings, surrounded by clusters of old wooden folding chairs. Worjyk even provided a barrel of beer and large bowls of pretzels and hard-boiled eggs to snack on. My parents gave me permission to be at the club on the night of the fight, after I had promised to stay there until daylight before coming home. They didn't want me wandering the streets late at night.

The members huddled around the radio, anxiously speculating about the coming bout. Worjyk was excited but nervous, chewing on the stub of his unlit cigar. In public it would've been considered unpatriotic to doubt Max's victory. But inside the club, Worjyk gave his honest and realistic assessment.

"Max had better be careful in the early rounds," Worjyk said. "This kid Louis can do some damage."

"Max has the better right," Johann chimed in.

"But that's about all he's got in terms of raw tools," Worjyk countered.

"You think Louis is going to win?" another fighter said.

"I'm not saying that," Worjyk said, lighting the stub of his cigar. "But think about it this way. Louis is eight years younger than Max. Eight years is a lot in the ring. Louis is an inch and a half taller, five pounds heavier; he's got a longer reach, a bigger chest, thicker biceps and forearms, and bigger thighs, calves, and ankles. And if that isn't enough, consider this: Louis has never been knocked down. Never."

Some nodded in agreement. Willy, who was a Nazi Party member, took offense.

"It sounds like you doubt that a white man can prevail over a black, Worjyk," he said. "It is the duty of every German to believe that Max can triumph in this noble cause. We must all be united."

"Look, this is a boxing match, not a political rally," Worjyk countered. "One of the things you gotta learn in this business is never to believe your own hype. Now we all know that Max has got the advantage in smarts and experience, and that counts for a lot in this game. But after fifteen rounds, it's not their brains that'll be duking it out in there. It'll be their bodies and their hearts."

"I heard a rumor that they only sold out half the tickets, because all the New York Jews are boycotting the fight," someone interjected.

"I heard a rumor that the Jews are plotting to slip Max some drugs before the fight, so he'll go down in the first round," another added.

"Yeah," Johann said sarcastically, "I'm sure his Jewish manager is part of the plot to make his own fighter lose."

"You never know with those people," Willy said.

I had mixed feelings about the fight. Of course I wanted Max to win. Yet on some level, I was very conflicted, because I also wanted to see him fall, to prove to the world that "inferior" races like Negroes and Jews might not be so inferior after all.

Neblig went around and topped off everyone's beer mug just before the fight started. I was almost seventeen years old, and most boys my age drank beer, but I had avoided all alcohol since beginning my training. I took a sip of beer and immediately felt it swimming through my body, making my brain tingle pleasantly. Neblig took a seat next to me, and we clinked beer mugs.

"I think Max's going to t-t-t-take him in ten," Neblig said. "He's g-g-g-gonna get him with a big right."

The radio broadcast started, and we could barely hear Germany's announcer, Arno Hellmis, over the roar of the crowd at Yankee Stadium.

The bell rang, signaling the start of the fight, and we all leaned forward toward the radio.

"And there's the opening bell," Hellmis said. "The fight of the century is under way."

In the first round, Louis connected with a series of punches that set everyone at the club on edge.

"Louis connects with another right to Max's head." Hellmis gasped. "Max's eye is already starting to swell and blacken."

"*Ach*, he'll never make it past the second round." Johann groaned.

"Shut up!" someone else shouted. "You'll bring him bad luck."

In the second and third rounds, Louis continued to do damage with his left jabs, and Max's face became badly bloodied. He seemed to be outmatched by the younger, stronger fighter.

"Max is putting up a courageous fight," Hellmis said, trying to defend Max. "But Louis fights more like a wild animal than a man. It's nearly impossible for a sportsman like Max to defend against such a savage and chaotic attack. It's been three rounds, and Max has yet to land a really solid punch on him."

The members grimly sipped their beer, waiting for something to cheer for. After a while, even Hellmis couldn't spin Max's poor performance into anything worth cheering about.

Then, in the fourth round, Louis finally dropped his guard after throwing a left.

"And Max connects with a solid right!" Hellmis said, his voice excitedly rising in pitch. "And another. Max's last two rights clearly stunned the Negro. Louis looks dazed and confused like a lost schoolboy. And there goes another solid right from Max, snapping back Louis's head. And wait! Wait a minute! I don't believe it, folks, Louis is down! Louis is down! For the first time in his career the Negro has been knocked down! He's struggling back to his feet now, after only a two-count, but Max has turned the tables in this fight!"

The men at the club cheered and kept refilling their beer mugs. I hadn't eaten since dinner, and the alcohol made my whole body feel numb while whirling scenes of the fight danced in my mind. Hellmis's words melted into distinct images, and I saw Max in his purple trunks looming over Louis with greater and greater authority and menace. The men around me laughed, cheered, and slapped one another on the back with every punch Max landed. The two fighters battled it out for eight more rounds, inflicting terrible damage on each other. Max's left eye was completely shut, his lip split, and streaks of his own blood had to be toweled off his face between each round. Yet his energy didn't flag; the momentum of the opportunity to upset Louis and get his shot at the title carried him forward.

Louis became dazed and tired and either from desperation or exhaustion delivered a low blow that brought on howls of outrage from Hellmis.

"Louis knows he is finished, so he is resorting to dirty tactics to stay alive. He is showing that the true colors of the Negro are brown *and* the yellow of a coward!"

Finally, in the twelfth round, Max delivered another

solid combination of punches that sent Louis down, first to his knees and then to the canvas.

"He's down again!" Hellmis screamed. "He's down! Louis is down! He's finished! *Aus! Aus! Aus! Aus! Aus! Aus! Aus!* Max has done it! He's defeated Joe Louis!"

The roomful of men leaped to their feet and cheered, wildly dancing, hugging, and chugging down their mugs of beer. I hugged Neblig, who lifted me up and screamed without a stutter. *"He did it!"*

Everyone spontaneously started clapping and marching out of the club and into the streets, chanting, "Schmeling! Schmeling! Schmeling! Schmeling!" Throngs of others poured into the streets to celebrate. We all swept into a nearby beer hall, where hundreds of people were celebrating, raising their glasses and singing. The room seemed to sway and throb with joyous revelers.

I settled myself on a long bench between Johann and Neblig, and they took turns refilling my beer mug. My vision blurred even more, and I slurred my words as I spoke, causing those seated around me to laugh and try to get me even more drunk. Every time my mug was empty, someone refilled it and proposed a toast to Max, insisting that we down our entire mugs in his honor. I happily obliged, and the beer slid down my throat with increasing ease. I sang and clapped along with the beer-hall sing-alongs and got swept up in the joy of the moment.

After an hour of steady drinking, I had to get up and relieve myself. I pushed myself up from the table, and my legs felt rubbery as I staggered into the men's room. A long troughlike urinal lined one wall. I undid my pants and had started to go when another drunken reveler came in and stood beside me to do the same.

"What a fight, huh?" he said.

"*Ja.*" I agreed.

"He really taught that Negro a lesson, I'll tell you."

"He sure did. *Ja.* He did."

"Too bad he can't fight a Gypsy next, or, even better, a Jew! It'd be fun to see Max take down all the mongrel races one at a time. Wouldn't it?"

My mind froze, and I suddenly realized that I was holding my circumcised penis out in full view for the first time. My stomach lurched as if the man's words had been a hard, quick punch to my gut. I quickly attempted to tuck myself back into my pants, fumbling with the buttons. Before I could finish buckling up, my stomach violently lurched again, and I vomited into the urinal.

"*Scheisse!*" the man said, jumping back to avoid the splatter.

I steadied myself by placing a hand against the wall. But then I heaved and threw up again, emptying myself onto the front of my shirt and the floor this time.

"You okay, buddy?" the man said, stepping back away from me.

"Yeah," I mumbled. "I'm fine."

I took one small step away from the wall. My mind re-focused enough to realize that I wasn't certain if I had pulled into my pants in time. I patted down the front of myself and discovered that my pants were only half unbuttoned, but I had managed to tuck myself inside. My hand came away wet, and I realized that I had urinated on myself. Then I felt my legs collapse beneath me and my body falling. The walls of the bathroom and the urinal turned sideways in my vision. And everything went black.

When my eyes finally fluttered open, I had no idea where I was. I vaguely remembered passing out and was relieved to discover that I was not still on the floor of the men's room of the beer hall. As my eyes adjusted, I realized I was lying on a cot in the locker room of the Berlin Boxing Club.

Neblig entered the room, carrying some of the folding chairs, which he stacked against the far wall.

"*Guten Morgen*, Herr S-s-s-s-stern!" he said sarcastically.

I tried to sit up, but my head felt like it was made of lead and dropped back onto the canvas of the cot. My stomach rolled. A sour taste filled my throat, nose, and mouth.

"What time is it?" I said.

"Around ten."

I saw my dirty clothing lying in a heap beside the cot, including my underwear. I quickly ran my hands over my body and realized I was naked under the blanket that covered me.

"Did you bring me back here?"

"*Ja*. You were in n-n-n-no condition to walk."

"Did you—um—how did I get changed and onto this cot?"

"I did it just like your m-m-m-mama." He laughed. "But

I didn't sing you a lullaby. And no k-k-k-kiss good night either."

He saw me staring at my pile of clothes.

"You w-w-w-were all covered in vomit, and you had p-p-p-p-pissed on yourself. Not your best moment."

I wanted to know if he had noticed my circumcised penis. If so, he gave no indication. He continued to arrange the folding chairs against the wall where they were kept for storage. Then he tossed me an old sweatshirt and warm-up pants from his locker.

"Here. They'll be b-b-b-big on you, but at least you won't smell like a beer-hall bathroom w-w-w-when you go home."

He walked back out of the room, and I quickly slipped on the pants, relieved to have my secret safely hidden again.

The Real Max?

ALL OF GERMANY GOT SWEPT UP IN MAX MANIA. HE flew home in grand style on the Hindenburg, the largest airship in the world and the pride of the Nazi fleet. Thousands turned up to greet him when he landed in Frankfurt, and the event was covered on live radio. Every newspaper and magazine featured photographs of Max and stories about the fight. Almost instantly Max's name and face appeared on products all over Europe as he endorsed everything from his favorite brand of almonds to shirt collars to motor oil. Max also acquired the rights to distribute the film of the Louis fight in Germany, and it quickly became the number one box office hit across the country under the title *Max Schmeling's Victory—A German Victory.*

The first fan to view the movie was Hitler himself. Max

sat directly beside the Führer as he watched the entire film and happily cheered every punch. All of the Nazi high command now vied to get close to Max, and he appeared to be happy to oblige them. The gossip pages of the newspapers ran endless photographs and articles about Anny and Max dining with Hitler or Goebbels and his wife, as if they were all the best of friends.

The Nazi press took every opportunity to position Max's victory as proof of Aryan superiority. German sportswriters and cartoonists depicted Louis as a coward or a savage and Max as a great and honorable Teutonic warrior. Max even wrote the introduction to a book called *Germans Fight for Honor, Not Money: Boxing as a Race Problem* by a man named Ludwig Haymann. I found a copy of the book in the locker room at the Berlin Boxing Club. I flipped open the book and read a random passage:

> *Cowardly by nature, Jews tend to avoid becoming boxers themselves and infest the ranks of managers and promoters. These positions allow them to utilize their natural skills as business cheats and fixers.*

This statement outraged me even more than the typical Nazi propaganda. Any true fight fan knew that the ranks of professional fighters were filled with Jews. The author argued that true Germans *fist*fought for honor while Jews and other mongrel races *prize*fought for money. Max's introduction to the book was a perfunctory greeting, praising

Haymann and encouraging German boys to pursue boxing. Max's words didn't carry any overt references to Haymann's anti-Semitic theories, but by introducing the book, he was clearly giving his endorsement to those views. I became so absorbed in the text, I neglected to hear Johann enter and start to suit up next to me.

"You can borrow that if you like," he said, making me jump with a start.

"Huh?" I said, quickly closing the book and putting it aside.

"The book," he said. "It's mine, but you can borrow it."

I was surprised that the book belonged to Johann. I hadn't known he was a Nazi. My first instinct was to refuse his offer to borrow the book. Yet I worried that he might suspect something of me if I indicated that I was not interested.

"Sure," I said, casually picking up the book again.

"But let me warn you, it's a total waste of time," Johann said. "I thought it was going to be a strategy book about how to win in the ring. But it's really just a bunch of Nazi propaganda. The only help that book would be in a fight is if the ref let me hit my opponent with it."

He laughed and exited the locker room. I was relieved to know that Johann had not become a Nazi. But the book raised more uncomfortable questions about Max. I tucked the book back into my bag and read the entire text that night, each sentence making me more angry and determined to one day prove that a German Jew could be a boxing champion. The book also left me even more confused about Max and his true alliances.

Max was so caught up in his new celebrity and the demands for his time that he didn't have time to train at the Berlin Boxing Club anymore. I was left to wonder if he was a completely different person from the man I had come to know. Perhaps all the attention from Hitler and Goebbels had transformed him into a full-blown Nazi. Could this be the same Max who was friends with my father? Who posed for paintings by banned avant-garde artists? Whose American manager was a Jew? Who had once claimed that there were no differences between men in the ring?

Who was the real Max? I feared what would happen if and when he returned to the club. Would he refuse to train me because he knew I was a Jew? Would he publicly denounce me and make me leave the club? Or perhaps he never would come back. Maybe he had moved beyond all of us.

That summer Germany hosted the Olympic Games in Berlin. In the weeks leading up to the event, the government made a concerted effort to clean up the city and hide all evidence of the regime's anti-Semitism. Acts of violence against Jews declined, and anti-Jewish propaganda posters were taken down and replaced by posters advertising the Olympics. Restaurants and hotels removed their signs that read NO JEWS ALLOWED. So when the community of international journalists arrived to cover the games, they saw little outward evidence of what really was going on.

Meanwhile every day the newspapers seemed to run

yet another photograph of Max being wined and dined by a high-ranking Nazi. In my mind Max and the city of Berlin were moving in opposite directions. While the entire country seemed to be whitewashing its racist and anti-Semitic ways, Max was revealing his true embrace of Nazism.

During the games, Max had to share the spotlight in the Berlin sports pages with the stars of Germany's Olympic team, gymnasts Alfred Schwarzmann and Konrad Frey, who each won three gold medals, and track star Luz Long. Long won a silver medal in the long jump, but he became most well known for helping his American rival Jesse Owens, a wiry Negro runner from Alabama. After Owens foot-fouled in his first two jumps, Long advised him to aim to begin his jump a few inches sooner. The advice worked, and Owens took the gold medal in the event.

Hitler had hoped to use the Olympics—like the Louis-Schmeling fight—as proof of Aryan supremacy. Jesse Owens foiled those plans, taking four gold medals, in the long jump, the 100 meters, the 200 meters, and the 4x100 meter relay team. Hitler refused to shake Owens's hand after his victories and left the stadium before the medal ceremonies each time he won. Yet even the German sportswriters had to write admiringly of the Negro's accomplishments, and he was embraced as a celebrity wherever he went, with fans crowding him for autographs and pictures.

Owens's performance further galvanized my obsession with the United States. The German Olympic team had been purged of nearly anyone of non-Aryan background.

On the other hand, the multiethnic U.S. team even included several Jewish athletes.

The day before the games ended, a thick envelope arrived at the gallery addressed to my father with Max's name and return address. I took the delivery but couldn't fathom what Max might've sent my father. I stood by while my father opened the envelope to reveal two tickets to the Olympics and a note.

"Dear Sig"—he read the note aloud to himself—*"I thought you and Karl might enjoy catching the last day of competition and the closing ceremonies. These are good seats, so cheer loud for Deutschland. Best regards, Max."*

My heart started racing. As much as I had divided feelings about whom to root for, I was dying to go to the Olympics. Max was instantly back in my good graces. Yet my father frowned at the note and the tickets in his hand.

"Tickets. Great," he said sarcastically. "This is just what we need."

He stared at the tickets, and then a small smile crossed his lips.

He went to the phone and had the operator connect him to a number in Berlin.

"*Guten Tag*, Herr Rolf, it's Sig Stern calling. [Pause.] Yes, it has been a long time. Listen, I just happened to come into possession of two prime tickets for the Olympic Games for tomorrow, and I thought you would want them. [Pause.] Yes. The seats are fantastic. [Pause.] Well, I had to pay double face value for them, so if you could go, I don't know, maybe twenty percent over that just to cover my costs, we could make a deal. [Pause.] *Wunderbar!* I'll have my son, Karl, drop them by at once."

I tightened my fists as I watched my father stuff the tickets, my tickets, into an envelope and scribble an address on the front. I couldn't believe he had just taken my tickets and sold them without a thought. Didn't he have any idea how much the Olympics meant to me? To everybody?

"Bring these over to Herr Rolf, and make sure you get the cash up front."

He handed the envelope toward me, but I refused to take it.

"Those tickets were for me—"

My father's face darkened.

"What?"

"Max said in his note that—"

"Perhaps you like the taste of paper better than bread?" he snapped. "It's all well and good for you to play your boxing games and scribble cartoons instead of trying to find more jobs to do. But we need money to eat, to live, far more than you need to go watch a bunch of men in shorts run around a track. Do you understand, Karl?"

I didn't respond.

"Do you understand?" he said, raising his voice and leaning his face close to mine.

"Yes, sir," I mumbled.

"Good," he said. "Now go."

He thrust the envelope into my hands and turned back to his desk.

For a minute I considered defying my father and going to the games with Neblig. Yet my intense desire to see the games gave way to a sinking feeling of desperation. We were living in an embarrassing state, stuffed into one room separated by bed sheets. Our meals were getting leaner and leaner. I knew my father was right. We could not eat the tickets for dinner. I swallowed my disappointment and delivered the tickets to Herr Rolf.

Good-bye, Winzig

THE WEEK AFTER THE CLOSING CEREMONIES, THE restaurants and businesses around our neighborhood rehung the signs reading WE DON'T SERVE JEWS in their windows, and *Der Stürmer* and other Nazi tabloids and magazines returned to the newsstands.

Despite my dedication to my training, I still found time to draw in my journal nearly every day, working on my cartoons and caricatures. Typically I drew late at night after I finished all of my chores, schoolwork, and deliveries, working by candlelight until I got too tired to hold my pen steady. One day I returned to Herr Greenberg's art supply store because I had run out of black ink. I hadn't been back to the store in several months, and I was shocked by the transformation. The once overstuffed shelves were now more than half empty, with just a few pads, pens, and paintbrushes scattered around, with large dusty spaces where other products used to be.

Herr Greenberg sat behind the counter, reading a book in Hebrew, looking slouched and defeated. A basket of small green apples stood beside the front counter along with a wooden bowl of brown eggs. Whereas in the past he would jump up to greet every customer, now he didn't even seem to notice as I walked in and approached.

"Herr Greenberg?" I said.

He finally glanced up from his book, and his eyes looked vacant and glazed over. When he saw that it was me, his face brightened, and he slowly rose from his chair.

"*Guten Morgen*, Karl. So good to see you," he said, shaking my hand. "It's been a while. How are your mother and father?"

"Fine," I said, noticing that his hand felt cold and frail.

"That's good. Please give them my regards."

"Of course," I said.

"Are you keeping up with your drawing?"

"Yes."

"You still want to draw the cartoons, *ja*?"

"I'm trying," I said.

"Good. The world could use more funny pictures. Now what can I do for you?"

"I just need some black ink."

"I think you're in luck. Black ink is one of the few things I still carry."

He came from behind the counter and moved to a nearby shelf. Typically he always had a small army of ink bottles of different sizes and colors lined up in tight rows like chess pieces. Now there were just two small bottles.

"How many would you like?"

I was hoping to buy several bottles, but I suddenly felt bad about depleting his already meager supply.

"Well, I would take both, but I don't want to leave you with none."

"Nonsense. That is why they are here, to be sold."

"Will you be able to get more?"

"Who knows?" He shrugged. "Because of the laws against doing business with Jews, none of my suppliers can sell to me anymore. I still carry a few things, but most of those come from Jewish-owned businesses, and they are having their own troubles getting supplies. I stock what I can."

He brought the ink bottles up to the counter and placed them into a small paper bag. I handed over the money.

"Could I interest you in an apple or perhaps a few eggs? They come fresh from my cousin's farm."

I noticed how threadbare his coat had become. His eyes looked watery and yellow and betrayed his desperation as he waited for me to respond.

"Sure. I'll take an apple."

"How about one for your sister? Just a penny more."

I hesitated. I didn't really have the extra penny to spare, but Herr Greenberg seemed to need it even more than we did.

"Okay," I said, selecting another apple from the basket.

Being in the store reminded me of Greta and our second kiss. I still carried her clover charm in my pocket. I still held on to the chance that one day we would be able to be together. I considered asking Herr Greenberg if she had been in to buy anything. But he seemed so lost and remote that it seemed unlikely that he would remember even if she had.

Before I left the store, Herr Greenberg approached me and placed his hands on my head, closed his eyes, and quietly chanted a short prayer in Hebrew. At first it felt strange to have the old man's hands on my head. But then, even though I didn't understand the Hebrew, I started to find the words and the light melody soothing. I watched his face, and as he said the prayer, his furrowed brow relaxed and his mouth curled into a small, determined smile, as if the words had given him some inner comfort and maybe even strength. When he opened his eyes, he said, "That was the Tefilat HaDerech; it's a prayer for a safe journey. Be careful out there, Karl."

I returned to the gallery to find it unusually quiet and still. Because of our close quarters, I could usually tell right away if someone was home and exactly what they were doing. I moved through the space and called out, but no one answered. I had to use the bathroom but found the door locked. I knocked. There was no answer, so I knocked again louder.

"Hallo?" I called.

"I'm bathing, Karl," my mother's voice finally replied.

"Are you okay?"

"*Ja*. I'm fine."

But her voice sounded anything but fine. She sounded indistinct and weary, as if she were speaking from a great distance. I paused by the door and listened but heard only the slightest ripple of water as her body shifted in the tub. I resolved to knock again in ten minutes.

I had turned to walk down to my room in the basement when I heard a faint sound coming from the main area of the gallery. I moved back to the line of curtains that served as walls and heard the sound of sniffling.

"Hildy?"

"Go away," she said.

"I got you an apple."

"I don't want an apple."

"Are you okay?"

"I said go away. I want to be alone."

I poked my head inside the curtain and saw Hildy lying facedown on her bed. A small writing journal was splayed out in front of her. She snapped the book shut. Behind her thick glasses, her eyes flashed with anger.

"I said go away! Can't I have any privacy?"

"Is Mama okay?"

"What do you think? Has she ever been okay?"

"Did something set her off?"

"I don't know. She was in there when I got home. Now, will you get out?"

I noticed a sharp smell like sulfur coming from somewhere in the room. I glanced down and saw Hildy's coat on the floor beside her bed, covered with a layer of yellowish goo.

"What happened to your coat?"

"I got hit in the shooting gallery."

"The shooting gallery?"

"Boys from the Hitler Youth, at the end of the day they wait for us across the street from our school, and when we come out, they throw rotten eggs at us and yell, 'Ten points to whoever can hit the first Jewess.'"

"Did you tell the teachers?"

"The teachers are more scared than we are. They just tell us to run fast and keep our heads down. This was the first time I got hit."

"I'm sorry, Winzig."

"You don't know what it's like to look like a Jew, Karl. You just don't."

"It's not easy for me either."

"It's not the same. You look normal. Everything about me looks Jewish—my nose, my hair, my skin, everything!"

"Come on, cheer up. I'll read you a Winzig und Spatz book or something. 'There's adventure in the air . . . ,'" I said, hoping she'd respond by finishing their call to action.

"Winzig und Spatz?" she said. "Those books are for babies. I'm eleven years old, Karl. No one in this family seems to notice. But I'm not a little kid anymore."

She was right. I hadn't really noticed, but over the past

few months Hildy had made the subtle transition from a
child to a preadolescent. Her face was thinner, and her legs
and arms were getting longer and skinnier like mine. I could
see the shadow of a woman just below the surface.

"I notice you, Hildy," I lied.

I sat beside her and tried to rest a hand on her shoulder.
She jerked away.

"Yeah, right. All you notice is yourself and your stupid
boxing."

"That's not true—"

"Do you know what yesterday was?"

"Yesterday was Wednesday. What does that have to do
with—"

"It was my birthday."

My heart fell in my chest, and my mouth went dry. How
could we all have forgotten? I felt a sharp pinch of anger at
myself, but even more so at my parents. She was their child,
after all.

"Oh, Winzig, I'm sorry."

"Yeah, right."

"Look, we can still have a party—"

"I don't want a stupid party. I don't want anything."

"Hildy . . ."

"I just want to be alone. There's no privacy in here."

"You can come down to the basement if you need some
privacy."

"I don't want to go to a basement or some stupid room
behind a curtain. I want to be in our old apartment. I want

things to be normal again."

She started to cry.

"Hildy, come on, it's okay—"

She sprang up off her bed.

"It's not okay, Karl. I know it's not; you know it's not; Mama, Papa, everyone knows it's not."

She ran out of the room and out the front door.

"Hildy, wait!" I called after her. But it was too late. By the time I got to the front door, she had already disappeared down the street.

I went back inside and looked into Hildy's room. Herr Karrote still sat on the table beside her bed, but other than that most of the childish decorations that had adorned her old room were gone. In fact the space had very few personal touches at all. I sat on the bed and picked up the journal she had been writing in, feeling slightly guilty for snooping. The book was filled with small poems and observations about our life, and they told the story of Hildy's escalating sadness and isolation. On one of the most recent pages I discovered the following poem:

Bald

My mother used to call them chocolate rings
But now they feel like rusted chains
Horrible dark brown things
If only they were blond and straight
No one would have cause to hate

My only hope is to cut them away
To become even uglier than I am today
Then maybe they'd leave me alone
And I could be invisible on my own

I closed the book and carefully placed it back on the bed. I hadn't realized the depth of pain and self-loathing Hildy had been experiencing. I was also struck by how mature and powerful her writing was. These were not the words of a child but of a young artist with some real talent. She had clearly moved beyond Winzig und Spatz. It was then that I noticed that her collection of Winzig und Spatz books was not on her shelf. Could she really have gotten rid of them? Something about that made me feel even more upset and helpless. I searched through her dresser, but they were not there. Finally I looked under her bed and found them hidden away behind a pile of old sweaters. I exhaled at the sight of the books, as if they had confirmed that the old Hildy still existed somewhere.

I replaced the sweaters covering the books, then picked up her wool coat and brought it to our jury-rigged kitchen. Using a bucket of water and a brush, I wiped away the egg, some of which had hardened inside the tight weave of the wool. I scrubbed the coat as clean as I could and brought it back to her room and laid it on the bed.

I went back to the bathroom door and knocked.

"Mama? Mama, are you okay in there?"

"Yes, Karl," she replied faintly.

I was going to say something to my mother about Hildy, but she sounded so lost that I feared it I might send her even farther over the edge. So I just turned and descended the stairs to my basement room, anger rising inside me.

I stripped off my shirt and did a set of sit-ups until I lost count and my stomach muscles burned. Then I switched to push-ups and again did so many that I lost count and my shoulders, chest, and arm muscles shook from the exertion. I kept going until the vibrating and burning in my body became so intense that my arms collapsed beneath me and my face fell onto the floor. I let my cheek rest on the ground as my breath heaved in and out, raising and lowering my exhausted body. I struggled to my feet and positioned myself in front of the small mirror I had hung on the wall beside my bed.

I stared at my reflection and for the first time took in the full physical transformation that my body had undergone over the past few years. My shoulders were broad and rounded; thick veins lined my nicely defined biceps and forearms; my chest and abdominal muscles formed a thin layer of armor over my midsection. My bony frame was now lined with muscles. The fearful look in my eyes was gone and had been replaced by determination and rage. Even my acne had cleared up. Yet for all of my physical strength, I never had felt quite so weak, because I was unable to wipe the tears from my sister's eyes or remove the grief from her heart.

That night I took out the new ink bottles I had bought at Herr Greenberg's and attempted to draw a Winzig und

Spatz comic strip to cheer her up. Yet all the ideas I came up with seemed too hollow, trivial, or unfunny. Every time I picked up my pen, it didn't lead me anywhere that seemed to matter anymore.

ONE DAY AT THE STATION A SHIPMENT OF CHEESE COMES IN FROM A FARM....

WINZIG COME QUICK! I'M STANDING ON A MOUNTAIN OF MUENSTER!

GO AWAY, SPATZ....

I'M TOO DEPRESSED TO COME OUT. I'M JUST A STUPID UGLY LITTLE MOUSE AND THAT'S ALL I'LL EVER BE....

The 1937 Youth Boxing Championship

"G-g-g-good. Hit that bag," Neglig said, holding the heavy bag as I slammed my fists into the fabric. I grunted with exertion, my forearms aching with each furious uppercut.

"Now try some j-j-j-jabs."

I switched to jabs, left, left, right, left, left, right, then right, right, left, right, right, left. Pounding over and over until it felt as if my wrists might snap off.

Worjyk wandered over and stood beside Neblig as I finished the set.

"Okay, that's it," Neblig said. I gave the bag a final left jab and a hard right cross and then stopped. The bag swung back and forth from the force of my last punch.

"You were really h-h-h-hitting hard today," Neblig said,

handing me a water bottle.

"You'd better be hitting hard, Knochen," Worjyk said. "You've got the tournament coming up."

"Tournament?" I said, out of breath.

"Yeah. You do want to compete for the youth championship, don't you?"

I stared at Neblig. Had he just said what I thought he had? Neblig smiled and nodded.

"We signed you up for the tournament," Worjyk said.

I let out a small pleased laugh and hugged Neblig.

"Don't start celebrating yet, Knochen," Worjyk said. "You're going to be going up against the best of the best, so don't get cocky."

"I won't let you down," I said. I extended my hand, and Worjyk and I shook.

Because the Berlin Boxing Club was not a youth-oriented club, I didn't get to fight as often as other boys my age. But despite my limited exposure, I never had been defeated in the ring. The city's formal boxing championship was a two-day tournament that brought together all of Berlin's best fighters under eighteen years old. Although nervous, I was also extremely excited. This was the opportunity I had been training for ever since meeting Max three years earlier.

The event was being staged at the Hesse Athletic Center, a small arena in the northern part of the city. The tournament's organizers had hoped to get Max to preside over the tournament, to serve as an honorary ring announcer or judge, but lately he always seemed to be "busy" hobnobbing with the Nazi elites or lobbying for a chance to fight Jimmy Braddock for the heavyweight crown. Despite the fact that Max had defeated Joe Louis, the American promoters favored giving the title shot to their homegrown star. German boxing writers were outraged, claiming the Americans were afraid of the championship belt going to a German. Max traveled back and forth to America, making appeals to the boxing authorities, and he had not returned to the Berlin Boxing Club in nearly a year.

A few days before the tournament I asked Worjyk if it bothered him that Max didn't come by the club anymore. Worjyk just shrugged his shoulders.

"Max comes and Max goes. That's how he's always been, Knochen. You should always remember that Max is out for Max. Sometimes I think that's what makes him a great fighter, but it also means he's not always the most reliable guy in the world."

I hadn't heard Worjyk or anyone else at the club utter even the slightest negative comment about Max. But his words certainly resonated with me as I tried to make sense of how Max seemed to drift in and out of my life without much thought, dangling himself like a toy in front of a kitten only to be pulled back at the last second.

Unlike the small gyms and clubs I had fought at in the past, the Hesse Athletic Center was a real arena that could hold thousands of spectators. Even before we opened the doors to enter, I could hear the muffled cheers of a boisterous crowd. My heartbeat quickened, and my palms began to sweat as Neblig, Worjyk, and I stepped inside. Several rows of folding chairs surrounded the ring; these were bordered by steep rows of bleachers set on metal risers. There was already a fight in progress, and more than a thousand people watched and cheered. The crowd awed and intimidated me. Some boys stomped their feet on the floor, making a loud, angry, clanging rhythm of support. We walked through an aisle between the stands, and the pounding caused the wooden floorboards to shake and jump beneath our feet. My pulse accelerated to match the rhythm of the stomping as the ring came into view, illuminated by six huge industrial light fixtures that hung down from the ceiling like gigantic steel eggshells.

A huge number of boys wore Hitler Youth uniforms, and there were groups of grown men, mostly fathers and older brothers of the fighters, dressed in other uniforms of the Reich. Early in my training Max had counseled me to never pay attention to the crowd. "When I fight in America, they love to root against me. They call me names and sometimes even spit at me when I'm walking in and out of the ring, but I just tune it all out. Remember, you are only fighting your opponent in the ring. If you let the crowd into your head, you're sunk. I just try to blur the noise and harness its energy to add power to my punches."

We made our way through the crowd to the locker room behind one of the risers. Several other boys were inside, getting changed for their fights. Like always, I had already changed into my boxing shorts so I wouldn't have to completely disrobe in front of anyone. I had also already tucked Greta's clover charm into my sock for good luck.

I sat on a low wooden bench while Neblig taped my hands and tied on my gloves. Worjyk gave me little tips and reminders about my technique, his usual unlit cigar hanging out of the side of his mouth.

"Remember to snap your hand back after your right jab, Knochen. You always leave yourself exposed for too long."

"I will," I said.

"Try to cut off the angles when you're on the attack. As soon as he shows weakness, make the ring as small as possible."

"I know," I said.

"And don't rely too much on jabs. You've got great reach, so it's a good weapon. But don't be afraid to throw in some power punches. You'll be up against some real fighters, and you may need to put them away fast."

"We've been over this a million times," I said.

"And we'll go over it another million times." Worjyk spat. "You fighters are all a bunch of stupid apes. That's why I've gotta drill this stuff into your heads."

Despite my protestations, it was a comfort to have him pacing and repeating his familiar instructions. Neblig finished tying on my gloves and then looked to Worjyk.

"N-n-n-now?" he asked.

Worjyk nodded, and Neblig reached into his bag and pulled

out a brand-new neatly folded silk robe. It was rich royal blue with white trim just like those the professional fighters wore. Neblig unfurled the robe, revealing the words THE BERLIN BOXING CLUB spelled out in large white letters on the back. I didn't know what to say. I had always wanted a robe but never even thought to ask my parents because of our financial situation. In fact it had been years since I had received any sort of meaningful gift from anyone. The last time had been when Worjyk had presented me with my boxing gloves. I had never seen anyone at the gym wearing such a robe, so I knew Worjyk had ordered it specially for me. My eyes misted over, and I had to choke back a huge lump in my throat.

"*Danke*," I managed to say. "Thank you both."

Neblig smiled.

"Forget about it, Knochen," Worjyk said dismissively. "I've been thinking about expanding my business to take advantage of the youth market. I figured this would be a great opportunity to advertise. Now let's get out there."

Worjyk gave me a pat on the back, Neblig slipped the robe over my shoulders, and we entered the arena. We went to weigh in near the registration table set up beside the ring. A large poster on the table displayed the pairings for the tournament, filled with every fighter's name. There were two main brackets, one on the left side of the page, one on the right, and the two fighters who won their brackets would square off for the championship. I glanced down this list of matchups and found myself scheduled to fight a boy named Meissner in the first bout.

As I scanned the other names, a jolt of cold adrenaline shot through my body. Gertz Diener was scheduled to fight later that same morning in my bracket. If we both won our first fights, we would face each other in the second bout. Conflicting fears and desires collided inside my head. First there was the core fear of exposure. Would Gertz denounce me as a Jew? Would he and the Wolf Pack attempt to physically attack me, as they had in the past? But more powerful than the fear was my lust for revenge. Would I actually get the opportunity to fight my nemesis fair and square inside the ring? In many ways my years of training had been motivated by the attacks of Gertz and the Wolf Pack. And yet up to now I had had to rely on surrogates to vent my frustrations. How I longed to land a punch on Gertz's smug Aryan face.

My first opponent, Meissner, was a slow, heavyset boy with meaty forearms and shoulders, who got easily winded when I danced around him. I was so excited and nervous about the possibility of fighting Gertz that I accelerated my pace of attack, trying to wear Meissner down and end the match quickly. My haste made me sloppy, and Meissner connected with a powerful right uppercut to my gut that almost sent me down. I quickly recovered and adopted a more conservative approach, attacking with a couple of jabs and then retreating to make him move.

After the first round, I was sitting in my corner getting instructions from Worjyk to slow the fight down when I saw Gertz enter the arena, followed by Franz, Julius, and several other boys from the Wolf Pack. Icy gooseflesh sprouted across my body at the sight of them. Gertz was dressed to fight, while the others wore Hitler Youth uniforms. They all took seats in one of the upper risers to watch me.

The bell rang, signaling the start of the second round. Neblig had to nudge me to snap me back to attention and up to my feet and into the ring. In the second round, I used a technique that Max called bicycle spokes, where I imagined Meissner was the center of a wheel and I relentlessly circled him, throwing a series of small but steady jabs and punches. Meissner grew impatient, having to constantly turn and shuffle his feet to keep up. His breath became more labored, and his punches lost their zip. After about a minute of circling, when I knew I had worn him out, I pressed forward with a more aggressive attack, working him into a corner with a combination of hard rights. I must have thrown fourteen unanswered punches, but he would not go down. Finally the bell rang, ending the round.

When I got to my corner, Neblig and Worjyk congratulated me on the round, but I saw Gertz and the others looking concerned. It suddenly occurred to me that if Gertz thought I was too good, he might reveal that I was a Jew to ensure that he wouldn't have to fight me. I decided that in the next round I needed to let Meissner score some points so that I didn't look as dominant.

In the next round I did not attack or use any real strategy. I even let Meissner score a couple of points. I had to be careful to let him connect with some punches, but none that would leave me too bruised or exposed. For the final minute, I went into defensive mode, dancing away from Meissner's lumbering attacks and waiting out the bell to end the fight. When the fight finally ended, the judges awarded me the victory, but I could tell by Gertz's confident reaction that he was not impressed by my performance. Worjyk berated me. "You looked like crap out there. Your footwork was awful. You let down your defenses a half dozen times. You're lucky he didn't destroy you!" I listened to all of his criticisms, knowing exactly what he was going to say before he got the words out.

After exiting the ring, I sat with Neblig and Worjyk and watched Gertz fight his first match. It had been a couple of years since I had gone to school with him, and in that time Gertz had grown several inches, and his boyish huskiness had evolved into a manly heft. He still wore his blond hair short and spiky and had a cruel slant to his expression. I wondered if he still spoke with a lisp. Gertz had good rhythm and a decent sense of strategy and easily outboxed his opponent. He scored a knockout with a jab-jab-uppercut combination in the second round. Raising his arm in victory, he stared at me with a confident smirk.

The next bout was not scheduled until after lunch. I couldn't eat anything but just sat with Neblig and Worjyk as they counseled me on how to fight against Gertz, but their words barely penetrated. The tension and excitement sent a thick pounding up the veins of my neck and into my head, blocking out all outside noise.

Finally, the lunch break ended, and Gertz and I stepped into the ring. I felt my stomach churn and then tighten in anticipation. The Wolf Pack sat in a row of chairs right beside the ring and loudly cheered as we approached each other. I had fought dozens of times in the years since they had used me as a punching bag and piss pot, but suddenly all my experience and strength seemed to drain out of my body. I stared into Gertz's eyes and saw my old self reflected in them. The skinny weak coward I had been jumped back into my skin. Just before we touched gloves to signal the start of the fight, Gertz leaned in and whispered: "Now everyone will see how to beat a Jew, Piss Boy."

He slammed his gloves against mine and then started dancing before me. I heard just the slightest trace of his old lisp when he called me Piss Boy, so the word "Piss" sounded more like "Pith." The fighting instinct rose up in me. Hearing my inglorious nickname ignited all the rage I harbored against him. And hearing the lisp gave me a quick jolt of confidence. He was still the same boy I remembered, who in the past had needed the whole Wolf Pack to confront me. Since then I had been trained by one of the world's greatest heavyweights and fought mostly against men, not boys. I knew I was no longer anyone's Piss Boy. I lunged forward, clapped my gloves against his, and whispered: "Or how to get beaten by a Jew."

The bell rang, and the fight commenced.

I spent the first minute of the round getting a feel for Gertz's style. He moved around a lot and had good command of his punches. But I quickly detected a flaw in his technique. There was a slight delay in his rhythm. His feet and hands weren't in sync, so he didn't punch and move fluidly. He always seemed to pause and set himself before an attack, telegraphing his punches. As a result, I was able to set my defense and time my counterpunches. He landed a few light jabs, and I could hear the Wolf Pack howling from the front row. Then I attacked.

I threw several combinations, favoring my left jab so he came to expect punches from that side; then I suddenly switched sides and came at him with my right. I landed a hard right cross to his head and savored the feeling of my fist's connecting with his jaw, the sensation of his neck snapping back against the force of my glove.

Gertz staggered backward and raised his hands to defend his face. I saw another opening and lowered my attack, landing two big uppercuts to his midsection. The second punch connected to that magical spot in the middle of his chest, and Gertz emitted a strangled gasp as his air supply momentarily got cut off. I delivered one more punch to the side of his head, and he fell to his knees. He sat there gasping for air as the bell rang, ending the round.

I took a deep satisfied breath as I saw that Gertz's coach had to help him to his corner. I walked over to Neblig and Worjyk, who waited for me by my stool. I looked over at the Wolf Pack and saw Franz and Julius conferring about something. With quickly dawning dread, I saw Franz rise from his seat and approach the judges' table. He spoke to an older man with large gray sideburns, who appeared to be the head man. Franz's dark eyes darted over toward me, and the man followed his gaze and nodded seriously.

The man rose from the judges' table and came over to our corner.

"What's the problem?" Worjyk asked.

"It has come to my attention that Herr Stern is a Jew. Is this true?"

Worjyk's face went white, but he recovered quickly.

"What does that have to do with—"

"Is it true, Herr Stern?" The man interrupted.

They all turned to look at me. Franz and Julius and the rest of the Wolf Pack stood nearby, watching too, and the whole crowd started to murmur, wondering what was going on. I finally nodded yes. The old man's eyes hardened. And without hesitating, he stepped into the ring and addressed the audience: "It has come to my attention that Karl Stern is a Jew."

Boos and catcalls rose up from the audience. The older man continued. "It is the policy of our athletic association to conform to the bylaws of the Reich, and therefore we cannot allow anyone of a mongrel race to participate in this tournament. Herr Stern is officially disqualified."

The crowd howled at the announcement. Various boys and men shouted, "Get out of here, you dirty bastard!" "Kill the Jew!" "Mongrel!"

I scanned the audience and saw the Wolf Pack leading a chant, *"Jude, Jude, Jude."* Soon most of the spectators joined in. Gertz sat in his corner with his head bowed. Pieces of garbage started to fly into the ring: wadded-up paper cups, banana peels, and apple cores. Finally my eyes found my own corner. Neblig was signaling to me to step out of the ring. But it was Worjyk that my eyes were drawn to. He stood immobile. His face had gone completely white. He looked as if he had just been stabbed in the back.

I quickly slipped out of the ring and ran back through the arena toward the locker room as spit, garbage, and insults rained down on me. A bottle struck the side of my forehead, leaving a small gash, but I kept running. I think Neblig tried to follow me but was cut off by groups of angry spectators, crowding into the aisles in my wake. I grabbed my gym bag and ran out of the arena, carefully dodging boys who tried to take swipes at me along my route.

I burst out into the street and sprinted down the sidewalk. I'm not even sure if anyone followed me, but I didn't look back. I ran for at least two miles at a full sprint before my knees buckled and I had to slow down. I had reached the park where Greta Hauser and I used to meet, and I leaned over with my hands on my knees, trying to catch my breath.

As I struggled to control my breathing, I could feel everything collapsing inside me. All of my years of training, discipline, and focus on boxing were eliminated in one single moment in the ring. My dream of becoming Youth Champion was gone. But worse than that, I knew I could not return to the Berlin Boxing Club. To do so would put Worjyk at risk for violating the government's policies about mixing with Jews. I could see from his expression that he would never allow me to return anyway. For all I knew, he might've been a high-ranking Nazi Party member. Boxing had been my one refuge in the storm, and I couldn't imagine my life without it.

I rummaged inside my gym bag and found the small rubber ball that Max had given me three years earlier as the very first phase of my training. I squeezed the ball with all my might until my knuckles ached and my hand turned white. And then I stood and threw the ball as hard and far as I could. I watched it land on the grass and then bounce and roll into the woods in the far distance. It was only then that I realized that I had left my new robe behind.

Ice Cream

THE FOLLOWING MORNING I SLEPT LATE, MISSING MY early-morning workout for the first time since I had commenced my training three years earlier. My father finally woke me and asked me to make a printing delivery to a new client who lived in an apartment above Café Kranzler on the corner of Friedrichstrasse and Unter den Linden. I could barely pull myself out of bed, and my limbs felt heavy as I slowly got dressed and then headed out to make the delivery.

Friedrichstrasse teemed with life, with men rushing to work and the cafés crowded with patrons lingering over breakfast and coffee. The client lived on the fourth floor of a large ten-story walk-up apartment building. The stairs creaked as I ascended the dark stairwell. On the way up I passed a heavyset old woman coming down the stairs, wearing her gray hair tucked under a blue kerchief. I had to let her squeeze past. She seemed to stare at me, and I cast my head down so she couldn't get a good look at me. When I finally reached the apartment on the fourth floor, I knocked and a man's voice called:"Who is it?"

"Delivery."

"Who?"

"I have a delivery. Some printing—"

The door suddenly opened a crack, and a hand reached out.

"Hand it to me," he said.

I looked into the shadows of the room but could not make out a face.

"I was told to get cash," I said. "Up front."

The hand disappeared for a moment and reappeared with a small wad of marks.

"Here."

I quickly counted the bills and then handed over the package.

"Now go," he said.

As soon as the hand disappeared back inside the apartment, the door slammed shut. I stuffed the bills into a special pocket my mother had sewn into the inside of my pants and walked back down the stairs.

As I emerged back onto Friedrichstrasse, people bustled all around me, window-shopping and eating at outdoor tables at the Café Kranzler. I watched a couple sharing a

Linzer torte, and my stomach groaned. It had been at least a year since I had had a treat like that. My parents used to meet their friends there for coffee and pastries. I couldn't remember the last time my family and I had eaten at any public restaurant.

I swallowed back my hunger and started to jog back toward the gallery, weaving in and around the pedestrians on the wide sidewalk, peering into the windows of shops and restaurants as I streamed by. Suddenly something made me stop in my tracks. Through the large plate glass window of an ice-cream shop, I saw Greta Hauser, sitting at the counter next to a boy I didn't recognize, each of them digging into large bowls of ice cream with whipped cream. My throat tightened, and my eyes burned.

The boy was tall and handsome with light brown hair. He wore a sharp gray wool suit and to judge by his clothes was from a prosperous family. Greta looked even more beautiful than I remembered her. She wore a plain white blouse and a blue and green plaid skirt. Her long blond braid draped over one shoulder. She laughed at something the boy said, and the braid swung off her shoulder and against her back. My face reddened, heat rising up my neck and across my head. How many times had I made her laugh? How many times had I touched her braid when we kissed?

I dug my hand deep into my pocket and felt for the clover charm. I gripped the charm tightly until it dug into my hand.

I impulsively moved to the door, entered the ice-cream shop, and walked right up to the counter where they were sitting. I hovered behind Greta for a moment before the boy looked up and noticed me.

"Can I help you?"

Greta turned, and her face went white as she beheld me. "Karl?"

I stared at her, unable to move or speak, my fists balled at my sides, anger seething inside me.

The boy stood and faced me.

"What's going on here? Do you know this guy?"

I continued to stare at Greta. Her eyes glazed over with tears. She looked frightened and confused.

I moved one of my balled fists over her bowl of ice cream, opened it, and dropped the clover charm onto the top of a pile of whipped cream.

Greta looked down into her lap.

"Hey, what the hell are you doing?" the boy said, pushing his hand against my chest.

I reached out and snatched his wrist, holding it firmly in my grip, squeezing until I felt his skin pinched tightly against the bone.

"Don't touch me," I said in a low, firm voice.

The boy tried to pull his arm back, but I held it tight for another moment. Finally I released his arm, and the boy fell back, knocking his bowl of ice cream to the floor, breaking the ceramic dish with a loud crash. Several patrons turned to stare at the commotion.

"Who the hell do you think you are?" he said, holding his wrist.

"She knows who I am."

I glared at her a moment longer, daring her to glance up. But she didn't look up from her lap.

I turned and walked out of the shop. I started running, but I could barely feel my legs moving. It was as if the sidewalk were sinking beneath my feet with each step, like the world was literally collapsing beneath me.

PART III
1938

"Great boxers must always maintain a certain amount of mystery about themselves. Your opponent should never feel as if he fully understands exactly who you are or what you are going to do at any given moment."

Helmut Müller, *Boxing Basics for German Boys*

The Last Picasso

SEVERAL MONTHS AFTER BEING DISQUALIFIED FROM THE tournament, I still had not returned to the Berlin Boxing Club. I never heard from Worjyk or even Neblig. I had been too embarrassed to tell anyone we were living in the gallery, so I'm not sure they would've been able to find me even if they had wanted to. I kept up my physical training out of force of habit more than anything else. Yet now the effort to push myself seemed hollow, driven only by a dull rage with no hope of satisfaction.

My anger and depression were made worse by my family's absolute obliviousness to my misery. They didn't even notice that my entire world had collapsed. Whereas in the past our family meals had been full of discussion and argument, now they were increasingly silent, as we exchanged only the most perfunctory remarks. The most startling transformation was my father. He had always been a talker, expounding on art or philosophy, or lecturing us on some modern idea he had heard about. Now he looked as sullen and angry as I felt.

I spent as much time as possible in my basement room either training or drawing in my journal. One evening after dinner I worked out on the heavy bag. I circled the bag, rotating sets of punches, first jabs, then uppercuts, then crosses, then combinations. I was so focused on mechanically driving my fist into the fabric that I didn't even notice my mother standing near the bottom of the stairs, watching me. I stopped when I saw her. She rarely came down to the basement since it had become my room.

"It must be nice," she said.

"What?"

"To be able to hit something like that, to have a release."

"I suppose."

"This boxing has been good for you," she said, sitting on my bed. She looked tired but smiled at me. "Sometimes I wish I had something like that."

"I don't really have it anymore," I confessed. "I was kicked out of the boxing league."

"I know."

"You do?"

"Yes. I have not been myself lately, but I can still figure things out, Karl. I know when you come and go. I'm still a mother. I'm sorry you can't compete anymore, but you still have your boxing."

"What do you mean?"

"You've barely missed one day of training in four years, and I don't expect you will anytime soon. It's inside you now. And I know you'll box again someday. There will be other tournaments."

"I wish I could believe you."

"There will be," she said, "because you want it so badly. That's how all great things get done. Do you know why I gave up painting?"

"No."

"Most people think I gave it up because of my family obligations, but that's not true. The real truth is I had no passion for it. My father was a portrait artist and wanted me to follow in his footsteps, so I did for a while. But I never really got any pleasure out of it beyond the pleasure that it gave him. Of course I love the world of art, but the process of painting was always a task for me and not a joy. On the other hand, you've been drawing in your journal for as long as you could hold a pen. I couldn't make you stop if I wanted to. And you have the same kind of passion for your boxing. That's why you have the makings to be great."

"Papa doesn't think so."

"He does."

"Then how come he never said anything to me? About anything?"

She sighed and seemed to consider her answer before responding.

"One of your father's modern ideas about parenting is to leave you alone and let you become the man you want to be, not the man he wants you to be. Do you remember when you were very little, perhaps four or five years old, and we used to dress you up in a tuxedo for the gallery openings?"

I hadn't thought about it in a long time, but suddenly an image formed in my head of myself as a young boy standing beside my father in a matching tuxedo. The memory gave me an unexpected feeling of warmth inside, like stepping into a hot bath.

"I even had a little matching blue silk scarf, didn't I?"

"Yes." She laughed. "You loved dressing up with your father like that. And he would parade you around the gallery with such pride. Do you know why he stopped?"

"No."

"One night at a gallery opening all your father's friends took to calling you Little Sig. You thought it was funny, but it upset your father. Later that night he said he never wanted you to dress you up in the tuxedo again. When I asked him why, he just said, 'Karl must be Karl.'"

"But then why does he always criticize all the things I want to do, like cartooning and boxing?"

"Both of those things have high risks. He still wants you to do what he thinks will be best for you. He's still a parent."

"He's a hard person to understand," I said.

"In some ways you're right. But in other ways he's very transparent. Your father tries to treat you how he wanted to be treated by his father. He believes in self-reliance and wants to instill independence in you. Also, he's tried to keep you and your sister out of trouble. Do you understand?"

"I guess."

"Good. Because now he needs you."

"Needs me for what?"

"He'll tell you. Get dressed and go to him."

My mother rose from the bed, kissed me on the top of my head, and then turned to move back up the stairs. It had been so long since she'd shown me any affection. I was struck by a powerful longing to be a little kid again, to run home from school to be enveloped by her embrace, to be comforted by her sweet voice when I woke from a nightmare, to let her bathe and dress me and take my hand as I accompanied her on her daily errands. Oh, how I loved her, and I needed to tell her so.

"Mama . . . ?"

She paused on the stairs. I was hoping to see the young vibrant mother I remembered from childhood. But when she turned back to face me, I saw only the withered, fragile woman that she had become.

"*Ja?*" she said.

"Nothing," I said.

She turned and slowly trudged back up the stairs.

I changed out of my workout clothes and went upstairs. I found my father waiting for me in their bedroom, hovering over a brightly colored abstract oil painting of a woman reading a book.

"Do you remember her?" he said, without turning to look at me.

"Of course. It hung in the living room of our old apartment for years. Right above the mantel."

"It was always my favorite. Picasso has magical eyes. He sees the world so differently than we do, but he is able to make us understand what he sees. That's what a truly great artist does."

Years earlier I had copied the Picasso into my journal, and it had struck me that the woman in the painting must've been reading something naughty and got caught in the act.

"There's beauty to it, and sexuality," my father said. "But also humor and mystery, even some darkness around the edges. So many ideas in one painting. It's no wonder those savages have banned art like this. Too many ideas. Too much beauty."

He folded a large piece of brown wrapping paper over the painting and carefully taped it shut.

"What are you doing?"

"I found a buyer for it," he said. "A Swiss dealer named Kerner, who says he's got a client who is mad for Picassos in Stockholm. It could fetch us enough to be able to to get to America."

"America?" My heart rose up. I'd had no idea my father had been working on an actual plan to get us out, and the idea thrilled me. Images of America, the promised land of boxing, movie stars, and comic books, flooded into my head.

"I have cousins in the United States, one in Florida named

Leo and one in New York named Hillel. They are the sons of
my father's brother," he continued. "They moved before the
Great War. We had not been in touch for years until now. I
don't know them well, but they've agreed to sponsor us. We
just need money to make the trip. I've sold nearly everything
I've been holding on to. This last Picasso should bring us just
about enough to get us what we need. But this dealer Kerner
is a man I don't trust. So I need you to come with me."

"Why?"

"Just to be careful."

"Careful about what?"

He finished wrapping the painting and turned to look
at me.

"We must be careful about everything these days, Karl."

We silently walked through the streets in the gathering
dusk. My father moved quickly, his eyes focused on a point in
the distance. We passed an iceman unloading a huge block
of ice with sharp metal tongs from his horse cart. Walking
by the open ice box sent a chill through me that enhanced
my tension and inner fear.

Kerner was staying at a small hotel downtown called the
Little Kaiser. My father took a deep breath before knocking
on the door. We heard footsteps approach; an eye peered
through the peephole; then Kerner opened the door and
grandly ushered us inside the suite. *"Willkommen!* Come in,
come in," he said, hugging my father warmly as if they were
old friends. Kerner was a tall man with a long, thin face and
a pencil mustache like Errol Flynn's. His long blond hair

was neatly slicked back against his scalp.

"And who is this?" he said in mock surprise. "Your muscle?"

"This is my son, Karl." my father said.

"He looks nothing like you, Sig. Sure the postman wasn't involved?"

Kerner was laughing, but his eyes were measuring me up. I had seen that look before in the ring when opponents tried to sneak looks at me before a fight. My hands instantly got cold and clammy and tightened into fists.

"Come in, come in," he said.

We stepped into the small sitting area that consisted of a couch and two armchairs positioned around a wide, low coffee table. My father unwrapped the painting on the table in the center of the room, and when it was revealed, Kerner clapped his hands with delight.

"*Fantastisch!* Look at those tits. My client will love it. He's a dirty old man, this guy."

My father winced but managed a weak smile.

"I'm just glad you were able to find a buyer who would pay my price."

"Yes," Kerner said. "There are still people with money to buy art out there if you look under the right rock. This is excellent, Stern. Always good doing business with you."

He extended his hand, and my father shook it as if sealing the deal.

"I will send you the money as soon as I'm back in Stockholm."

"Send me the money?" my father said, releasing his hand.

"I assume you want Swiss francs? Or would you prefer U.S. dollars?"

"We agreed that I would be paid my portion up front."

"Did we?" Kerner said, furrowing his brow as if trying to remember the conversation. "I don't recall us discussing that."

"I'm certain we did," my father said.

"Well, it is an awkward misunderstanding. But I'm afraid I don't have the cash."

"That is unfortunate," my father said.

"But I will send it to you straightaway. As soon as we get back to Switzerland."

"We?"

"Yes," Kerner said. "Oh, I'm sorry, I forgot to introduce my associate, Gustav."

A beefy man dressed in an ill-fitting blue suit emerged from the bedroom of the suite and came to stand behind Kerner. He moved his jacket aside to place his hands on his hips and in doing so revealed a flash of the gray steel of a revolver stuck in the side of his belt.

"Gustav and I will be traveling back to Switzerland this afternoon"—Kerner continued—"with the Picasso. Now you and your *boy* should run along and not do anything stupid."

"This is what you've sunk to, Kerner? Highway robbery?"

"Call it what you will," he said.

"You won't get away with this," my father said.

"No?" Kerner said. "And what can you possibly do about it, Stern? Your government has banned this painting. If they knew you had it, they would only take it away. Besides that, you're a Jew and a black marketeer. They would shoot you like a rabid dog. At least with me, you know it will wind up in the hands of a true art lover. We both want to make sure this pretty bitch finds a loving home."

My father stood silent for a moment, his face reddening with anger. Then he suddenly lunged forward, grabbed the painting, and hoisted it high over his head as if to smash it.

Kerner stepped forward to block him. I was too stunned to know how to react.

"Stop!" Kerner shouted.

Gustav pulled his gun and leveled it at me. My body froze, and my eyes locked on the dark hollow of the barrel. My father stared at Kerner, the painting shaking in his hands high above his head.

"You really want to see your son shot over a painting, Stern?"

My father's eyes quickly darted from Kerner to Gustav to the gun and then to me. He slowly lowered the painting and tossed it to the ground.

"There will be a special place in hell for opportunist pieces of garbage like you when this is all over."

"Who said this will ever be over?" Kerner said casually.

"Take a good look at these men, Karl," my father said. "This is what the scum of the earth looks like."

My father grabbed my arm and quickly led me out of the room.

"Gute Nacht!" Kerner said as we retreated.

Gustav kept the gun pointed at us until we were back out the door.

We did not speak at all as we walked away from the hotel in the thickening darkness. My father did not go directly home but strayed down along a path by the Spree River. The current of the river moved quickly, and the water looked black with glints of silver in the moonlight. He finally came to stop at a small park overlooking Museumsinsel, Museum Island, an island in the center of the city with a series of museums built in the last century. He sat on a park bench facing the island and stared at the dark outlines of the domes and statues of the buildings. After a moment, I sat beside him.

"Kaiser Friedrich Wilhelm the Fourth had those built," he said, finally breaking the silence, "to house all the art treasures of the kingdom. Hard to believe the government once valued such things enough to build those magnificent palaces for them."

"What are we going to do?" I asked.

"I don't know," he replied.

"What are you going to tell Mama?"

"For now I'm just going to tell her that everything went fine, at least until I have another plan in mind. I can't leave her without hope."

My father again lapsed into silence. I felt uncomfortable

sitting there with him, unsure of what to say. I was horrified at my father's powerlessness. But I also felt a strange sense of satisfaction, at sharing in this moment of my father's despair, two men bound together through cruelty with no one else to rely on. We sat like that for another fifteen minutes, in the cool darkness. Finally my father rose, and we walked home together.

The Mongrel

AFTER THE PICASSO INCIDENT, I HOPED THAT MY FATHER would come to rely on me more and that he would treat me more like an adult. Yet in the aftermath he only became even more remote and secretive. I never even found out exactly how he explained the incident to my mother. They seemed to close into themselves even more deeply with each passing day.

Several weeks later a package arrived for me at the gallery. I almost never received any personal mail, so I couldn't imagine whom it might be from. The return address on the thick white envelope bore a name I didn't recognize, Albert Broder. I took the package down to the basement, slit open the side, and spilled the contents onto my bed. The envelope contained a large collection of boxing magazines and comic books. Finally a small piece of gray notepaper fluttered onto the basement floor. I picked it up and read:

Dear Karl,

I'm sorry I have not reached out to you sooner, but it took me a while to track down an address for you. I thought you would enjoy these magazines and comic books, especially a new one from America called Action Comics. It has a great new crime-fighting hero named Superman who I think you will like. Things have not been the same here since you left, for more reasons than you know. I miss your comradeship. Please come visit if you get the chance.

Your friend,
Albert Broder
(aka Neblig)

I felt my chest tighten with emotion. Neblig had not given up on me after all. I still had a real friend who had spent the time and energy to track me down. It had been six months since my last fight, and I wondered what Worjyk and the other members thought of me.

I dug through the pile of magazines until I discovered

Action Comics. The cover featured a striking image of the new hero called Superman, a muscular man with dark black hair and dressed in a blue jumpsuit and a flowing red cape, hoisting an automobile over his head and smashing it into the side of a rocky hill. A group of men, presumably gangsters, ran away in fear as shattered glass and pieces of the car flew off in all directions.

I was instantly transfixed by the story. Like me, Superman was an alien, an outsider from another planet that had been completely destroyed. His physiology was different from that of normal humans, just like what the Nazis said about the Jews. Only instead of being corrupted, Superman's blood gave him superior strength and intelligence. He even had dark, wavy hair like a Jew. And his alter ego, Clark Kent, wore glasses and looked like one of my father's intellectual friends. Also like me, he transformed himself from a humble, meek, ordinary man to a muscle-bound warrior. Despite their strength and heroism, both Superman and Clark Kent were misunderstood outsiders.

One line in the comic book really stuck out and sealed my devotion to this new hero. The writer described Superman as "Champion of the Oppressed." He was no ordinary detective or soldier, fighting crime or rescuing damsels in distress. No, he was the protector of the weak and those most in need. He was the champion of justice. Someone who would stand up for helpless old men whose stores were vandalized and little girls who had rotten eggs and apples thrown at them.

I read and reread the comic book a half dozen times that day. The character of Superman seemed so much bigger and more significant than the childish comic strips I had been drawn to in the past. I was so overwhelmed and inspired by the story that I immediately set out to create my own superhero. I grabbed my pen, ink, and journal and in one fevered burst sketched out everything, including my character's uniform, logo, weapons, and the entire story of his origins. Everything about the character came to life almost instantly, springing from the deepest corners of my imagination. I wrote and drew for five straight hours, working and reworking different ideas. When I was done, I had given birth to the Mongrel.

When I finally put my pen down, I felt physically drained but satisfied in a way I never had been in my cartooning before. I wanted to share my new creation with someone. Yet I knew my parents wouldn't understand. I feared my sister would be too frightened by the dark implications of the story. There was only one person who I thought could fully appreciate my new hero.

In the darkest corridors of the third Reich evil scientists experiment on human lab rats....

We will mix the blood of all the mongrel races

And perform a transfusion on a baby and create a monster...

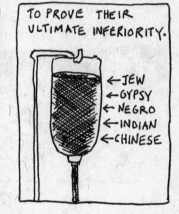

To prove their ultimate inferiority.

←Jew
←Gypsy
←Negro
←Indian
←Chinese

But the experiment fails... the baby is getting stronger!

And far more intelligent than a normal baby!

THE NAZI DOCTORS ORDER A NURSE TO KILL THE BABY WITH POISON...

BUT SHE CANNOT COMMIT THE HEINOUS DEED.

I WILL NOT HARM THIS BEAUTIFUL CHILD.

SHE BUNDLES THE BABY BOY INTO A BASKET AND SETS IT DOWN IN THE RIVER....

THE BOY DRIFTS FOR THREE DAYS AND NIGHTS...

UNTIL HE WASHES ASHORE NEAR A HUMBLE SHACK.

HE IS DISCOVERED BY A KINDLY OLD BOXING COACH WHO ADOPTS HIM AS HIS OWN...

AND TEACHES THE BOY THE SECRETS OF THE WARRIOR ARTS.

THE BOY GROWS EVER STRONGER AND MORE INTELLIGENT.

WHEN HE REACHES MANHOOD, THE BOY TRANSFORMS HIMSELF INTO A MASKED HERO KNOWN ONLY AS...

THE MONGREL

PROTECTING THE WEAK AND POWERLESS EVERYWHERE!

Return to the Berlin Boxing Club

I APPROACHED THE LARGE BRICK BUILDING, A WAVE OF nauseous tension sweeping through me. It had been half a year since I had been there, and everything looked the same, but different, clouded by my anxieties about how I would be received. I assumed that every member of the club must've heard about my disqualification at the tournament for being a Jew. These men had helped me on my journey from boyhood to manhood; they had been my comrades and friends. I felt bonded to them through our shared effort and pain. Would Worjyk bar me from even walking in? How many of the boxers I had sparred and trained with were also Nazis? How would they react to me now? Would they spit on me or try to beat me up? Surely Neblig wouldn't have invited me back if he'd thought I would get that kind of reception. Yet my doubts lingered as I ascended the stairs, past the other floors filled with whirring machinery manufacturing cloth.

As soon as I got to the landing on the top floor, I could tell something was wrong. The gold lettering on the club's door had been chipped and peeled away, so I could barely read the faded outline of where the words "The Berlin Boxing & Health Club" used to be.

I tentatively poked my head inside the door and was shocked by the extreme transformation. All the boxing equipment—the rings, the heavy bags, the weights, even the old posters from the walls—had been removed. The space was now filled with a series of long tables with dozens of women sewing and cutting brown wool blankets. The only decorations on the walls were a large industrial clock and a framed portrait of Hitler. The women all wore plain blue smocks and kerchiefs over their hair and intently stared down at the work in their hands. Piles of completed blankets stood stacked against the wall behind each worker. A foreman in a long white lab coat walked around the room holding a clipboard and observing the women's work. Every so often he would stop to inspect one of the completed blankets to make sure the stitching was right. No one looked up as I stepped into the room.

Then I noticed Neblig circling the tables, pushing a large dustbin on wheels, picking up the small scraps of fabric and thread that the women had cut away. He wore simple brown worker's overalls and a wool cap. When he finally glanced up and saw me standing by the door, a smile dawned across his face.

"Karl!"

He stepped away from his dustbin and came over to greet me, warmly shaking my hand and gripping my shoulder. The foreman frowned and approached.

"Herr Broder, you know we don't allow visitors inside the manufacturing rooms."

"*Ja*, Herr Schinkel, I'm s-s-s-sorry. May I take my lunch b-b-b-break now, s-s-s-sir?"

"Okay," the foreman replied. "But no more time than usual."

"Of course," Neblig said. "K-k-k-karl, I'll meet you downstairs in a minute, at the corner store."

I went back out and waited for Neblig at the corner store where we used to buy our milk shakes. The store had not changed at all since I had last been there, except there was now a sign in the front window that read: NO DOGS. NO JEWS. NO GYPSIES. A few moments later, Neblig jogged down the street to join me.

"So g-g-g-good to see you, Karl."

"You too," I said.

"Come on, I'll b-b-b-buy you a vanilla shake."

He started to walk into the store, but I gestured to the sign. He glanced at it and nodded.

"Wait here. I'll get them t-t-t-to go."

He went inside and emerged a few minutes later with two shakes, which we drank while we walked.

"Worjyk sold the c-c-c-club weeks ago," he explained.

"I was lucky that the factory owner k-k-k-kept me on as a janitor."

"But what happened to the club?" I asked. "Was Worjyk in some kind of financial trouble?"

"No. He had his reasons for s-s-s-selling. G-g-g-good reasons."

"I don't understand."

For a moment I feared that the demise of the club was tied to my exposure as a Jew. Would the Nazis have shut him down simply for having a Jewish member?

"He was hoping you'd come b-b-b-back so he could speak with you d-d-d-directly. But he left me this letter f-f-f-for you to explain in case you didn't."

Neblig reached into the front pocket of his overalls and removed a worn and creased yellow envelope that looked as if he had been carrying it for quite a while.

Dear Knochen,

By the time you get this letter, I will have left the country. I have joined a group of Jews who are settling in Palestine. They say we will all have to become farmers when we get there, but I'm sure there will also be a need for boxing coaches in the Promised Land. For obvious reasons I was not able to stand up and defend you at the tournament. I regret that, and I always will. I hope you can find it in your heart to forgive me. You have all the makings of a great fighter: good footwork, a quick jab, great reach, and the heart of a lion. And always remember, Jews are born fighters. David beat up Goliath pretty good, right? I hope you and your family remain safe and well both in and out of the ring.

Yours truly,
Abram Worjyk

My eyes stared at the page, not quite believing what I had just read. Even more shocking than the revelation that Worjyk was a Jew was the fact that he had already fled the country, making me even more nervous about my family's own situation.

"He had no idea that you were J-j-j-jewish until that moment at the t-t-t-tournament," Neblig said.

"Did he leave because of me? Because he thought the Nazis would come after him?"

"No. He had been plotting his escape for months, m-m-m-maybe years. When I t-t-t-tried to find you, I was kind of hoping you'd be g-g-g-gone too."

Then it all spilled out. I told Neblig the whole story of our diminished financial situation, the theft of the Picasso, and my fast-receding hope of ever getting to America. I had never spoken to anyone about these things, and it felt good to unload all my anxieties despite the fact that I knew Neblig would not be able to help.

Finally he asked, "What about M-m-m-max?"

"What about him?"

"Couldn't your father ask him for a l-l-l-loan or s-s-s-something? Aren't they f-f-f-friends?"

"They were friends, but I don't think they've spoken in a couple of years, since I started my lessons. And it's hard to tell what kind of friends they really were. My father had lots of friends back when times were good, but they all seem to have disappeared. Besides, my father is still a proud man; he could never go begging like that."

"What about you?"

"Me?"

"Y-y-y-you were about as close to Max as anyone at the club. He was c-c-c-cordial to everyone but never really befriended any of the other m-m-m-members. It was just a place for h-h-h-him to work out, to find s-s-s-sparring part-ners. But you were different. He really t-t-t-took an interest in you. Why d-d-d-don't you ask him for help?"

"I haven't heard from him in months. I wouldn't know how to reach him."

"He's in America now, training for his rematch w-w-w-with Joe Louis. But that's only a couple of w-w-w-weeks away. After that, win or lose, he'll b-b-b-be coming back to Berlin. He stays at the Hotel Excelsior on Stesemannstrasse. You c-c-c-could write to him."

"I don't know," I said. "I don't feel right about it."

"Don't let pride g-g-g-get in your way. Pride is a luxury

that s–s–s–sometimes you c–c–c–can't afford." He put a hand on my shoulder and held my gaze. "That's something I've had to l–l–l–learn the hard way in my life."

I paused, letting his words sink in. "I'll think about it," I finally said.

"G–g–g–good. Now I have to get b–b–b–back to work. But I'm afraid I have another small piece of b–b–b–bad news for you."

"What is it?"

Neblig took a deep breath.

"Barney Ross just lost the welterweight championship."

"What? To who?"

"Henry Armstrong. It was a brutal b–b–b–battle. Armstrong really gave him a beating. Ross's trainers were begging him to th–th–th–throw in the towel, but he w–w–w–wouldn't quit. And he was n–n–n–never knocked down. He made it through fifteen r–r–r–rounds and stayed on his f–f–f–feet, even though he knew the f–f–f–fight was lost. The story I read said that it was the most courageous f–f–f–fight the writer had ever s–s–s–seen."

"Will there be a rematch?"

Neblig shook his head.

"Ross retired right after the match."

"Retired?"

"*Ja*. It's probably a g–g–g–good thing too. Most fighters t–t–t–try to stay in the ring t–t–t–too long."

I felt a sickening emptiness in the pit of my stomach. For years Ross had been my real-life Superman, a scrawny, poor outcast who had transformed himself through sheer force of will and determination into a hero. I had always held on to the belief that if there were a Jewish World Champion, things would never get too bad for the Jews in Germany, as if his very existence were a shield for us all. Now he had been defeated, and worse still, he was retiring. I was so stunned by the news about Ross and Worjyk that I didn't even think to show Neblig my comic book. He had already returned to his job at the factory when I remembered it was in my rucksack.

I went home that night and flipped through my old boxing magazines, rereading all the stories about Ross's magical rise and career. I took small solace in the fact that Henry Armstrong, the man who had taken his crown, was a Negro and therefore also was a symbol of the strength of the mongrel races.

Yet I felt horribly conflicted, because now my last hope seemed to rest with Max Schmeling, a man who was being held up around the world as a symbol of Aryan supremacy and was preparing to do battle again with his own mongrel opponent, Joe Louis. Lying in bed, I felt the weight of responsibility bear down on me as it sank in that my relationship with Max might be my family's only hope of escape.

The Rematch

Several months earlier Joe Louis had captured the heavyweight title by easily defeating the Cinderella Man, Jimmy Braddock. German sportswriters accused the Jews of manipulating things to let Louis have the fight instead of Max, so the championship could stay in America. Boxing fans and writers around the world seemed to agree that Louis could not be considered the legitimate champion unless he beat Max, the only man to have defeated him in the ring. With mounting fears of another world war on the horizon, the rematch at Yankee Stadium was no longer about two men but about two nations and two worldviews: fascism versus democracy, racial purity versus diversity, oppression versus freedom.

Most Germans believed Max's victory to be inevitable—

and all part of Hitler's plan of Aryan ascendancy. To them, Max was racially superior, had more experience and intellect, and had beaten Louis once already. Yet some brave sportswriters were more pragmatic and questioned if Max, who was two years older than the last time they had fought, could go the distance with the much younger Louis, who was entering his prime.

The fight began at three A.M., Berlin time, and just as before, the entire German nation stayed awake to listen. Lights glistened in nearly every home and apartment building; and restaurants, beer halls, and theaters stayed open late and were filled with noisy patrons. If you walked down any street, you could hear the radio broadcast buzzing through the air from all directions.

By 1938 street violence against Jews had become so brazen, commonplace, and ignored by the police that most Jews, including my family, no longer ventured out after dark unless it was absolutely necessary. So I was forced to listen to the rematch, unlike the previous fight, with my father and sister on our family radio in the front room of the gallery. My mother retreated to the bathroom to soak in the tub, claiming she had no interest in the fight.

My father sat stoically in the one nice upholstered armchair we had brought from the old apartment, while I perched on a wooden stool directly next to the radio. Hildy sat on the floor, sketching in one of her notebooks. I wished I could read my father's mind to know what he was thinking and whom he was rooting for. Nearly all Jews in Germany were now pulling for Joe Louis, hoping that a symbol of Nazi strength would be brought low. Some feared that a Schmeling loss would trigger yet more anti-Semitism and reprisals. Still other Jews continued to consider themselves patriotic Germans and would never consider rooting for anyone but their countryman. Despite my resentment toward Max, I couldn't help but still root for him. He had shown me kindness and attention at a time when no one else had, and I still held out hope that he would help me.

Images danced in my head as announcer Arno Hellmis's rapid-fire words spilled out of our radio speaker. Even Hildy paused in her drawing and looked up as the bell sounded, signaling the beginning of the fight.

"There's the bell starting the first round. Both fighters move to the center of the ring . . . Max in purple trunks and Louis in black with white trim. Both fighters are circling, throwing jabs, getting a feel for each other. And now Louis goes on the attack, throwing a quick combination that seems to have taken Max by surprise. He's got Max backing up . . . and Louis lands a hard right to Max's jaw . . . and another to the gut and another! Max is up against the ropes, and the punches keep coming from Louis. Get out of there, Max!"

Hellmis's voice rose in pitch as the crowd's cheers swelled around him. He could barely talk above the din or keep up with the action. As Max struggled, Hellmis shouted warnings and encouragements to his fighter like a concerned friend rather than an announcer.

"Louis lands another brutal shot to Max's body . . . and another! Now he's firing punches at Max's head, one after the other. For heaven's sake, Max, get your hands up! He has Max up against the ropes. And he lands another! And Max's knee is buckling! Stay up, Max! Stay up!"

The crowd roared louder, and in my mind I saw Max teetering on the verge of collapse.

"The ref is pulling them apart now . . . that last hit to the body really got to Max. And now Louis moves in again and lands another right to the jaw, and Max goes down! He's down! Get up, Max! He gets back to his feet, but Louis attacks again, and Max is down again! But he pulls himself back up! He's on his feet again! Careful, Max! Get your hands up! And Louis delivers another crushing right, and Max is down for a third time!"

A gasp went up from the crowd, and Hellmis seemed on the verge of tears.

"He's on his knees, trying to get up, but it looks like he might be down for good! Yes. That's it. The fight is over. Max Schmeling is beaten! It seems impossible, but it's true. Max is—"

The radio signal went dead. The Nazi authorities had cut the broadcast as soon as it was clear that Max had been defeated. The entire fight, the rematch of the century, lasted not even one round, barely two minutes.

We all sat staring into a blank spot in space where we had been seeing the fight in our mind's eye. A thin crackle of static was the only sound. Finally my father rose and switched off the radio.

"Good," he said flatly. "Now both of you off to bed."

Hildy and I obeyed, retreating to our rooms without any further discussion.

Once down in the basement, I lay on my bed and tried to comprehend what had just happened. I almost didn't believe what we had heard. It was inconceivable that Max would not only lose but be defeated so quickly and totally. I tried to picture what it looked like, with Louis raining down punches and Max falling not once but three times.

My father's reaction communicated all I needed to know about his feelings for Max and the possibility of his reaching out for any sort of help. I knew it was up to me. I tried to compute how the loss might influence Max's reaction to my plea. If he had won, I reasoned, he would have been even richer, more powerful and influential, and it would have been even easier for him to assist us in some way. On the other hand, if he had become champion, it would have been more difficult to make contact with him, with everyone demanding even more of his time. Perhaps with this humbling loss, he would look more kindly upon a request to help someone weak and powerless. There had even been some whispered rumors that if he lost, he would be thrown in jail by the Nazis for disgracing the Reich.

I sat at my desk and tried to compose a letter to Max. I struggled to think of a way to begin. Should I tell him I was sorry about the loss to Louis? Should I ask how he was feeling? Should I tell him how hard things had gotten for my family? I wrote several drafts, filled with awkward false starts, before I finally composed a very short note in which I simply asked if I could come see him at the Excelsior Hotel when he came back to the city. I reasoned that it would be easier to explain everything in person.

I finished writing at four A.M.and snuck out of the gallery to drop it in the mail slot on the corner. Our neighborhood was eerily quiet and empty, unlike the night of Max's first fight with Louis, when the streets of Berlin had been filled with revelers till well past dawn.

As I approached the mail slot, a group of three angry drunk brownshirts came around the corner, grumbling about the fight. I froze as they walked right toward me.

"The Negro must've fouled him, just like Sharkey did."

"It was the Jews," said another. "I'm sure of it."

"They probably poisoned him somehow."

"That's why they insisted the fight be held in New York City," said the third, "so they could pull their dirty tricks."

"Damn kikes."

They brushed right past me, and one of them grazed my shoulder. He stopped and said, "Watch it."

"Sorry," I muttered.

He angrily glared at me. I held my breath as he looked me up and down.

"Come on," one of the others said. "Let's go."

He abruptly turned away and kept walking into the night.

I exhaled. Clearly my non-Jewish looks had saved me. I

shuddered to think what might have happened if my sister or my father had been with me.

I deposited the letter in the mail slot and quickly retreated to the gallery.

Broken Glass

IN THE DAYS IMMEDIATELY FOLLOWING THE FIGHT, WILD rumors circulated in the Nazi press that Max had been poisoned or that Louis had used brass knuckles inside his gloves. One German paper even speculated that Max had died from his injuries in the ring and that the Jewish American press was conspiring to keep it a secret. In truth Max had simply retreated to a New York hospital to be treated for his injuries. Eventually photographs emerged of Max in his hospital bed, and he was quoted in interviews saying that he had been defeated fairly.

Several weeks later he returned to Berlin. This time there was no fanfare, no dinners with Hitler or Goebbels, no endorsement deals, no parades in his honor. The homecoming barely got a mention in the sports pages of the paper. I did find one small photo of Max and Anny getting out of the back of a car together and entering the Excelsior Hotel. So at least I knew he had not been jailed.

The photograph also confirmed that he was staying at the location where I had sent my letter. Yet after several weeks I did not receive a reply, so I wrote him again, and again, and again, one identical letter every few days, hoping that one of them would get through. But I never heard back. I imagined my letter lost in a vast sea of fan mail. Or worse, perhaps Max was just coldly ignoring my pleas.

That summer and fall every week seemed to bring a new piece of bad news for the Jews of Germany, like logs being thrown onto a flame that was burning hotter and wilder. In July all Jews were required to carry special identification cards at all times. Jewish doctors were downgraded to the status of medical attendants and were no longer allowed to treat Aryan patients; and Jewish lawyers were forbidden to practice law. Incidents of anti-Jewish vandalism steadily rose and became more and more brazen. A group of Nazi thugs destroyed the great synagogue in Munich. Eventually we were even required to have a *J* stamped on our passports.

The Nazi repression of the Jews seemed to march in step with their global aggression as first they annexed Austria and then the Sudetenland, a portion of Czechoslovakia with a large German population. The world seemed to be letting the Nazis get away with anything they wanted.

My father and mother reacted to each piece of news in the morning or afternoon editions of the paper with growing dismay and dread. My father would read a story and mutter: "They can't do this."

"They already have," my mother would reply.

Then two horrible events hit in quick succession. First fifteen thousand Polish Jews were expelled from Germany and sent back to Poland. As my father read the headline aloud at the breakfast table, my mother grabbed the paper from his hands.

"You see," she yelled. "They're running us off like nothing more than animals. Like you'd herd a cow."

"So what do you want me to do about it?"

"Something! Anything!" my mother replied.

"You think I'm not trying?"

"Try harder!" she snapped.

"Thanks for your support," Papa spat back bitterly. "All you do is sit in the bath all day. You think that helps?"

"I have to find some escape. I can't stand sitting around watching you do nothing!"

"You're such a genius? You think of something!"

He quickly rose from the table and walked out of the gallery. He was gone all day. After sundown I started to worry that he was gone for good. It was not uncommon for men unable to provide for their families to simply disappear. Maybe he had decided to leave us to fend for ourselves, or worse, perhaps he had been arrested for selling degenerate art or something he had printed. We all went to bed that night without any word from him. I couldn't sleep. I nervously watched the clock as the minutes ticked by, hoping and waiting for him to come back.

Finally, at 1:30 A.M., I heard the front door swing open. The smell of him blew in with the wind as he stepped inside. The faint odor of cigars and cheap peppermint schnapps shot through the gallery and into the basement. I heard snippets of his argument with my mother in harsh whispers.

"So you still have money for liquor and cigars, but not to help your family."

"I'm trying to do business. Businessmen drink. Art collectors drink."

"So do the whores on Friedrichstrasse."

"That's enough, Rebecca!"

They went back and forth for nearly an hour in the same circle of accusation, anger, and frustration until they ran out steam and lapsed into bitter silence, and I was certain that they had both fallen asleep.

The next morning, the paper brought even worse news. A Polish Jew living in France named Herschel Grynszpan, whose family had been deported from Germany back to Poland, had entered the German Embassy in Paris and shot and killed a German diplomat named Ernst vom Rath. As my father silently read the story, his face turned white, and he quietly handed the paper over to my mother, who reacted with a similar petrified silence.

That night we were just finishing dinner when there was a knock at the door. We all froze. There was another another knock and then the urgent voice of a man.

"Sigmund? It's Dolph Lutz."

"Lutz?" my father said, rising to answer the door.

He opened the door, and Lutz quickly stepped inside and closed it.

"I'm sorry to disturb you," he said. "But I had to warn you."

My mother, Hildy, and I came to the front of the gallery to join them.

"Warn me?"

"The Nazis have taken to the streets and are attacking Jews and Jewish businesses."

My mother gasped and covered her mouth.

"What about the police?" my father asked.

"We've been ordered to stand down."

"Stand down?"

"*Ja*. Look, I really have to go. I suggest you just lock your doors and windows and turn off the lights, so no one thinks anyone is here."

Lutz moved back to the door.

"I will try to check on you later, but I can't make any promises. I'm sorry," he said quietly, and then slipped back outside.

My father double locked the door behind him and turned out the lights.

"Get to the back room," he instructed, "and don't make a sound."

We all huddled together in the back room, afraid to talk or even move. We must have sat like that for nearly an hour, listening to one another breathing. My sister coughed, and we all shot her angry glances to suppress it. At first the street was quiet. An occasional car drove past like it was any other night.

Finally we heard loud voices approaching in the distance. The first distinct sound I heard was laughter. Then the voices grew louder and more menacing. None of us dared get up to look out the front window, but we could hear jackboots clomping on the sidewalk, crashing sounds, screams, cries, and beer hall chants.

Finally a group stopped directly in front of the gallery.

"I think this is a Jew store," a young man's voice shouted.

"Yeah! I think they had jewelry in there."

"No, it was an art gallery," another chimed in.

"It's been closed for years, though."

"Yeah, but I bet they've got lots of money hidden in there."

"Open up, Jew!"

A loud pounding came at the door. Hildy cried and pressed herself close to our mother.

"Keep quiet!" my father whispered.

"Open the door or we'll break it down!"

More loud pounding and jiggling of the handle. Then a barrage of kicks and punches against the old wood, until I couldn't imagine the door holding out much longer.

"Wait! Wait!" one of them finally said.

There was a beat of silence. Were they going to give up?

Then a massive crashing sound erupted from the front of the gallery as the large plate glass window smashed. My father stood up.

"Stay here!" he directed my mother and Hildy. "Karl, you come."

We had no weapons in the house, so my father grabbed a mop handle and thrust it into my hands and then took a rusty old hammer out of one of the desk drawers for himself.

"Come on." He gestured to me to follow him.

"Sig, be careful!" my mother said.

He boldly stepped forward and led me down the dark makeshift hallway between the curtains to the front of the gallery. When we emerged into the front room, we saw our plate glass window had been shattered by a tossed garbage can that lay on the floor tipped up against the couch. A group of young men poured through the window like angry bees from a hive. There were four of them, dressed in neatly pressed brown shirts and black leather jackboots. They all carried clubs, and their eyes were wild with bloodlust and the thrill of their violent adventure. The leader was a tall man with wavy blond hair whom I thought I recognized from the neighborhood, but I couldn't be sure in the half-light.

My father raised the hammer over his head.

"Get out of here! This is our home!"

"You have no home in Germany anymore, Jew!" the leader said.

My father's eyes narrowed, and he squared his shoulders and seemed to stand even more erect.

"I am a German!"

He suddenly rushed at the man, howling at the top of his voice.

The men were taken by surprise by my father's attack. The leader was barely able to dodge my father's hammer blow. It grazed the side of his arm, ripping through his shirt and cutting a thin bloody line down his forearm. He growled in pain.

"You'll pay for that."

All four men moved toward my father with their clubs. I stood dumbstruck for a moment as I watched him fend them off with expert self-defense moves he must have learned in the army. He swung the hammer at them in quick wide chops, keeping them at a distance, until the four of them spread out and charged him at once. Papa was able to toss two of them to the ground before the other two grabbed him and pulled him down.

I ran at them with my mop handle and tried to beat them away from my father, who was now on the bottom of the pile, receiving a vicious series of whacks from their clubs.

Two of them broke off from the pile and came after me. I had never fought with a stick, and it felt awkward in my hands. I was not quite sure how to attack or defend with it. I wished I could square off against them in a boxing ring, where I'd know exactly what to do. So I stupidly tossed my weapon aside and attacked one of the men with a quick combination of punches. I landed only two blows before the other man hit me over the head with his club and I went down hard. I tried to cover myself as they both pounded me with their clubs and kicked me.

I saw that my father had somehow managed to disarm

one of the attackers. He had him pinned on the ground by the throat with one hand while he fought off the other with the hammer in his free hand. In that moment my father seemed mightier than Superman, Barney Ross, or the Mongrel. Unlike our attackers, who looked wild and out of control, almost frothing at the mouth, my father appeared composed, focused, and determined.

Then the man beneath my father writhed under his grip, crawled one of his hands along the floor, and grabbed a jagged shard of glass, a deadly six-inch triangle.

"Papa!" I screamed.

But before my father could react, the man plunged the piece of glass into my father's side.

My father gasped in agony and released the man's neck. The man stuck the glass deeper into his side and then stood over him and kicked at my father's face. I lunged over to try to protect him, but the two other men pulled me back down. I felt the edges of their boots stomping on the back of my head and neck until everything went black.

Drop Cloth

I FELT THE BACK OF MY HEAD THROBBING AGAINST THE floor and my eyeballs pulsing beneath my closed lids, pushing up against the painful blackness. When I finally opened my eyes, a dark image hovered above me. Slowly the image came into focus, and I saw Hildy staring at me with a look of terror.

"He's waking up!"

I struggled to sit up. My head felt heavy, and my vision whirled in dark circles. It took a moment for the room to come back into sharp focus. All the curtains had been ripped down, leaving the gallery exposed as the one raw room it really was. Furniture had been overturned and destroyed, pillows slashed and dishes broken. The floor was covered with a layer of feathers, splintered wood, and shards of glass.

Through the darkness, I finally saw my mother sitting against the back wall, cradling my father in her arms. Deep red blood stained the entire side and front of his white shirt.

I pulled myself to my feet but almost immediately fell back down from the dizziness. I touched the side of my head and felt several large contusions jutting up along the back of my skull like a patch of small half-cut oranges. A deep warm gash ran down just behind my left ear.

"Karl, stay down," I heard my father call out in a weak voice. "Give yourself a minute for your head to settle."

"Sig, please don't try to talk!" my mother said.

But despite his weakness, my father took charge.

"Hildy, come bring your mother some of my shirts for her to use as bandages."

Hildy fetched a couple of his shirts from the ground, and my father sat up.

"Tear them into strips," he commanded.

My mother did as instructed and tore the shirts into long strips.

"Good, now wrap them around me, here," he said, indicating his midsection.

He grunted in pain as my mother tightened the bandages.

"Sig," she gasped, "I don't want to hurt you."

"It's okay. It needs to be tight to stop the bleeding," he said. "Wad up a piece of the cloth and put it in my mouth."

My mother folded a small section of the shirt, and my father bit down on it and gritted his teeth as she continued to wrap and secure the bandages. Finally she finished, and he spat out the cloth and exhaled, breathing heavily.

"Good. Now, get me and Karl glasses of water."

Hildy retrieved the glasses and brought one to each of us. The water helped revive me and made my legs feel solid. I struggled to lift myself to a standing position.

"We've got to take the glass out to stop the bleeding," my mother said

"No. If we try to pull it out, it'll only cause more damage. I've got to get to a real doctor."

"We can't drag you through the streets like this," she said.

"Call Steiner, Hartzel, or Hein Voorman," he grunted, and gripped his side in agony. "They have cars and they owe me. See if one of them can come take me to a doctor."

My mother ran to the back of the gallery and made some phone calls, returning a few moments later.

"Hartzel said he'd do it, but it might take him a while to get here."

"How long?" my father said.

"He didn't say."

We all sat together huddled around my father and waited for the car to arrive. Loud, angry noises of the riot continued to ebb and flow outside. Fresh blood soaked through my father's makeshift bandages and ran along the side of his pants. His breath became more labored with each passing minute, and his eyes fluttered open and shut.

"Sig, stay awake!" my mother said whenever he appeared close to dozing off.

My own face and neck throbbed, and the raw contusions seemed to spread and connect with one another, making my entire head feel like one large bruise. Just blinking my eyes caused sharp sparks of pain to pop inside my head like little firecrackers. Both of my thumbs also ached. In my hasty attack, I had completely forgotten the most basic rule about how to make a fist with the thumb tucked safely over the knuckles. I was lucky I hadn't broken anything.

After forty-five minutes of tense waiting, we heard a faint car horn from outside. My mother ran to the window.

"It's him!" she said. "Karl, help me get your father up."

My mother and I hoisted my father to his feet. He groaned in pain as we pulled him up and dragged him out the front door to the waiting car. Blood had soaked through the entire bandage, so it looked like a crude crimson sash. Our street was littered with garbage and broken glass, but the roving band of Nazis seemed to have moved on to another area.

My father gritted his teeth and took short, harsh breaths as we awkwardly lowered him into the backseat of the car.

Hartzel, the Bavarian landscape painter whom my father had shown at one of his last gallery openings, sat in the driver's seat, nervously tapping the steering wheel and peering out the windshield.

"Thank you so much for coming," my mother said.

"We'd better go," he replied quickly.

"Hildy, you and Karl sit in the front seat, I'll be in back with your fathe—"

"We can't take the children," Hartzel said.

"What?" my mother said.

"It would make us too conspicuous. We'd be stopped. I'd be arrested. We'd all be arrested."

"I won't leave the children!"

"They'll probably be safer here anyway," he replied. "The rioters have moved on. Right now this street is quieter than the rest of the city."

"I won't do it!"

"Rebecca, he's right," my father said from the backseat. "Karl is a man now. He can take care of things." He looked me in the eye, and I gave him a small nod.

"We'll all be in greater danger if we travel together," he said.

"But, Sig—"

"No arguments, Rebecca. I've got to get help."

"We'll be fine, Mama." I chimed in.

My mother stared at me and my sister, weighing her choice.

"Okay," my mother finally said.

She got into the backseat next to my father.

"Here, cover yourselves with this," Hartzel said, handing them a paint-splattered drop cloth over the front seat.

"How will he breathe with this over his head?" my mother said.

"I can't drive around with him bleeding out in the open," Hartzel said. "We wouldn't make it two blocks."

"He's right." My father interrupted. "Just do it, Rebecca."

Our mother sat beside our father and positioned the drop

cloth over their bodies. Before covering themselves completely, my father called out: "Wait. Children, come here."

Hildy leaned inside the car, and she hugged and kissed my mother and then my father.

"Don't be scared, my little beauty," my father said to her. "I'll be fine. And Karl's the toughest guy on the block now."

I kissed my mother and then reached out to shake my father's hand.

"Don't worry," I said. "We'll be okay."

"Come closer, Karl," my father said.

I leaned in, and he tenderly touched the side of my face and kissed me on the cheek. I could not remember the last time I had been kissed by my father, and it felt strange.

"I finally got to see you fight," he said. "You must be something in the ring. Take care of your sister, okay?"

"I will," I said.

I felt a rush of emotion toward my father like I'd felt the day my mother had visited in the basement. I wanted to tell him that I loved him, but the words got stuck in my throat.

"Good-bye, Karl," he said.

I covered them both with the drop cloth so they were completely hidden and shut the door. My parents slumped down in the seat under the cloth, until they looked like they could pass for a pile of painting supplies instead of two living, breathing human beings. Then Hartzel drove off into the night. Almost as soon as they rounded the corner, a loud crash came from down the block in the other direction.

"Let's get inside," I said.

An Evening Stroll with Our Aunt

IT WAS ONLY TEN P.M. BY THE TIME WE GOT BACK INSIDE, though it felt as if it were past midnight. We made our way downstairs to the basement, because I figured that would be the safest place for us. Anyone breaking into the gallery would see that it had already been ransacked and I hoped would also assume it had been abandoned.

Hildy was terrified, and as we sat in the darkness, she peppered me with questions that I couldn't answer. "Where are they going to take Papa?" "Will he be okay?" "How long will we have to stay alone?" "What are we going to do?" I tried to keep her calm, but my lack of any concrete information or plan made her more and more hysterical.

Then we heard another loud crash. A baby cried from an apartment nearby. The sound of shouts, laughter, and chants swelled as another wave of men and boys poured down our street. A brick was thrown through our already broken window, shattering most of the remaining glass. Hildy shrieked in terror.

"Shhhh!"

"They're going to kill us," she cried.

"Keep quiet!"

"I want Mama!"

"Please, Hildy. Pull yourself together."

"I can't!"

"Keep your voice down or they'll hear you."

"I want my mama!"

"I'm here. It's okay."

"It's not. They're going to get us."

"I'll protect you."

"You can't—"

"I can. I'll get us out of here."

"How?"

"I think I know a place we can hide."

"Where?"

"Just stay down here. I've got to go back up and make a phone call."

"I want to come with you! Don't leave me!"

"No. Just stay here. It's okay."

I stood up to go upstairs, and she screamed, "Karl!"

I clamped my hand over her mouth.

"Quiet!" I hissed.

Her breathing calmed a bit, and I removed my hand.

"You can come with me, but you have to promise to be quiet. Can you do that?"

She nodded.

We both slowly made our way back up the dark staircase to the main floor. I searched around in the darkness until I found my father's address book.

"I need you to light a match for me so I can look up a number," I said. "Can you do that?"

Hildy nodded. I found a box of matches, and she lit one. Her eyes were wide with terror as I flipped through the book until I found the name I was looking for: "BERTRAM HEIGEL." I picked up the phone.

Twenty minutes later the front door gently opened, and the strange high voice of the Countess called out, "Karl?"

The Countess stepped over our broken furniture and inside the main room.

"Are you here?"

Hildy and I emerged from the back dressed in our sweaters, scarves, hats, and overcoats. We had both packed our rucksacks with some books and a few possessions we were able to find in the wreckage.

"Thanks for coming," I said.

"Of course," he said. "A girl like me always likes a night on the town."

I stepped into the light, and the Countess gasped.

"Karl, my dear boy, you look awful."

"It's not so bad," I said.

Through the darkness, I could see that he had dressed in

his long blond wig and makeup with a kerchief tied around his head. He wore a simple blue dress under his overcoat. I was not sure why he had dressed as a woman, but I was glad he had. A woman walking with two children would be far less likely to be attacked than a man.

"Hildy," I said, "this is the Countess."

"Aren't you a darling?" the Countess said, approaching and taking her by the chin and staring at her in the dark. "I bet you're Daddy's little princess."

Hildy nodded nervously.

"I do like to be called the Countess, but you may call me Aunt Bertie, if you like. I've always wanted a little niece just like you."

Another loud crashing noise erupted from the street. We all flinched.

"So, it's just a few blocks to my apartment," the Countess continued. "And if anyone asks, you're my niece and nephew and we're just out for a stroll, returning from a lovely dinner party, like a silly game of pretend. Do you think you can do that?"

Hildy nodded.

"Okay then, let's be off."

We emerged onto the street and made our way toward the Countess's apartment building. Along the route we saw that dozens of Jewish stores and homes had been attacked. We passed Herr Greenberg's art supply shop, and tubes of paint and colored pencils lay trampled on the ground in front of the store, so great swirls of color mingled with the broken glass of his front window. Multicolored boot tracks led off in all directions like trails of blood in the woods that a hunter would track to find a wounded animal. I saw streaks of red mixed in and wondered if Herr Greenberg's blood had been spilled along with his paint.

The Countess held Hildy's hand as we moved quickly down the sidewalk. A group of boys, who appeared to be my age, emerged from around a corner and approached us. I instantly recognized one of them as my old friend Kurt Seidler. I hadn't seen Kurt in more than two years, since the day I had been kicked out of our school with all the other Jews. Kurt and his friends were not wearing Nazi uniforms, but I noticed they were all carrying items that they must have looted from Jewish homes or businesses. One of the boys had a silver teapot, another held a small radio tucked under his arm, and Kurt himself gripped a set of brass Sabbath candlesticks, one in each hand.

I pulled my hat low over my face as we approached. The boys were smiling and talking excitedly. As we passed, Kurt addressed the Countess.

"Hey, anything left to grab up ahead?"

"No," the Countess said quickly.

I carefully glanced up, and Kurt suddenly caught sight of me. A flash of recognition dawned on his face. His eyes locked on mine. My pulsed quickened as I wondered what he would do. We stared at each other for a long moment, and then he quickly looked away.

"Come on, boys," he said. "Let's check it out anyway."

Kurt and his friends moved on. I exhaled and glanced over my shoulder at them. They seemed so overwhelmed with the excitement of the night that they almost appeared to be skipping down the sidewalk. A sharp wave of nausea hit me. I wondered what had become of my other friends. Were they out looting and attacking Jews too?

"Wasn't that Kurt Seidler?" Hildy asked.

"I don't know," I said. "Let's go."

We moved on down the block and saw a group of brownshirts kicking at an elderly Jewish man lying in the street. Hildy cried out when she saw them, and the Countess pulled her close. I heard the Jew's muffled cries as we passed: "Please, stop." The brownshirts were so focused on their task they didn't notice us passing by on the opposite side of the street.

We finally made it to the Countess's apartment building, which was on a quiet residential street in a neighborhood where few Jewish people lived. As a result, the street was completely untouched and still, as if it were just any other night.

As we entered the apartment, I noticed that the front rooms seemed different. Several pieces of furniture and some artwork appeared to be missing. The Countess noticed my quizzical expression.

"I've had to redecorate a bit over the past couple of years. Leaner times call for a more sleek style. But I've kept my boudoir intact. Here, Hildy, come take a look."

The Countess led us into the bedroom, which was

dominated by a large vanity covered with cosmetics and multicolored perfume bottles. Feather boas and scarves hung over the edges of the mirror. He sat Hildy on a small embroidered chair in front of the vanity.

"I've never seen so much makeup," Hildy gasped.

"Not all of us are as naturally beautiful as you are, my dear. You can play with whatever you like. Karl, come help me in the kitchen."

I followed the Countess into the small kitchenette, where he helped me clean and bandage my wounds. Then he poured some milk into a saucepan on the stove to make hot cocoa.

"Does she know I'm a man?"

"No. I don't think so. I didn't say anything."

"Good. Don't. She'll be more comfortable if she thinks I'm a woman. All little girls want their mothers when they need comfort, *ja*?"

"I need to find them," I said. "I need to know if my father's okay. He lost a lot of blood—"

"In the morning," he interrupted. "There's nothing to be done tonight. It's a madhouse out there."

"I need to at least call the hospitals."

"I don't have a phone in the apartment anymore. And it's too risky for you to use the public phone in the lobby that you called me on earlier. Too many prying ears. None of us would be safe. I'll find a safe phone for us to use tomorrow. We'll find them. Don't worry."

He mixed pieces of dark chocolate and sugar into the

simmering milk and then poured three cups, and we returned to the bedroom.

Hildy was flipping through a big stack of phonograph records that were lined up on a shelf beside the vanity.

"You have so many records."

"They're my lifeline. I sold my radio months ago. I got sick of hearing all the bad news and the rotten music they play these days."

"I've never seen such a big collection of jazz singers."

"Yes. Unfortunately, no one is allowed to play this kind of music anymore. Isn't that ridiculous? As if Louis Armstrong were some sort of political operative. But I still listen to them late at night with the volume turned low."

A large old wooden phonograph sat nearby, and the Countess started picking out thick black discs and putting them on, one by one. We listened to the crackling music as we drank our hot cocoa. Some of the Jazz Age cabaret songs were funny, some were sad, and many of them had a world-weary quality.

"All these songs are from the good old days, which didn't seem so great at the time but are looking better and better. This one was always my favorite. It's by Josephine Baker. Do you know who that is? She's a wonderful Negro singer from America. She used to play the cabaret here, and there'd be a line around the corner. Used to do a crazy dance wearing only bananas!"

"Peeled or unpeeled?" Hildy giggled.

The Countess put on the scratchy old disc, and a voice

emerged that was fragile and sexy at the same time. The lyrics struck me as ominous, like she was singing about a Germany she knew was slowly dying.

She's a little bit sad and a little bit smart
Something of an angel and something of a tart
She likes danger, dancing, brawling and booze
She's got everything to gain and nothing to lose

She's my Berlin baby
A brightly falling star
My Berlin baby
Always goes too far

Let's eat and drink and dance and sing
Who cares what else tomorrow brings
The morning may just not begin
So grab a little sin

She's my Berlin baby
A brightly falling star
My Berlin baby
Always goes too far
Always goes too far
Always goes too far

The last strains of the music faded, and the needle scratched as it reached the end of the record. The Countess lifted the needle and turned off the machine. Hildy had fallen asleep on a small purple velvet couch. The Countess gently placed a pillow beneath Hildy's head and covered her with a blanket.

"She can sleep here. You take the couch in the living room."

He handed me a pillow and a blanket from a closet.

"Thank you," I said. "You were brave to come out and get us."

"You were the brave one, Karl. You figured out the plan and took control. I just answered the call. You're just like your father."

I experienced an unfamiliar feeling of pride at being compared with my father.

By the time I retreated to the living room and settled down on the couch it was well past midnight. As I lay back, my mind raced with concerns and anxieties. How would I track down my parents? Had my father received treatment in time? How long would the anti-Jewish rioting last? Would it ever end if the police and the government didn't care to stop it? How would we escape this nightmare?

I grabbed my rucksack and took inventory of the few things I had been able to salvage from the gallery: a small pile of my sketchbooks and journals, the little money I had stashed under my mattress, my prized copy of *The Ring* magazine with the cover story on Barney Ross, the book *Boxing Basics for German Boys*, and the first issue of Action Comics with the origin of Superman. I opened Hildy's rucksack and looked inside. She too had taken some of her journals, her favorite dress, and a sweater that our mother had knitted her. I was relieved to see that she had also taken Herr Karotte and the very first Winzig und Spatz book. These items from our old life gave me some small measure of comfort. The Nazis had broken our windows and torn apart our furniture, but they had not destroyed our selves. I set the books aside and finally drifted off to sleep.

The Feint

THE NEXT MORNING THE COUNTESS FOUND A FRIEND A few blocks away who agreed to let us use his phone. It was too dangerous to risk returning to the gallery, because bands of brownshirts still roamed the streets, looting whatever they could find and harassing any Jews they came across. Some of them forced the Jews to sweep or scrub away the mess in the streets as if they had caused it themselves.

The Countess's friend was an old gentleman, named Herr Braun, who had a large white mustache and wore an ascot and a silk jacket. He lived in a freestanding brick town house that had once been quite grand but, like his fine clothing, had begun to fray. Hildy stayed in the apartment while the Countess and I went to make the calls to try to find our parents. With Herr Braun's help, we made contact with every hospital and clinic we could think of, but no one could find a record of Sigmund Stern's being admitted for treatment.

"If they were smart, they found a private doctor," Herr Braun said.

"Were your parents friendly with any doctors?" the Countess asked. "Jewish doctors?"

"None that I can think of."

"Well, I'm certain that's what they must have done," the Countess said, with a little too much forced confidence.

"There were many arrests last night," Herr Braun said. "I was listening to reports on the radio this morning. They might've been pulled over and arrested."

Instantly the worst images of my parents rotting in a dirty jail cell flooded into my head. What would happen to Hildy and me if they had been arrested? Would we be arrested too?

"There's no need to panic the boy," the Countess said.

"I'm just trying to be realistic," Herr Braun said.

"Why would they arrest them?" I asked.

"For inciting the riots," he replied.

"Inciting the riots? What did they do to incite the riots?"

"Nothing of course," Herr Braun said. "But the news reports are blaming the Jews for starting the trouble themselves. There's even talk that the government intends to have the Jews pay to repair all the damage. And there may be more trouble tonight. I would suggest that you stay indoors until this all blows over."

"You and your sister are welcome to stay at my flat as long as you need."

"What if it doesn't blow over?" I said.

Neither man responded.

"I need to find my parents."

"I wouldn't recommend making any more calls," Herr Braun said. "It's not good to be asking too many questions. You might bring suspicion on yourself . . . and us."

"Suspicion of what?"

"It doesn't matter. Suspicion of anything."

"Let's just lay low for a while, Karl," the Countess said gently. "I'm sure things will quiet down after a couple of days. And then we'll find them."

"No. I've got to find them now."

"It's too risky," Herr Braun said.

"I know someone who can help," I said.

"Who?" the Countess asked.

"Just someone. He lives not too far from here."

"Why don't you call him first?" the Countess asked.

"No. I have to see him in person."

Since Max had ignored all my letters, I feared he wouldn't take my calls. I needed to confront him face-to-face.

"You shouldn't be out on the streets alone, Karl," the Countess said.

"I'll be fine," I said. "I don't look Jewish. No one will bother me."

• • •

The Excelsior Hotel dominated an entire city block, and the management boasted that it was the largest hotel on the European continent. The building featured six hundred guest rooms, nine restaurants, several shops, a seven-thousand-volume library, and a specially built underground tunnel connecting it to the Anhalter Bahnhof, the railway station across the street. The hotel had its own security force and even published its own daily newspaper. It was a city within the city, and as I approached on foot that day, it seemed as imposing as an armed fortress.

I had thought through several different scenarios to breach the hotel's security and find Max, from posing as a telegram delivery boy to hiding myself on a food service or laundry cart like a slapstick scene from a Marx Brothers movie. I even considered bribing one of the maids or janitors with the little cash I had left. In the end, I realized that the risk of any of those ideas was too great and the chances of success were slim. So I decided to simply use the direct approach.

I entered the main lobby, a great gilded room adorned with massive gold light fixtures and overstuffed furniture, and approached the front desk, where a line of smartly uniformed clerks manned their stations. I walked up to one who looked approachable.

"Can I help you?" the clerk said.

"I'm here to see Max Schmeling?"

The clerk's eyes narrowed.

"Is he expecting you?"

"Well, no, but—"

"I'm sorry, but Herr Schmeling does not take unplanned visits from fans."

"I'm not a fan. I'm a friend. He's an old friend of my family."

"Really?" he said doubtfully.

"And he's my boxing coach."

"Your boxing coach? I didn't know Herr Schmeling needed to take on students."

"I'm the only one. Or I was. We used to train at the same place, the Berlin Boxing Club, and—"

"Listen, I don't think Herr Schmeling has time to be disturbed today—"

"Just call him. Please. I'm certain he'd want to see me if he knew I was here."

"And why didn't you call ahead and let him know you were coming?"

"I was just passing by and thought I'd say hello. I think he'd be quite displeased if he knew I was turned away. He's always spoken so highly of the staff here. I'd hate for him to have to complain to the management about one of the employees."

I squinted as if struggling to read the clerk's name tag.

"That would be a shame, wouldn't it, Herr Preysing?"

The clerk frowned and picked up the phone.

"Name?"

"Karl Stern."

He stepped away from the desk and dialed. It occurred

to me that Max might not even be there. He and Anny might be in their country home. The desk clerk spoke into the phone in a low voice, but I could still hear what he was saying.

"Room seven-oh-one, please. *Danke.* [Pause.] *Guten Morgen*, Herr Schmeling. This is Heinrich Preysing at the front desk, so sorry to disturb you, sir. But there is a young man here who wishes to see you and claims he's a family friend and your boxing student. Yes, his name is Karl Stern."

There was a long pause, which felt like an eternity. I watched the clerk's face as he listened and nodded. A tight little smile crossed his lips, and I felt sure that Max had instructed him to turn me away and my final hope would be dashed. I felt sick to my stomach. My mind grasped for another plan to track down my parents, but there was no other plan.

"Of course, Herr Schmeling. Good-bye."

He hung up the phone.

"Take the elevator to the seventh floor and make a left. Herr Schmeling and Frau Ondra's apartment is number seven-oh-one."

"Danke sehr," I said.

I made my way across the vast lobby. A thin man with dark, neatly parted hair sitting in a wing chair reading a newspaper glanced up at me as I passed. Did he suspect something? He returned to his paper, but as I continued walking, it felt as if a hundred eyes were following me and I expected that at any moment someone would shout,

"Jew," and a hotel detective would come and throw me onto the street. But I made it across, entered the elevator, and breathed a sigh of relief as the door closed behind me. A uniformed elevator operator manually pulled a brass handle and made the car rise to the seventh floor. He pulled open the door, and I stepped into the hall, which was lined with a long yellow carpet with a maroon filigree design. I followed the numbers on the doors until I stopped at 701 at the very end of the hallway. The room had large double doors and a doorbell rather than a plain door knocker like the other rooms. I took a deep breath and rang the bell.

As I waited, I tried to think of what I would say to him, but no words came to me. Should I mention the letters I had sent? Should I ask him if he'd recovered from his injuries? Or should I not make any small talk and just ask him for help right away? Panic rose in me that I'd lose my nerve altogether. Finally I heard someone approach from the other side, the door swung open, and there was Max, casually dressed in wool slacks, a white button-down shirt, and suspenders. It struck me that I had only ever seen him dressed for fighting, working out in the gym, or in a formal suit or tuxedo. Something about the casual attire put me off-balance, like I was seeing the real Max for the first time. His expression was neutral as he saw me, not angry, but also not with his normal easygoing smile. His eyes looked serious, perhaps even a little annoyed at being interrupted.

"Karl," he said, extending his hand.

"I'm sorry to just drop in, but—"

"Not at all, come in," he said, ushering me inside the entryway and closing the door behind us. Before the door shut, I saw him peer over me and glance down the hall, like he was checking to make sure no one had seen us.

"Look, I've got other guests right now. If you'll just wait for a few minutes, I should be done shortly."

He led me to a small sitting room just to the right of the front door. Even from my brief glimpse of the hallway, I could tell the apartment was large, at least three or four bedrooms, and richly decorated with the finest furnishings. I sat in an upholstered wing chair and waited. There was a small crystal bowl filled with green peppermint hard candies on the side table beside my chair. I hadn't eaten all day, and the sight of the candy made me dizzy from the lack of sustenance. I took a handful and quickly stuffed them into my mouth and crunched them with my teeth so I could swallow them as quickly as possible before Max returned.

The room also had an antique writing desk against one wall. On the desk were two framed photographs, one a formal portrait of Anny Ondra, the other a personally autographed picture of Adolf Hitler. A jagged piece of the hard candy stuck in the side of my throat, and I had to cough to dislodge it.

I heard Max reenter another room and resume talking with his guests. There appeared to be two other men in the room.

"They have to give me a rematch, don't they?" Max said.

"It's not the Americans I'm worried about," another man

said. "It's our own beloved government."

"They won't want to risk another defeat," the third man said. "It would embarrass the Reich."

"Embarrass the Reich." Max spat. "I won one and Louis won one. I'm the only man to ever defeat him. I know I can give him a good fight."

"We know that, Max. But Hitler doesn't want a good fight; he only wants victory."

"It's my only chance to regain the title."

"I don't think they care about the title. You've already been World Heavyweight Champion. So that's enough. It's not worth the risk to them."

"I need to get some fights in Europe. Prove to everyone I can still compete."

"Don't worry about it, Max. We'll be able to set something up."

"What about Louis?"

"That'll take some time."

"Think of what the purse would be for a title fight against Louis," Max said. "You've got to get me that fight. I'm getting older every day, you know. I'm not like a fine wine that just gets better with age. I'm more like a good strong cheese. I can only be aged so long before I start to stink."

The other men laughed.

My ears burned. My father had been stabbed. Jews were being robbed and beaten at will. My entire world was collapsing, and Max and his colleagues just sat around talking about boxing and money, like it was any other business day.

Was it possible he didn't know what was going on?

Finally Max ushered his friends out of the apartment. The entire time I had been there, I never saw them and they never saw me. They were just disembodied voices. After closing the front door, Max came down the hall to find me.

"Sorry to keep you waiting, Karl."

I saw him quickly glance at the portrait of Hitler that had been staring at me the whole time. His eyes found the photograph and then quickly moved away.

"Here, let's go into the living room to talk, *ja*? Anny is away in our country house, so I've been trying to get some business done."

He led me to a large, marvelously furnished room overlooking the railway station and the city. One of the daily newspapers sat on a glass table in the center of the room with the headline JEWISH RIOTS ERUPT ACROSS THE REICH. There it was, sitting in front of him. He did know.

"Have a seat," he said, gesturing to one of the couches.

But I couldn't sit. Something about the headline in the paper left me frozen, my legs locked in place. And all the emotion, frustration, and rage of the past two days boiled to the surface. I had always been respectful of Max and careful of what I said to him. But now I couldn't stop myself.

"How could you let this happen?"

"What do you mean?"

"This!" I said, gesturing to the paper. "You know what's going on out there, right?"

"Yes," he said, slowly sitting across from me. "It's . . .

extremely unfortunate."

"Unfortunate? Is that all you can say? Is that all you can do?"

"I'm not sure what you expect—"

"You're a powerful man."

"But I'm only one man," he said, keeping his voice quiet and measured.

"People would listen to you."

"I'm afraid it's not that simple."

"What's not simple?"

"You don't understand."

"Then make me understand."

"Do you think I approve of what's going on?" His voice rose, sharp and defensive. "Do you think this is my doing?"

"Then why don't you speak out?"

"People just don't speak out these days."

"But you're Max Schmeling."

"I would be thrown in jail as quickly as anyone."

"I don't believe that."

"Look at what happened to von Cramm."

"Gottfried von Cramm? The tennis player?"

"Yes. He criticized the government, and they framed him for something else and threw him in jail. His career is over. His life is over." He was almost pleading with me, desperate for me to understand.

"Von Cramm is not you. You're bigger than he is."

"There's a lot you don't understand."

"You're right. I don't understand how you can have all

these Jewish friends and then have dinner with Hitler and Goebbels."

"I'm not one of them. I've never joined the party." He stood and paced the room, making abrupt gestures with his arms to emphasize his points. "What am I supposed to do when the leader of our country asks to see me? Say no? Sorry, I can't make it tonight. I've got more important plans."

"Maybe."

"These are difficult times, Karl. Very difficult. And you may find this hard to believe, but everyone needs to be very careful. Even me." He moved closer and leaned toward me. "Do you know what Anny wanted me to do after I lost to Joe Louis? Do you?"

"No."

"Stay in America. She called and said, 'Don't come home, Max. It's too dangerous for you.' She was convinced they would send me to prison for losing and shaming the Reich."

"Then why did you come back?"

"I'm a German," he said. "Whatever is going on now will pass."

"That's just what my father said."

"Sig has always been a smart man. Your father and I are both survivors. He understands. Listen, Karl, you've been an excellent boxing student, but there's one thing I never taught you. And it might be your most important survival strategy in the ring. It's called the feint."

"The feint."

"Yes. A feint is a trick. Whenever you fake a punch or

try to give your opponent the impression that you've been punched or hurt so that you can mount your own attack. Whenever you mislead someone in the ring. That's a feint. It's the same in life. Sometimes you have to give the impression you are doing one thing in order to do another and survive. You should never give your opponent a clear picture of your real intentions."

Everything he said made complete sense, but those few words suddenly changed my view of him and of every other German who thought they were feinting through the rise of Hitler and the Nazis. For my entire life Max had always represented strength, but now I saw only weakness and self-interest. My eyes burned and my throat tightened as I stared at him.

"Last night our home was attacked by a gang of thugs. Everything was looted or destroyed, and the police did nothing to stop it. My father and I were beaten, and he was stabbed in the stomach. I'm not sure if he was able to get treatment. I have no idea where he or my mother might be right now. For all I know, he may be dead or they may have been arrested. I have no money. No family to turn to. My sister and I are hiding at a friend of my father's, but we have no real place to live and nowhere to go. How is the feint going to help me with that?"

Then I did something that I hadn't done in many years and certainly never in front of Max or anyone at the Berlin Boxing Club. I broke down and cried.

The Excelsior

MAX SENT ME WITH HIS DRIVER IN HIS MERCEDES-BENZ sedan to pick up Hildy and bring her back to the Excelsior, where he said we were welcome to stay as long as we needed to. When I got to the apartment, Hildy was sorry to leave the Countess, who had pampered her all day, letting her try on his best gowns and experiment with his makeup. Hildy and the Countess embraced as we left.

"Good-bye, Aunt Bertie," she said.

"Good-bye, Princess Hildegard," he replied in his strange high-pitched falsetto. "I want you to have this so you'll always remember me."

He gave her a small, round jeweled compact, with deep red rouge on one side and a mirror on the other.

"For me?"

"For you."

"I can't take this."

"Please, dear, I insist. A proper lady always needs to be prepared for anything."

"Thank you again," I said, shaking the Countess's hand.

The Countess pulled me toward him and hugged me close. I had not been that close to the Countess since the very first day when he tried to touch my cheek and I pulled away. This time I returned the embrace.

"You're a good man, Karl. I'm sure your father is proud of you."

We walked back down the stairs to the waiting car. And as we got inside, Hildy said: "Why was he so nice to us?"

"He?"

"Yes. He."

"You mean, you knew?"

"I'm not a fool, Karl. Why did he help us?"

"He and Papa were in the war together. Papa saved his life. He was a hero, you know."

"I didn't know that," she said. "But I'm glad I do now."

She gave a small smile, but then her face grew serious. She looked out the window and played with the jeweled compact the entire ride, opening and closing the lid with a little snap.

Max's driver drove us around to the back entrance of the hotel. Max was waiting by the loading dock where the hotel staff received deliveries. He looked both ways as we got out of the car and quickly ushered us into a service hallway.

"Welcome to the Excelsior," Max said to Hildy.

"*Danke*, Herr Schmeling," she said.

"I'm sorry we couldn't take you through the lobby, but I don't want to raise any suspicions."

"We understand," I said.

"Come this way."

He led us down the dark hallway until we came to the large metal service elevator. A janitor waited there for us, holding open the heavy metal grate that served as a door.

"Thanks, Hermann," Max said to the janitor as we all stepped inside the elevator. Hildy jumped as the janitor closed the door with a loud clang, then pulled a lever. The elevator started to rise. We all rode in silence until we reached the seventh floor and the janitor pushed the lever and it slowed to a halt.

"Seventh floor," he said, pulling open the grate.

We all stepped out. Max turned back to the janitor to shake his hand.

"Thank you again," Max said.

I noticed Max furtively held a wad of bills in his palm that he discreetly passed to the janitor as they shook hands.

"Of course, Herr Schmeling," he said, taking the bills and quickly stuffing them into his pocket.

The rest of the morning, Max made phone calls trying to track down my parents. He had contacts with the police and the local government, but no one seemed to know anything. He briefly left the apartment to make an inquiry at a local police precinct where he had a friend.

"Stay inside the apartment," he instructed. "It would be best if as few people as possible know you are up here."

Hildy and I spent the day sitting and waiting in a guest bedroom, feeling frustrated and helpless. At around midday we heard the front door to the apartment open and a woman's voice call out.

"*Hallo*. Housekeeping."

Hildy and I stared at each other. Her eyes went wide with fear.

"*Hallo?* Herr Schmeling?" we heard the voice call again.

"Good," another woman's voice said quietly. "They must be away."

We heard the maids flip on the radio in the living room and talk casually with each other as if they were alone.

"What'll we do?" Hildy whispered to me.

I tried to think. I couldn't let them find us. Max had instructed us not to be seen. And our presence would seem even more suspicious since we hadn't answered when they called out. We couldn't risk trying to sneak out of the apartment, because we would have to walk right past them. And we didn't really have anywhere to go.

"Come," I whispered back.

I grabbed Hildy's hand and went to the door of our room, peering down the hall to make sure the coast was clear. Then I pulled her down toward the master bedroom, farther away from the front of the apartment, where the maids were cleaning. I quickly scanned the bedroom for a place to hide. Behind the curtains? Under the bed? Surely they would clean those areas. Max and Anny had a huge walk-in closet. I opened the door, and inside I discovered rows of hanging clothes, racks of fancy men's and women's shoes, a tall armoire, and an enormous steamer trunk covered with travel stickers from around the world.

I opened the trunk, which was empty and just big enough to hold Hildy.

"Get in," I said.

"How will I breathe?" she said.

"I'll leave it open a crack so air can get in."

"What about you?"

"Don't worry. I'll figure something out. Just get in and keep quiet. And whatever happens, don't come out unless I tell you it's okay."

I pushed her inside and gently closed the trunk, leaving it open just a crack. I scanned the closet, looking for other ideas. Should I try to create a wall of Max's suits and hide myself inside? That would never work. I opened the doors to the armoire, which was filled with shelves from top to bottom, leaving no room for me to hide.

I heard the maids' voices approaching. I quickly used the shelves of the armoire like steps on a ladder and climbed up and hid myself on the top of the outside, which was hidden by a decorative piece. I reached over the top and closed the armoire doors, and I curled myself up in a tight ball, hoping that my entire body was hidden from view from below. Then I waited. The top of the armoire was dusty, and I could feel my nose start to itch and twitch.

It seemed as if hours had passed until finally the maids entered the master bedroom and started to clean. I heard small snippets of their conversation over the din of the vacuum cleaner.

". . . my bus passed through some of the Jewish neighborhoods on the way over here this morning."

"*Ja*, mine did too."

"What a mess, huh?"

"They deserve it."

"I used to work with a Jewess. She wasn't so bad."

"A Jew maid. That's something you don't see very often."

My entire body started to perspire, and I could feel the moisture building up on my face and dripping down my nose, mingling with the dust. I felt a sneeze coming on and did everything in my power to hold it in.

One of the maids opened the door to the walk-in closet and stepped inside to vacuum and dust. I closed my eyes and held my breath. I heard the whirring of the machine moving back and forth over the floor. Then she opened the door of the armoire and refolded some of the clothes inside. My body was drenched in sweat. I felt droplets of moisture drip off my nose and onto the top of the armoire. I thought for sure a drop would fall on her and give me away.

Finally she closed the armoire door and walked out of the closet. I stayed absolutely still for another half hour as they finished cleaning. When I felt confident they had gone, I climbed back down and opened the trunk. Hildy fell out onto the floor, gasping for breath.

Max returned an hour later with no news about our parents. I told him what had happened, and he cursed himself for forgetting to cancel the maid service.

Healthy Instincts

Max continued his search by telephone with no luck.

All night there were more scattered riots and attacks on Jews all over Germany. Hildy and I shared a guest bedroom in the apartment, but neither of us slept. I heard her tossing and turning in the bed next to mine. Neither of us spoke, for fear that letting our anxieties out into the open air would somehow make them more real. My mind was filled with horrible nightmares about what might have happened to our parents. And every time I heard a noise from within the hotel, I saw images of Nazi thugs stuffed into the elevator and winding their way up the Excelsior stairs to come get us.

When morning finally came, I wanted to go out and

look for my parents on foot, but Max thought it was too dangerous, so he offered to drive around with me to search for them with his driver in his car. Despite her protests, he insisted that Hildy stay behind in the hotel and gave her strict instructions not to answer the door or telephone. The front desk would collect any messages that came.

Even though I had lived through the worst of it, the scenes of devastation were more startling in the harsh light of day. Rows of shops had been vandalized, synagogues burned; scraps of ripped-apart books, broken furniture, and glass littered Jewish neighborhoods like a fresh layer of snow. I scanned the streets, looking for my parents or any familiar faces, but it was hard to get a glimpse of anyone. The Jews who braved being out in public were cleaning or repairing their shops with their heads bent low as they attempted to sweep up the mess or put plywood up to cover broken windows. There were some uniformed Nazis about, watching with satisfied expressions on their faces. But most of the ordinary Germans I saw would just walk by the destruction with their eyes averted as if trying to pretend it wasn't there. It seemed as if much of the city of Berlin were purposefully avoiding eye contact.

We finally arrived in front of the gallery. From the car it seemed deserted, but I couldn't see much of the dark interior through the broken glass. Max and I got out and carefully stepped through the smashed door into the front room. I tried to flip on the light switch, but the bulbs in the main room had been broken in the melee. In the half-light I saw our possessions scattered all over the room and the small puddle of blood where we had been attacked. Max knelt down beside the blood to examine it.

"Your father?" he asked.

I nodded.

I moved toward the back room, stepping over piles of clothes and books. Our makeshift office and kitchen had also been pulled apart. Then I heard the sound. It was a faint wheezing noise, coming from the bathroom.

"*Hallo?*" I called. But there was no response.

I moved to the bathroom door. There was no light on inside. I pushed the door open, and the noise got louder. I saw a figure in the shadows of the room.

"Who is that?" I called.

Max hurried back to join me just as I flicked on the light, which by some miracle still worked.

There was my mother, fully dressed and sitting in the bathtub with no water, clutching her knees, and breathing heavily. Her red-rimmed eyes were frozen open with fear, staring into a blank spot in space.

"Mama."

She did not immediately turn to look at us.

"Mama!" I said, approaching and shaking her shoulder.

She turned and finally seemed to see us.

"Karl?"

"Yes. It's me, Mama."

"Karl . . . is Hildy . . . ?"

"She's okay," I said. "She's at Max's hotel."

She looked at Max and seemed to acknowledge him for the first time.

"Come out of there, Mama."

We hoisted her out of the tub, but she seemed dazed and disoriented.

"Where is Sig?" Max asked.

"They took him," she said.

"Who took him?"

"The Gestapo."

"Do you know where?"

"No," she said. "I—I—"

She started crying.

"Come," Max said. "Let's get you back to my apartment. We'll track him down from there."

"No," she wailed. "I should be here. I should wait. . . ."

She was bawling hysterically. I tried to lead her away by the arm, but she pulled away from me.

"I can't leave," she said.

"Mama, please," I said. "We've got to get out of here."

"No," she cried.

"Yes," I said, grabbing her by the shoulders and staring into her eyes. "We're not safe here anymore. We've got to go. We've got to go now. Hildy needs you. I need you. Now come."

My words seemed to sink in, and her sobbing subsided. I fetched a glass of water, which she drank in one long gulp. And her breathing relaxed to a normal pattern.

"We really must be going," Max said, glancing toward the front window.

"We must gather some of our things," she said, picking through the piles of objects. She picked up a few tattered old books, an atlas, a large book of photographs of European landmarks, an anthology of prints by Dutch masters, random things.

"Mama, there's nothing here worth taking."

"Do as I say, Karl!" she snapped. I was surprised by the ferocity and clarity of her reaction. She handed me the books and started to gather more things.

Max and I helped her pack some of our possessions up into a cardboard box and an old suitcase, and finally we were able to coax her out of the gallery and out toward the waiting sedan. Two young women strolled down the sidewalk toward us as we emerged. They noticed Max, and one whispered and pointed to the other. Max kept his eyes locked on the car and helped usher my mother into the backseat. The two young women stopped to stare as Max and I slid inside the car and drove away.

When we returned to the apartment, Hildy ran into my mother's arms, and they held each other without speaking for several minutes. Max and I awkwardly stood by, not wanting to break their spell. My mother held one arm around Hildy's waist and stroked her head with the other, while Hildy buried her face against my mother's chest. This seemed to revive both of them, and my mother was finally able to sit and tell us what had happened.

"Hartzel drove us to the Hessendorf Clinic, but there were groups of Nazis being treated there for minor cuts and bruises, so we had to move on. We finally got to the Jewish Hospital across town about a half hour later. By then your father had lost a lot of blood and was hallucinating. The ward was full of other Jews who had been attacked, ordinary-looking people, women, children with gashes on their heads and broken bones. They took him right away and removed the glass from his side and stitched him up. He was lucky that it hadn't punctured any major organs or he would've surely been a goner. He was given a blood transfusion, and after a few hours he was feeling a little better."

"As soon as he was thinking clearly again, he wanted to go back and find you. But it was one thirty A.M., and the doctors convinced him that he needed to rest until morning. They gave him morphine for the pain, and he fell asleep. I was awake all night worrying, thinking about you. I tried to call, but the phone lines at the hospital were down."

"In the morning your father's wound was still quite tender, but he insisted we go back to the gallery to make sure you were okay. Of course, when we got there, you were gone. And we both panicked because we had no idea where to look for you. We were trying to figure that out when a car pulled up with a group of Gestapo officers. They were dressed in ordinary suits, and at first I thought that they were a group of insurance agents coming to assess the damage. Isn't that ridiculous? But that's what they looked like at first glance, a bunch of harmless insurance agents. Then I noticed their expressions, dark and hungry. And one of them had on those black boots under his pants.

"They started questioning us about our political beliefs and kept trying to get your father to confess that he was a Red agitator. Of course, your father laughed at that, which they did not appreciate. They searched the gallery, and when they found the old printing press in the basement, they put your father in handcuffs and arrested him. They said the press had been used to print forbidden political material and that he was a traitor to Germany. Then they put him in their car and drove off. There was nothing I could say to stop them and no one I could turn to, no police, no lawyer, no neighbors. I have no idea where they took him. But I was afraid to try to follow them. I needed to find you, but I had no idea where to look for you either. So I just waited. The minutes turned to hours, and my mind filled with the worst thoughts that weighed me down like stones until I couldn't move."

She glanced down at the daily newspaper on the coffee table, which carried the headline GOVERNMENT CONSIDERING MEASURE TO MAKE JEWS PAY FOR RIOT DAMAGE. She picked up the paper and scanned the article and read a few excerpts aloud. "Reich Minister Goebbels commented that the demonstrations reflected the healthy instincts of the German people. He explained, 'The German people are anti-Semitic. It has no desire to have its rights restricted or to be provoked in the future by parasites of the Jewish race.'"

She put the paper aside and muttered to herself, "Healthy instincts . . ." Then she looked up at Max and said, "You've got to help us get out of here."

The *Amerika*

SINCE HIS LOSS TO JOE LOUIS, MAX'S INFLUENCE IN government circles had completely evaporated. As a result, he made little headway when he attempted to find out my father's whereabouts through official channels. In most cases Max was simply ignored, which would have been unthinkable when he was riding high just a few months earlier as the most celebrated man in Germany. I could hear the frustration in his voice as he worked the phones, trying to cut through the silence and bureaucracy.

"Now you want me to write a letter to your supervisor? But I thought you were the supervisor? What kind of idiocy is this? Do you know who I am? [Pause.] Yes, sir. I'm sorry I raised my voice, but if you could just— [Pause.] *Ja*. I will write to your supervisor."

Yet in some ways Max's new anonymity turned out to be a benefit. He had become far less conspicuous and was able to go about his business without a constant spotlight on him. In fact Reich Minister Goebbels had specifically told the sportswriters to keep Max out of the papers, so as not to remind the German people of his humiliating defeat.

And Max was still a rich man. After a couple of days of fruitless inquiry, he paid a small bribe to a government official, who was able to find out that my father was being held by the Gestapo at Gerlach Haus prison and had been charged with some sort of political crime. He was not allowed visitors. Gerlach Haus was the center of Gestapo interrogations in Berlin and had a dark reputation. It was rumored that late at night screams of torture victims could be heard from the street outside. The official advised Max and my mother not to ask too many questions about him or run the risk of being judged guilty by association, even though my father wasn't guilty of anything to begin with.

We all stayed at the Excelsior for several days. Hildy and I tried our best to stay out of Max's way. It was awkward for me to be around him without the common bond of boxing and with the heavy question of my father's fate hanging over us all. We had been at Max's apartment for a week when my mother called Hildy and me into her room and shut the door. We all sat close on the bed, and she gave us another update on her lack of progress. When she finished, I asked: "Well, what are we going to do next?"

"Max is going to help me keep searching. He's agreed to let me stay here for as long as I like."

"Don't you mean *us?*" Hildy said.

"No." My mother shook her head. She took a breath and said, "You and your brother are going to America."

"America?" Hildy said. It was the first she had heard of the plan.

"You're going to live with your father's cousins for a while."

A rush of adrenaline shot through me at the thought that my dream of going to America actually might be about to come true. But the feeling was blunted by the fear of leaving our parents behind to an uncertain fate. As much as I wanted to go, I couldn't abandon my parents.

"I'm not going to leave without you and Papa," I said.

"Neither am I," Hildy added.

"All the arrangements have already been made."

"Then unmake them," I said. "I have to stay and help find Papa. Hildy should go."

"What?" Hildy cried. "I don't want to go alone."

"Listen, you both have to be reasonable."

"I'm a man now," I said. "I can help."

"I know. That's why I need you to go with your sister. I won't have her making the crossing alone."

"But what about Papa?"

"He would want you both to go. Of that I'm certain."

"But—"

"No buts, Karl. It took an incredible amount of effort to make these arrangements. And they can't be changed. Hildy, you'll live with your father's cousin Hillel and his wife, Ida, in Newark, New Jersey. They have a son who is about your age. I think his name is Harry. Karl, you'll be staying with Cousin Leo and his wife, Sarah, in Florida."

"Florida?"

"Yes. A city called Tampa."

"Why can't we be together?" Hildy asked.

I wanted to ask the same thing. For as grown up as I thought I was, I also felt disappointed and apprehensive that Hildy and I would not be together in the New World.

"Neither one of them could take both of you. And it won't be forever. We're extremely lucky they agreed to sponsor you at all."

"How long?" my sister asked.

"I don't know, Hildy." Our mother sighed.

"But what about you?" I asked.

"I'll join you as soon as we can free your father."

"I don't want to live in America," Hildy whined. "I want to stay with you."

"You don't have a choice. The arrangements have been made."

"But how can we afford—" I started to say.

"Max has been kind enough to lend us the money we need and arrange the transport."

Our passage was booked on a ship coincidentally named the *Amerika*, leaving from Hamburg the very next day. It all happened so quickly, I didn't have a chance to return to the gallery to retrieve anything else or even say good-bye to anyone. The only people left in Berlin I cared about were Neblig and the Countess. I wrote them both letters and also sent Neblig my copy of the origin of the Mongrel. I figured I could make contact with them again once I was settled in Tampa.

Max and our mother escorted us to Hamburg via a private train car. Our mother nervously watched the door of the compartment the entire ride. She nearly jumped out of her skin when the conductor arrived to collect our tickets.

About an hour into the journey Max went to use the restroom, leaving us alone. A few minutes later two Gestapo officers appeared at the door of our private car. My mother gasped at the sight of them but tried to compose herself as they stepped inside. One was tall with glasses, the other short and round. Both wore black dress uniforms and hats with the death skull insignia.

"Guten Morgen," the tall one said. "Papers, please."

"Certainly," my mother said. She handed over her passport.

I noticed my mother's hands shaking and shot her a glance as if she could make them stop.

"And the children," the short one said, gesturing to me and Hildy. His eyes lingered on Hildy.

Hildy looked down into her lap.

My mother nodded, and we each handed over our passports.

The men opened the books. Each had a prominent red *J* stamped on the inside.

"And where are you going?" the tall officer asked.

"Hamburg," she said.

"And is that your final destination?"

"The children are going to America."

"America. I hear it's a very good place for mongrel children like these," the tall one said. "And why are you not joining them?"

My mother bit her bottom lip, considering her answer. She obviously could not talk about my father, which would put us all in danger.

"I have business to conclude here," she replied.

"What kind of business?" the tall one asked.

"What kind of business?" my mother repeated.

"*Ja*. It's a simple question," the tall one said.

My mother stared at him for a long moment, biting her bottom lip.

Just then Max reentered the train car.

"Is there something wrong?" he said.

The short officer's eyes widened at the sight of Max.

"Herr Schmeling," the short officer said excitedly, "it's an honor."

He extended his hand, and he and Max shook. The tall officer seemed less impressed. Max extended his hand, and the tall officer shook it slowly.

"We were just getting to know your friends," he said dryly.

"Her husband is a business associate of mine," Max explained.

"How interesting."

"I can assure you everything is in order," Max said.

"Herr Schmeling," the short officer said "would you mind signing an autograph? It's for my son."

"Of course," Max said, removing his fountain pen and a small pad from his jacket pocket. "His name?"

"Rudolf," the man answered.

The tall officer suddenly laughed.

"Rudolf! That's *your* name. His son is Friedrich."

Rudolf blushed.

"Okay, I want one for me too," he said. "What's the big deal?"

"No problem," Max said.

He signed the autographs.

"There you go," Max said, handing the autographs to the short officer.

"*Danke.*"

"And one for your children?" Max asked the tall one.

"I don't have children," he said curtly.

"Then one for you?" Max offered.

"No," the tall officer replied. He turned back to my mother. "May I ask what kind of business you and your husband are in?"

My mother's eyes widened, and she hesitated. Hildy curled her hand into mine.

"Her husband is an art dealer." Max jumped in. "And Frau Stern is a decorator. They've been helping my wife, Anny, and me decorate our country house."

"Is that so?" the tall one said.

"*Ja.*" Max continued. "In fact Magda Goebbels was so impressed by their work the last time they visited that she and the Reich Minister are considering using them to do their Berlin home."

"Reich Minister Goebbels?"

"We've already met several times about the project," my mother said.

"He's planning to build a small film screening room right in their home," Max added. "It's going to be quite spectacular."

The tall one hesitated, took a long look at my mother and Max, and then turned to his counterpart.

"Come on, let's go."

He abruptly turned and exited the train car. Rudolf shook Max's hand again and followed the tall officer out. We all exhaled as the door closed and we were alone again. In that instance, the feint had worked.

We arrived at the Hamburg docks just in time to board the ship and barely had time to say good-bye.

My mother held me close and whispered in my ear: "Karl, I'm counting on you now to be a man and take care of things. You have the books?"

My mother had carefully packed away the large books she had taken from the gallery: the atlas, the old book of photographs of European landmarks, a collection of prints by Dutch masters.

"Yes," I said. "I have them."

"Those books are special, Karl. Guard them very closely.

If anything happens to me or your father, I want you to bring them to a man named Louis Cohen in New York."

"Louis Cohen," I repeated.

"He's a book dealer who owns a shop called The Argosy in Manhattan. I wrote all of his contact information on a piece of paper that I put inside the atlas. He's a good man. Can you remember that?"

"Yes. Are they valuable?"

"Not the books. Long ago your father hid things in the endpapers that Louis Cohen will help you sell. I packed you extra glue and endpapers in case you have to reseal them. Be careful with these books. They are our future."

"I will," I said.

She hugged me tightly and kissed me on the top of my head just like she did when I was a little boy.

"You make me very proud, Karl."

"I love you, Mama. And tell Papa—"

My words were cut off as I choked back a sob rising in my throat. I hugged my mother closer.

"I will," she said. "I will."

I held her a moment longer, and then she turned to Hildy.

Hildy ran into her arms, and my mother held her close and stroked her hair. My mother whispered into Hildy's ear, and my sister nodded, her moist eyes staring out, trying to absorb the words.

I turned to Max.

"Say hello to America for me," he said. "I think you will like it over there. It's a young country, full of energy and different people. But be careful. Sometimes the young can be stupid and reckless. Do you know what I mean?"

"I think so."

"Try to keep up your training. You've got the tools to be a great fighter."

"I will," I said. But in truth I had no idea if I'd ever box again.

"I will take care of your mother. Don't worry. And we'll find a way to free your father."

"Thank you," I said, although I could sense uncertainty under his forced confidence.

I extended my hand, and we shook. He held my grip and looked me in the eye.

"All Germans are not the same, Karl," he said. "This will pass."

The words rang hollow as the voice of my father echoed in my head saying the exact same thing.

Hildy and I boarded the ship. We walked up the gang-plank and onto the deck. We scanned the crowd waving from the dock, but our mother and Max had already disappeared.

The ship pushed back from its moorings and groaned to life. The massive engines whirred, and tugboats crept alongside, easing the vessel out of the harbor.

The sun was just going down, and the fading landscape onshore was bathed in dark orange. Hildy and I stood side by side. watching our homeland recede into the distance. She sidled up close to me and took my hand, leaning her head against my shoulder. Her dark eyes looked out at the crowd on the dock from behind her thick glasses. She blinked back tears and held my hand tightly. We didn't speak for a several minutes. Until finally I whispered: "There's adventure in the air . . ."

She looked up at me through tear-streaked eyes and answered: "And cake to be eaten."

We stood there holding hands on the deck, as tugboats slowly guided us out to sea. Despite my sadness at leaving my parents behind, a feeling of weightlessness came over me as I watched Nazi Germany recede into the distance. Eventually we were clear of the harbor. The tugboats moved away and headed back toward the docks, and the ship slowly turned to the open sea. Hildy and I stood in the same place but turned to watch the land move farther and farther into the distance until it finally disappeared from sight.

Late that night I lay awake in our little cabin, staring at the ceiling, while Hildy slept curled up in the other bunk against the opposite wall. The ship gently rose and fell, but my thoughts were back onshore in Germany, wondering where my parents were at that moment and if they were safe. And then my mind kept drifting to the books and what my parents had concealed inside them. I thought that if I knew what they had hidden, it would make me feel as if they were close by, like they were speaking to me. Finally my curiosity got the best of me. I quietly climbed out of bed, careful not to wake Hildy. I flipped on a small lamp and laid the three books on my bunk. I retrieved a straight razor I had packed in my toilet kit.

First I opened the front cover of the enormous atlas. I took a deep breath and then, using the razor, I gently sliced along the edge of the endpaper, tracing a perfect line around the perimeter. After completing the cut, I very carefully lifted the endpaper off to reveal several pieces of artwork beneath. I immediately recognized two drawings by Rembrandt and several etchings by Albrecht Dürer.

I repeated the same surgical procedure on the other two books, each revealing several wondrous works of art from different eras, including several studies by Rodin, a small landscape by Matisse, a drawing of a boy by Picasso, and several works by my father's expressionist friends, Otto Dix, Max Beckmann, and Ernst Ludwig Kirchner. The collection was worth a small fortune.

When I removed the final endpaper, I gasped at the sight. It was a drawing by George Grosz of a man dressed in a tuxedo holding a champagne glass up in a toast. I knew, even without the telltale scarf, that it was an image of my father. I felt my throat constrict and my eyes well up at the sight of him in all his glory. I saw so many attributes in the drawing that I had never noticed about my father before: confidence, humor, strength, and, perhaps most important, the pure joy of being alive. My papa. It had taken me seventeen years to start to understand him, and now, when I needed and wanted him the most, we were forced to be apart.

I lifted off the drawing to reveal another sketch by Grosz. This one was a study for the painting he had made of Max Schmeling that had set my whole boxing career in motion. The image of Max, while so familiar, also looked different to me. For the first time I noticed that his hands were held up in a defensive pose, as if he cared as much about self-preservation as triumphing.

Without Max we never would have been able to escape from Germany. Yet I wondered how much, if anything, he would have done for us had I not confronted him. Then I remembered the Countess. No one had displayed more courage than he had in our rescue, braving the worst of our night of terror to guide us through the streets and then selflessly harboring us in his apartment. He could have easily been arrested himself or even killed. In many ways the Countess had more strength than anyone I had ever known.

I placed the two drawings by Grosz side by side. On the surface they appeared to be such opposites, my father a man of culture and intellect, Max a warrior, dedicated to physical strength and sport. And yet they were both what my father would call moderns, men who didn't want to be encumbered by old traditions and labels. They each strove to define themselves as individuals, and each failed because of the Nazis.

As I stared at the drawings, it struck me that I might not see either one of them again. A deep heaviness filled my chest, and my eyes stung with tears as I tried to see myself in each portrait but realized that I didn't fit perfectly into either frame. I would have to try to hold on to the best elements of both. But I would have to become my own man.

ONE DAY AT
THE STATION
FEFELFARVE
HATCHES HIS
MOST EVIL
PLOT YET...

I'LL GET RID OF THOSE
VERMIN WINZIG AND SPATZ
ONCE AND FOR ALL!

HE SETS NETS NEAR
EVERY WINDOW TO
CATCH SPATZ

AND PUTS OUT MOUSETRAPS
ALL OVER TO GET WINZIG.

THEN HE SCATTERS
POISONED FOOD
EVERYWHERE

POISON

BUT HE IS TOO
LATE. OUR
HEROES HAVE
ALREADY ESCAPED
TO A NEW
WORLD CALLED...

Author's Note

This is a work of fiction set against the backdrop of real historical events. Max Schmeling did rescue two Jewish boys on Kristallnacht. Though this is not their story, the incident inspired me to explore the history of Schmeling and the Jews of Berlin. Any similarities between the Stern family and the family of the rescued boys are purely coincidental.

Because of his loss to Louis, Schmeling was no longer protected by the government and was drafted and served as a paratrooper during World War II. He was old to be a paratrooper, and there were strong suspicions that he had been forced into the dangerous duty as punishment for losing to Louis and never officially joining the Nazi Party. After the war, he and Anny Ondra put their lives back together, and he eventually became a successful businessman as one of Germany's leading Coca-Cola executives. After reuniting on the television show *This Is Your Life* in the 1950s, Max and Joe Louis became friends and stayed in touch until Louis's death in 1981. Louis had fallen on hard times, and Schmeling helped to pay for his medical expenses and burial costs and served as a pallbearer at his funeral. He rarely spoke about his heroic actions during Kristallnacht. He and Anny Ondra were married for fifty-four years and had no children. Max Schmeling died on February 2, 2005, just a few months shy of his hundredth birthday.

Sources

I consulted dozens of sources during the writing of this book. For background on Schmeling and his fights with Louis, I relied upon David Margolick's *Beyond Glory: Joe Louis vs. Max Schmeling and a World on the Brink*; *Max Schmeling: An Autobiography* (translated and edited by George von der Lippe); and *Ring of Hate* by Patrick Myler. Two books in particular offered wonderful insights into the heyday of Jewish boxing: *Barney Ross: The Life of a Jewish Fighter* by Douglas Century and *When Boxing Was a Jewish Sport* by Allen Bodner. For general facts and timelines of Nazi Germany, I utilized *The Holocaust Encyclopedia* by Walter Laqueur and *The Holocaust Chronicle* by John Roth, Ph.D.

YouTube proved to be an invaluable resource as I was able to watch newsreels of 1930s Berlin, films of both Schmeling and Louis bouts in their entirety, as well as many other fights from the era. I even found clips of Max and Anny Ondra's film *Knockout*.

The Neue Galerie in New York City is a wonderful museum devoted to German and Austrian art of the early twentieth century. There I was able to view works by most of the great expressionist artists mentioned in the book and sample great Austrian cuisine at the Café Sabarsky.

I reveled in revisiting the work of comic book and comic strip pioneers Wilhelm Busch (*Max und Moritz*), Jerry Siegel and Joe Shuster (*Superman*), Bob Kane and Bill Finger (*Batman*), Ham Fisher (*Joe Palooka*), Rudolph Dirks (*The*

Katzenjammer Kids), George Herriman (*Krazy Kat*), Lee Falk (*Mandrake the Magician*), Harold Gray (*Little Orphan Annie*), and many others. For general background on the history of cartooning I relied upon *100 Years of American Newspaper Comics*, edited by Maurice Horn. And I would be remiss if I did not mention the inspiration I took from Art Spiegelman's epic graphic novel series *Maus*.

By far the most valuable insights I gained came from talking to people who lived in Germany during the period. I'm deeply indebted to Gerald Liebenau, Ursula Weil, and Rose Wolf, who shared stories with me about their childhoods living in Nazi Germany. They made history come alive in a way that no book or film ever could.

Acknowledgments

First, I want to thank my editor, Kristin Daly Rens. When I found out we would be working together, the only piece of information I had about Kristin was that she was a German speaker. I have been extremely pleased and privileged to discover that she is also a brilliant and creative editor.

My agent, Maria Massie, of LMQ, is a wonderful advocate, adviser, and friend (not an easy trio of roles to juggle). I also want to thank Kassie Evashevski, at UTA, who bravely navigates the trenches of Hollywood for me. My assistant Barbara Clews is always an enormous help to me and bravely endures my grouchy moods when I get in to my office after an early-morning writing session. Many friends read early drafts of the manuscript. But I want to especially thank Martin Curland, whom I can always count on for good and honest insights. I also want to thank Keith Fields, who taught me the rudiments of boxing despite my almost chronic lack of rhythm and discipline.

My parents are unwavering in their love and support of me and my writing. My sister, Susan Krevlin, read to me and drew with me when I was a little boy and helped to nurture my love of books and art. My darling daughters, Annabelle and Olivia, are my greatest loves *and* distractions. And I wouldn't have it any other way. Finally I want to thank my other greatest love, my wife, Stacey, to whom this book is dedicated. Every book in my life begins and ends with her.

The Berlin B★xing Club

Letter from the Author

Dear Reader,

I hope you enjoyed the book. I thought I'd take a minute to tell you something about how this story came to be written. Believe it or not, it took about ten years from conception to publication.

I first became interested in Max Schmeling while I was working as a writer for a show on the History Channel. I had known about Schmeling and his legendary fights with Joe Louis—and like most people, I assumed Schmeling was a Nazi. As I dug deeper, I learned that not only was he *not* a Nazi, but he had actually sheltered two Jewish boys on Kristallnacht, the night of state sanctioned anti-Jewish riots in Berlin, and then helped to get them out of the country. I'm always intrigued when a character from history reveals something totally unexpected, and it fascinated me that one of the most famous and revered men in Nazi Germany wasn't a Nazi at all.

So I set out to write a book about someone who was labeled a Nazi but wasn't, and someone who was labeled a Jew, but didn't consider himself Jewish. To me, this really gets at the poisonous heart of totalitarian regimes: People are not allowed to be who they want to be.

In this "Extras" section, I've included a timeline I created while writing and researching the book that traces the rise of the Nazis alongside Max's boxing career and the life of Karl's other boxing hero, Barney Ross.

I've also included an essay about my failed career as a cartoonist. While reading that part, you should keep in mind one of my favorite quotes by John Lennon: "Life is what happens to you while you're busy making other plans." This has certainly proved true with me. Thanks again.

All the best,
Robert Sharenow

The Berlin Boxing Club Timeline

1905
September 28, 1905—Max Schmeling is born in Klein Luckow in Germany's Brandenburg province.

1909
December 23, 1909—Future Jewish boxing champion Barney Ross is born Dov-Ber Rosofsky on New York's Lower East Side.

1922
The Ring magazine founded by Nat Fleischer.

1923
July 1923—Benny Leonard and Lew Tendler, both Jewish lightweights, fight for the world championship. Leonard wins.

1924
August 2, 1924—Max Schmeling defeats Kurt Czapp in his first professional fight.

1926
August 24, 1926—Max Schmeling defeats Max Dieckmann in the first round in Berlin to capture the German light heavyweight title.

1927
June 19, 1927—Max Schmeling captures European light heavyweight crown by defeating Fernand Delarge of Belgium.

1928

April 4, 1928—Max Schmeling defeats Franz Diener in the fifteenth round to capture the German heavyweight title.

November 1928—Schmeling relinquishes German heavyweight title.

1929

June 6, 1929—Schmeling defeats Spain's Paulino Uzcudun in fifteen rounds in New York.

September 1, 1929—Barney Ross wins first professional fight against Ramon Lugo.

1930

June 12, 1930—Max Schmeling earns the world heavyweight boxing crown by beating Jack Sharkey after Sharkey delivers a controversial low blow.

1931

July 3, 1931—Max Schmeling defeats Young Stribling in the fifteenth round by TKO (technical knockout) in Cleveland.

1932

June 21, 1932—In a fifteen-round rematch, Jack Sharkey defeats Max Schmeling to claim the heavyweight title in a controversial decision.

1933

January 30, 1933—Adolph Hitler is sworn in as chancellor of Germany.

February 27, 1933—Nazis burn the Reichstag, the German parliament building, to create crisis. On the following day, Hitler is granted emergency powers.

March 11, 1933—Storm troopers attack Jewish-owned businesses, sparking a wave of violence against German Jews.

March 24, 1933—Enabling Act of 1933 is passed—Hitler is granted dictatorial powers by Germany's parliament.

March 26, 1933—Barney Ross defeats Tony Canzoneri to capture the junior welterweight championship.

April 1, 1933—Nazis stage boycott of Jewish businesses.

April 7, 1933—Nazis enact laws ordering the dismissal of non-Aryan teachers and civil servants.

April 11, 1933—Nazi decree defines non-Aryans as anyone descended from non-Aryan parents or grandparents. One parent or grandparent classifies the descendant as non-Aryan, particularly if the parent or grandparent was Jewish.

April 26, 1933—Nazis create the Gestapo, secret state police.

May 10, 1933—Nazis stage book burnings across Germany.

June 8, 1933—Max Baer defeats Max Schmeling in ten rounds by KO in New York.

July 14, 1933—Nazi Party is declared the only legal political party in Germany. Jewish immigrants from Poland are stripped of their German citizenship.

September 29, 1933—Nazis prohibit Jews from owning land.

October 4, 1933—Nazis prohibit Jews from being newspaper editors.

October 19, 1933—Germany leaves the League of Nations.

1934
January 26, 1934—Germany and Poland sign ten-year non-aggression pact.

February 5, 1934—Non-Aryan medical students are barred from taking licensing exams.

February 13, 1934—Schmeling loses to Steve Hamas in twelve rounds in Philadelphia.

May 17, 1934—Jews not allowed national health insurance.

May 28, 1934—Barney Ross defeats heavily favored Irishman Jimmy McLarnin to earn the welterweight title, becoming the first boxer to hold two world titles simultaneously.

June 13, 1934—Schmeling fights Paulino Uzcudin of Spain to a draw in twelve rounds in Barcelona.

June 30, 1934—Hitler conducts a purge of the SA leadership in what comes to be known as "The Night of the Long Knives."

July 22, 1934—German Jews are prohibited from getting legal qualifications.

July 1934—Zionist movements begin organizing illegal immigration of Jews from Central and Eastern Europe.

July 25, 1934—Austrian Chancellor Engelbert Dollfuss is killed in a failed coup attempt by Austrian Nazis.

August 2, 1934—German President von Hindenburg dies. Hitler becomes Fuhrer.

September 11, 1934—Hitler appoints Bavarian Justice Minister Hans Frank to his cabinet and charges him with aligning German law with Nazi ideology.

September 17, 1934—Barney Ross loses to Jimmy McLarnin in a split decision.

1935
January 13, 1935—France returns the Saar region to Germany.

March 1, 1935—Germany takes possession of Saar region. Nearly all Jews apply to become French or Belgian citizens.

May 10, 1935—Schmeling defeats American Steve Hamas in Hamburg (TKO in ninth round).

May 21, 1935—Nazis ban Jews from serving in the German military.

May 28, 1935—Barney Ross defeats Jimmy McLarnin in the last of their three fights.

July 7, 1935—Schmeling defeats Paulino Uzcudin of Spain in Berlin (by decision in twelve).

August 6, 1935—Jewish artists and performers in Germany are forced to join Jewish Cultural Unions.

August 18, 1935—Civil marriages between Aryans and non-Aryans are forbidden.

September 15, 1935—Hitler decrees the Nuremberg Race Laws against Jews. Only those with pure German blood can be true citizens.

October 10, 1935—Rabbi Leo Baeck issues a prayer of mercy to be read on Yom Kippur. The Nazis ban the prayer and arrest Baeck.

1936
February 4, 1936—Swiss Nazi leader Wilhelm Gustloff is murdered by Croatian Jew David Frankfurter to protest the mistreatment of German Jews.

March 7, 1936—German forces invade the Rhineland.

March 9, 1936—Pogrom—a violent anti-Jewish riot—against Jews of Przytyk, Poland.

June 19, 1936—Max Schmeling stuns the world by knocking out Joe Louis in the twelfth round at Yankee Stadium.

June 17, 1936—Heinrich Himmler named chief of German police.

August 1936—At the Olympic Games in Berlin, ten Jewish athletes win medals.

1937

January 30, 1937—Hitler associates Jews with Bolshevism.

March 15, 1937—Joint Boycott Council organizes a mass anti-Nazi rally in New York.

March 21, 1937—Pope Pius XI issues a statement against extreme nationalism and racism.

June 22, 1937—Joe Louis becomes world heavyweight champion by knocking out Jimmy Braddock in the eighth round in Chicago.

August 1937—Attacks on Jews in Poland increase.

November 25, 1937—Germany and Japan sign a political and military agreement.

1938

January 21, 1938—Romania revokes citizenship of many Jews and curtails Jews' rights.

March 13, 1938—Germany folds Austria into the Reich (the Anschluss).

March 28, 1938—Germany no longer recognizes Jewish community organizations.

April 16, 1938—Schmeling defeats American Steve Dudas in Hamburg (KO in sixth round).

April 26, 1938—The Decree Regarding the Reporting of Jewish Property is issued, paving the way for the confiscation of the property of German Jews.

May 16, 1938—First group of Jews sent to forced labor at Mauthausen concentration camp.

May 31, 1938—Barney Ross loses world welterweight championship to Henry Armstrong. Ross retires.

June 15, 1938—1,500 Jews interned in German concentration camps.

June 22, 1938—More than 70,000 people crowd into Yankee stadium to watch the second Louis/Schmeling fight. Louis knocks out Schmeling in the first round, sending the former champ to the hospital.

June 25, 1938—Jewish doctors are barred from treating Aryan patients.

July 8, 1938—Munich's Great Synagogue is destroyed.

August 17, 1938—All Jewish men in Germany are required to officially add Israel to their name. Jewish woman are required to add Sarah.

August 26, 1938—Zentralstelle Für Jüdische Auswanderung (Central Office for Jewish Emigration) is established in Vienna under the leadership of Adolph Eichmann.

September 27, 1938—Jews barred from practicing law in Germany.

September 29, 1938—The Munich Agreement: the French and English allow Germany to annex Czechoslovakia.

October 5, 1938—German passports for Jews required to be marked with a J for *Jude*.

October 6, 1938—Germany annexes the Sudetenland.

October 28, 1938—Germans expel 15,000 Polish-born Jews to Poland.

November 7, 1938—In reaction to the expulsion of Polish Jews, Polish Jewish student Herschel Grynszpan shoots German diplomat Ernest von Rath in Paris, who dies two days later.

November 9–10, 1938—Kristallnacht (The Night of Broken Glass): Nazi pogrom signals for many the starting point of the Holocaust.

November 12, 1938—German government fines Jews one billion Reichsmarks to pay for damage caused by Kristallnacht.

November 15, 1938—Jewish children prohibited from attending German schools.

December 3, 1938—Decree on Eliminating the Jews from German Economic Life is issued by Goring.

1939
July 2, 1939—Schmeling knocks out Adolf Heuser in Stuttgart in the first round to win the European heavyweight title.

September 1939—Germany invades Poland. Great Britain and France declare war, signaling the official beginning of World War II.

Max Schmeling is drafted into the German army, serving as a paratrooper.

1940
April 24, 1940—Schmeling's Jewish manager Joe Jacobs dies of a heart attack.

June 1940—The Germans capture Paris.

1941
December 7, 1941—The Japanese bomb Pearl Harbor.

1945
World War II ends.

1947

September 28, 1947—Schmeling defeats Werner Vollmer (KO in the seventh round).

December 12, 1947—Schmeling defeats Hans Joachim Dragerstein in Hamburg (KO in the tenth round).

1948

May 23, 1948—Schmeling loses to Walter Neusel in Hamburg (by decision in ten).

October 2, 1948—Schmeling defeats Hans-Joachim Dragerstein in Kiel (KO in ninth round).

October 31, 1948—Schmeling loses to Richard Vogt in Berlin (by decision in ten). His last professional fight.

Max Schmeling retires from the ring.

1954

Max Schmeling visits America and has a reunion with Joe Louis.

1957

Max Schmeling wisely invests in the German Coca-Cola franchise and eventually becomes a successful businessman.

1960

Joe Louis and Max Schmeling are reunited on the television show *This Is Your Life*.

1967
January 17, 1967—Barney Ross dies in Chicago.

1981
April 12, 1981—Joe Louis dies in Las Vegas, Nevada. Having lost all his money, he was working as a greeter at a casino. Max Schmeling helped pay for the funeral and served as a pallbearer.

1987
Anny Ondra, Schmeling's wife of 54 years, dies in Germany.

1990
Joe Louis inducted into the International Boxing Hall of Fame (66 wins, 3 losses, 54 knockouts).

1992
Max Schmeling inducted into the International Boxing Hall of Fame (56 wins, 10 losses, 4 draws, 39 wins by knockout).

2005
February 2, 2005—Max Schmeling dies at the age of 99.

Confessions of a Failed Cartoonist
By Robert Sharenow

One of the most pleasurable aspects of working on *The Berlin Boxing Club* was creating the illustrations and cartoons. My boyhood dream was to become a cartoonist, but I had not really picked up a drawing pen and pad in more than twenty years, save for an occasional doodle or birthday card. Through my lead character, Karl, also an aspiring cartoonist, I got to rediscover the joy of drawing and in some way fulfill at least two of my personal ambitions by birthing my own comic strip (*Winzig and Spatz*) and superhero (The Mongrel), which both appear in the book. For me it was some small redemption for one of my life's bitter disappointments.

Growing up I had an unusual passion for comic strips, comic books, and political cartoons. To me, the comic strip was one of the highest forms of narrative art. I particularly reveled in the worlds of Charles Schulz's *Peanuts* and Hergé's *The Adventures of Tintin*. While Hergé's intricately drawn and plotted creation provided adventure and escape, Schulz offered a roadmap of the human condition. Charlie Brown, Lucy, Linus, and Snoopy were as real and three-dimensional for me as any characters in the history of fiction. With just a few panels Schulz conveyed story, character, humor, and emotion. The Peanuts gang cheered and comforted me and gave me rich insight into the workings of the world, reflecting my own struggles with family, love, hate, friendship, longing, success, and failure. So from an early age, I drew caricatures and formulated ideas for original comic strips and comic book heroes.

Later I attended Brandeis University, where I drew political cartoons and a comic strip called *Feedback* for the school newspaper. Like Gary Trudeau's original *Doonesbury* strips at Yale, *Feedback* was loosely based on the lives of my roommates and friends. When my friend Eric protested apartheid in South Africa, so did one of my characters. When my roommate Dan was put on academic probation because of excessive library fines, so was one of my characters. When fraternities tried to come onto campus, one of my characters joined and one of my characters tried to block them. In perhaps my most forward-thinking moment as a cartoonist, one of my characters even came out of the closet. This was in 1987, a full decade before Ellen DeGeneres portrayed the first openly gay character on television. Although, to be honest, one of my gay friends insisted he was my most underwritten character and that I shouldn't be too proud of myself. By my junior year, *Feedback* had developed a loyal following of readers, and I was, in some ways, living out my childhood ambition.

Every college cartoonist dreamed of being the next Gary Trudeau and having his or her college strip become the *Doonesbury* of our generation. While I was at Brandeis grinding out *Feedback*, Yale's newspaper cartoonist Sabin Streeter had a compilation of his comic strip *Hollenhead* published and nationally distributed by Plume. To say I was jealous would be a vast understatement. I envied Streeter with a passion that bordered on mania. Someone bought me a copy of his book, and I steadfastly refused to read it. I even hated the guy's name. Sabin Streeter? Who was he trying to impress with that pretentious literary moniker? (I now realize that it probably was—and is—his real name and not a pseudonym like Dr. Seuss or Mark Twain.)

At the same time, my jealousy of Streeter was counterbalanced by my already formidable collection of self-doubts.

Why weren't my strips funnier? Why couldn't I draw better? Why hadn't I studied harder in high school and been able to go to Yale? Then it surely would've been my comic strips published in a book, not his.

Sometime during my junior year, *Newsweek* contacted the newspaper and left a message saying that they intended to reprint one of my cartoons. I hardly believed it when my editor in chief gave me the news. Later that day, someone from *Newsweek* called me to work out the delivery of the art and payment for my services. Payment? They were going to pay me? I couldn't believe it. Being published in a national magazine was thrilling enough, but to be paid for it was a whole other ballgame. I had turned pro.

That one phone call from *Newsweek* seemed to reinforce everything I'd hoped for about my talent and my prospects for the future. Now I was convinced it was all going to happen for me and I would knock old Sabin Streeter from his perch as the voice of college America. Surely a book contract and a national syndication deal would follow.

Soon, thanks to my publicist (also known as my mother), my entire family, friends, neighbors, and even some strangers knew that one of my cartoons was going to be published in an upcoming *Newsweek*. I was mildly annoyed by my mother's bragging, but secretly happy that she was letting everyone know about my accomplishment.

One week prior to the issue coming out, I received my first check as a professional artist. I can't remember what the amount was, maybe $50 or $100, but it seemed like a fortune. I had been paid to do something that I would've done for free! What could be better?

One week later, just two days prior to my big publication

day, *Newsweek* called again.

"The magazine's decided not to run your comic strip."

"What?"

I must've misheard him.

"Yeah. I'm sorry. The issue got really full. It didn't fit the layout anymore. These things happen."

Over the next thirty seconds, I felt like vomiting, crying, lying in the fetal position and sucking my thumb, and/or screaming, all at once. But instead I just stood there, phone in hand, mouth agape, wondering how my mother was going to retract her global notification.

Finally, I recovered my composure enough to ask.

"Can I keep the check?"

"Sure," he said, with touches of both sympathy and pity.

I hung up the phone a broken man. Not only did I feel my Doonesbury dreams evaporating, but I would now face years of friends and relatives asking, "So when is the *Newsweek* with your cartoon coming out?" The agonizing answer was, Never.

I continued to write *Feedback* until I graduated, but something had been taken out of me. All the doubts I had about my ability to draw seemed to be reinforced by *Newsweek*'s supposed formatting crunch. In truth, drawing was always a struggle for me. I never really buckled down and took art classes like I should have, so I never had a great command of the discipline of drawing. I frequently felt frustrated because my illustrations never quite matched my imaginings. I always seemed to be writing dialogue and characters that outpaced my ability to draw them.

Writing was the part of the process that always came easier to me. But to be a novelist or any kind of writer seemed like an even more absurd ambition, given that I had never taken a writing class and was not a particularly gifted student. Also, everyone at Brandeis seemed to want to be a novelist, while being a cartoonist was a relatively unique ambition, with a thinner playing field of competitors. If I couldn't win that race, how would I ever get a novel published?

More than twenty years have passed since the *Newsweek* debacle. In that time Charles Schulz died and the golden age of the newspaper comic strip died with him (as did the golden age of newspapers). I've had the great good fortune of having two novels published, two more than I ever expected.

When I first conceived *The Berlin Boxing Club* and the character of Karl, I thought about illustrating the book myself, and I was seized by the same insecurities that had plagued me as a college student. But then I bought a sketchpad and pen and started to draw again. I was still not a very good artist, but I could not believe how much fun it was. How could I have let so many years go by without doing this? Soon, if my daughters asked me to play with them, I would ask them to draw with me instead. I quickly filled several sketchbooks with comic strip ideas, caricatures, and cartoons in much the same way I had when I was a kid. But this time the drawings were all done from the perspective of my character, Karl.

Some critics have praised the illustrations in the book while others have thought them to be crude and not very good. I believe they are very authentic because I still possess the skills of a fifteen-year-old, self-taught artist, which is what Karl is, too (funny how it worked out that way).

One of the harsh truths of adulthood is that you stop doing many of the activities that gave you pleasure in your youth. I don't play baseball, stuff quarters into pinball machines, or jam with my old band mates anymore. And I may never illustrate another book. But through *The Berlin Boxing Club* I learned to love drawing again, and I enjoy it without any of the frustration, ambition, or bitterness that I used to feel creating *Feedback*. So I have to thank my character, Karl, because without him I may never have picked up my pad and pen again in the first place. I may even try to find Sabin Streeter's book and give it a read.